THE LORDS OF DAIR

—by—

Helen Wieselberg

G. P. Putnam's Sons • New York

SBN: 399-12117-X

Library of Congress Cataloging in Publication Data

Wieselberg, Helen.
    The lords of Dair.

    I. Title.
PZ4.W653Lo 1978 [PS3573.I376] 813'.5'4 77-17313

For EBW, EW and LB
without whom this book would have no author
and for TOM
without whom this author would have no book

THE LORDS OF DAIR

I

The Duke of Dair's dark eyes became two glittering pistols pointed at my own, and suddenly his voice was gunfire.

"My God, woman!" he roared, "Do you think I have no pride?"

Then he was gone, and the great carved door to the North Courtyard closed with a crash between us.

The moment haunts my dreams. Even now.

* * *

"Before there were Saxons in Britain, or Normans to conquer them, a fortress atop the great rock outcropping called Crag Cavage commanded the one level land route from Dairminster west to the Irish Sea," my *Guide to the Welsh Border Castles* informed me as the train crept out of London into slow, relentless rain.

"Today, devotees of eighteen-century architecture vie for invitations to Dair Manor, the extraordinary Adam country house that rises among vast formal gardens at the foot of the huge crag," the book continued. "For Dair may be seen by invitation only; it has never been deeded to The National Trust."

I had my invitation. A letter from old Mr. Singleton of the auction firm of Singleton Abbs, hand written as required by some code of etiquette remembered from a bygone era, saying simply:

To Whom It May Concern,
This will introduce our representative, Ms. Deborah Guest, who will prepare a preliminary list of the items you wish to auction in the fall.

Yours faithfully,
WALTER SINGLETON

"Ms." was not Mr. Singleton's style, of course, but I had burst into tears at his letter introducing me as Mrs. Gavin Guest. As the train mercifully gathered speed, taking me farther and farther away from London, I realized that I had been divorced from Gavin for three days.

Through fresh tears, I forced myself to read on about the glories of Dair. "Rembrandts, Romneys, Gainsboroughs," my guidebook announced. "Whole rooms furnished with works from Chippendale's own hand. Ceilings carved by Grinling Gibbons, porcelains from the court of Kubla Khan, tapestries and rugs from the France of Madame Pompadour, a golden lion believed to be the work of Cellini . . ."

They would probably have a press conference after the ceremony, I thought, checking my watch to see how much time remained before Cindy Sanders became the second Mrs. Gavin Guest. She would probably wear white satin, as she had at her four previous weddings. I remembered somebody teasing her about that at a party Gavin and I had gone to, and I remembered her shouting back, "White satin goes with me hair and me pearls, love!"

10

"... a celebrated fleet of antique cars ... widely considered the finest private collection of Renaissance sculpture in Britain ... Etruscan antiquities said to outrank the Louvre's ... a library which is occasionally open to scholars. ..."

And a mystery older than the house itself, I thought. Perhaps as old as the ruins of Castle Cavage high on the looming crag behind the white elegance of Dair. Perhaps as old as time.

I looked at my watch again and saw that the end of the world had come. Back there in London, Cindy and Gavin had a headline-making marriage, a thousand friends to toast their future, and a future.

While I, alone in a railroad carriage bound for the Welsh border, had nothing at all.

I was weeping blindly when I felt someone's hand stroking my hair.

"It'll never last," Alaric Meade whispered to me. "I give it six weeks."

"Rick," I began, "didn't you go to the wedding?"

"Attending my own wedding to Cindy was quite enough, thanks."

"Is she going to be dreadful for Gavin?" I remember asking.

"I sincerely hope so," Alaric Meade replied. "Now tell me why we're both on the same train to the wild Welsh mountains."

"I talked Mr. Singleton into sending me to a stately home called Dair Manor. I'm to count the spoons and whatever else they mean to auction off this fall."

"So they're having the auction after all."

"Yes. Had you heard about it before now?"

"Deb, darling, people have been giving odds for and against it since Christmas. It's the battle of the century. I suppose I'll hear of nothing else all weekend."

"Are you going to Dair Manor, too?"

"Oh, I virtually commute. Whenever there are revels at

11

Dair I'm expected to be first to arrive and last to leave, and this weekend there's a very big bash indeed."

"What kind?"

"It's May Day. They get rather picturesque about it. You'll probably find the whole drill fascinating, but I've been through it so often I honestly dread it. Although I will concede that Dair has the best chef in Britain. They pay him a king's ransom, of course."

"You always know everything, Rick. How do you manage it?"

"If I told you, you'd rush right out and start publishing a scandal sheet of your own."

"How dare you describe *Nobility* as a scandal sheet?"

Alaric Meade could always cheer me up in a matter of minutes, and he had often taken the time and trouble to do it. I'd always been grateful and more than a little surprised. When a man is so handsome, one doesn't really expect kindness from him, too. But in addition to his red hair and fine gray eyes, Rick had a smile that always made me think, *That's what sunshine would feel like if they added peppermint.*

And so, less than half an hour after I had noted the world's end, I—Ms. Deborah Guest, Britain's most unwilling thirty-year-old divorcée—was smiling. The tears were now just wet streaks on my face and damp little bumps on the fresh white pages of my guidebook.

"You're not the first woman who has shed tears over Dair," Rick said, closing the guidebook firmly over two sheets of cleansing tissue. "Do you know much about the Cavages, Deb?"

"Only what's in the file at Singleton's."

"That should be rather a lot."

"Oh, it is. But it's mainly about things, not people. I guess all I really know about the Cavage family is that they seem to have their secrets."

"If they do, *Nobility* has failed utterly in its duty to the reading public."

"I mean old secrets, Rick. In the file there's a perfectly bewildering correspondence between somebody at Singleton's and an Oxford undergraduate named Cavage."

"Thaniel Cavage?"

"No. I think his name was William."

"Thaniel's grandfather."

"I suppose so. The letters start in 1914. Who is Thaniel?"

"The present Duke of Dair. Kendra's husband. But you were saying Old Billy Cavage had written Singleton's some baffling stuff."

"Well, yes. I made photocopies of some of it, it was so odd."

"I think I should remind you that I edit a scandal sheet, Deb. Have you got those copies with you?"

"Yes, I do. And I'm sure it's all right for you to see them, since they date back to the First World War."

"Mr. Singleton may not agree, but where are they?"

I pointed to the document case Singleton's had given me, and Rick fetched it down from the baggage rack. I opened it, saying, "First of all, there were lots of old newspaper cuttings that said things like NEXT DUKE WILL TELL ALL."

"I still use that one. It sells another five hundred copies, probably all to immediate families of dukes."

A photocopy of a cutting from *The Daily Mail* of February 6, 1914, stared up at me.

"Here it is again," I said, handing the paper to Rick.

" 'Viscount Mabry, heir apparent to the fourth Duke of Dair and a student at All Souls College, Oxford, today pledged to "make public the full story of the ghost at Dair immediately upon my succession to the title." In conversations with a member of the press, Lord Mabry, who prefers to be known as William Cavage and whose family is as old as the ruined Welsh border castle ...' " Rick mumbled, half aloud.

Looking up, he said, "They always do this, Deb. Every time Daddy's complaining about the bills."

"No doubt they do. But this one still meant it five months later. Look."

I gave him my photocopy of the memo old Mr. Singleton's father had written, on what must have been the first typewriter in London, in July 1914: " 'If there is a secret room, as his young Lordship vows, it is not in Dair Manor, where all exterior measurements match interior measurements exactly, and every inch of cellar and attic space has been explored thoroughly by Ellis and myself. This winter, when His Lordship's father, the Duke, retires to Positano, we are promised a chance to explore and measure the Old Place on the rock.' "

"And the Old Place would be Castle Cavage. Have you ever seen it, Deb?"

"Lived in London all my life, and I've never even toured the Tower."

"Neither have I." Rick laughed. "But I have seen Castle Cavage. You've been to the Edinburgh Festival, of course."

"Of course. Gavin always worked then. Edinburgh's a godsend for performers."

"Well, take the rock Edinburgh Castle stands on. It's almost the size of Gibraltar. Now cantilever that out over a riverbed, so it looks as if there's nothing to hold it up. That's where they built Castle Cavage, starting about a thousand years ago. Of course, they don't live in it anymore. Haven't since they got to be dukes and built themselves something a bit fancier."

"Dair Manor?"

"Yes. It's palatial. But the Old Place is still very much there, looking down on everything. And it's not really a ruin, you know. It's just deserted. I'll try to show it to you when we get there, Kendra permitting."

"Is this the same Kendra I keep reading about in *Nobility*?"

"She may be the only woman in the world named Kendra. It's a combination of her parents' names: Ken and Sandra Pace. From Oklahoma City, by cracky. Kendra. Duchess of

14

Dair. Well, now, did Mr. Singleton ever get inside that secret room?"

I handed him my photocopy of the next document in the file—a letter dated January 1919: " 'My dear Mr. Singleton,' " Rick read. " 'I sincerely regret my inability to permit any further exploration and measurement of these premises at the present time or in the foreseeable future. Signed, William Cavage.' "

Across this letter, someone—was it at Singleton's or at Dair?—had drawn the letter X.

"Is this all you know about the Cavages and their resident ghosts?" Rick asked me. He was no longer smiling.

"Ghosts? I thought Old Billy, as you call him, was going to spill the beans about just one."

"He may only have known about one. I've heard about two."

"Rick, be serious, please. You don't believe in ghosts any more than I do."

"These have some rather distinguished credentials, my dear. They're mentioned in Boswell's *London Journal* and Pepys' *Diary*."

Then, as the wet skies darkened and the west wind hurled torrents against our streaming windows, Alaric Meade told me—as if it were common gossip that every schoolboy knew and only I did not know—something of the strange story surrounding the lords of Dair.

"Cavage is one of the oldest noble houses in Britain," Rick began. "The first knighthood was conferred on them in about 1285."

"Did they do something very heroic?"

"Heavens, no. They were virtually forced to accept knighthood by the Crown, as many landed families were at that time."

"I always thought knighthood was a reward for killing dragons or rescuing damsels in distress."

"Not in the reign of our late King Edward the First. A very efficient executive, even by present-day standards." Rick

15

chuckled. "If you owned property worth more than twenty pounds, he wanted you on his team. So he told you to get yourself a horse if you didn't already have one, and be ready to ride off in the service of the Crown on command. In return, you could call yourself Sir, and hope somebody else would do the same."

My husband of ten years had been married for less than an hour to a film actress with white satin hair, a rope of Oriental pearls that Singleton's had sold her at auction for thirty-three thousand pounds, and an international reputation for near-total stupidity—yet here I was, actually giggling about life in thirteenth-century England.

Hurt, bewilderment and the unbearably clumsy attempts a few friends had made to assure me they were "on my side" lay behind me now in London. The drudgery of cataloguing perhaps thousands of objects, with only my tape measure and tape recorder for company, awaited me at Dair. But what a marvelous interlude Alaric Meade made of the afternoon that carried me from one loneliness to the next.

Rick hadn't always been a magazine editor, raking in a fortune every month by telling the world what celebrities were wearing, eating, chatting about and doing to the insides of their houses. He'd had some poems published when he was at Oxford, then he'd turned his hand to writing plays. Once or twice he'd had a small production by an admiring but impoverished group in North London called the Contemporary Drama Society. Gavin had a part in the second one: quite a good part, with graceful and witty language—and no pay.

About a year later, everything was arranged for an off-Broadway production in New York. Rick and the two young men who were sure they could raise the necessary money were in Manhattan, shopping for the right theater. I had given up my job as shop assistant for an antiques dealer in Belgravia, packed up everything Gavin and I possessed and told our landlord he could have the flat on the first of the month.

Rick's cable arrived on the twenty-seventh: NO SHOW. SORRY. He went to work at *Nobility* a week later.

I was never sure, but I think he lent Gavin money once or twice. I'm almost certain he never wrote another play. I'd read of his marriage to Cindy Sanders and their subsequent divorce. But, aside from meeting him occasionally at the more fashionable auctions at Singleton's, I had been out of touch with Rick for years.

"So the Cavages have been going off to fight for king and country," he continued, "with their suits of armor and their coats of arms for about seven hundred years."

I nodded. My thoughts were beginning to turn to what a staggering amount of furniture one family could accumulate in about seven hundred years, but Rick regained my full attention like a shot.

"And yet in all those seven hundred years—among his other titles, Thaniel's the twenty-sixth Knight of Cavage, so it's twenty-six generations—*not one of the Cavages has ever been killed in battle!*"

His red hair was reflected in the blackness of the rain-drenched window like a bonfire in the night, and a fiery light flickered deep in his gray eyes. *"Not one,"* he said again.

"How very fortunate," I murmured.

"And how seemingly impossible," Rick added, "that one family could go through everything from the last battle of the Crusades to the last gasp of Empire without a casualty."

"The Cavages are the luckiest family I ever heard of," I told him. "They lead charmed lives."

"Exactly so. Charmed lives."

"Do you think there's something supernatural about that?"

"Frankly, yes," Rick answered. "Don't you?"

º   º   º

Old Mr. Singleton hadn't wanted to send me to Dair Manor.

"I know you keep getting foolish little jobs redecorating

17

tea shops and picking up props for fashion photographers and helping—"

"I've been an actor's wife for ten years, Mr. Singleton," I cut in. "I've had to earn every extra penny I could."

"Not any more, though," he snapped.

When I stopped crying he said, "What I mean, Mrs. Guest, is that you're an absolutely first-rate art historian. With the academic background you've had, and your extraordinary ability to remember anything you've seen for even a second, and that extra sense you're blessed with . . ."

"What extra sense?"

"My father had it. I wish I did. He could go to a church fair, spend a few pennies for an old cookery book and find a lost letter from Emily Brontë inside it."

"I've never done anything even remotely like that." I sighed.

"But you have! When all those miserable nineteenth-century Dutch seascapes were unpacked last year, the rest of us just looked at them and groaned. We'd never have known there was a Pieter de Hooch in the lot if you hadn't insisted on taking it to the National Gallery for X-ray."

"Oh, well. I just seemed to—know," I whispered.

"Just like my father. What I'm trying to tell you is, you could become very expert in almost any field. Even if you didn't choose to specialize, you'd still be very valuable to a firm like this. You're really much too talented to spend the next three months emptying old cupboards in the Duchess of Dair's attic. It's work for a clerk."

"That's really all I'm good for, Mr. Singleton. To vanish into an attic with all the other discarded rubbish." I tried to smile. "Who knows? There might be another Emily Brontë letter there."

"Oh, all right," Mr. Singleton grumbled. "Nobody has ever really catalogued what's at Dair. It might as well be you. They've got so much they probably don't know the extent of it themselves."

"Are they going to auction everything?"

"The Duke's letter isn't at all clear on that point. He is retaining us, he says"—Mr. Singleton referred to the brief note scrawled on the white index card imprinted with the single word "Recipe," which had been hand-delivered by a liveried chauffeur the previous day—"to dispose of 'certain of the contents.' So your guess is as good as mine."

"I find it puzzling that he wrote to you on a recipe card," I ventured.

"It's a good deal more puzzling that he wants us to sell for him. As recently as last year he was high bidder on that Hispano-Suiza that turned up in Inverness. Ten thousand pounds spot cash. And, of course, the Duchess buys all sorts of things."

How true, I thought, remembering the watchword in the Goods Received rooms whenever a tiara was going on the block. *"It's almost flashy enough to suit the Duchess of Dair."* I said only, "I didn't realize she had bought anything but jewelry in the past few years."

"Then let's hope jewelry's not what they want to sell. She's much our best customer for that sort of thing."

"I'll find out, Mr. Singleton. And thank you for letting me have my own way about this."

"Oh, nonsense, girl. I hope the job takes your mind off . . ." He paused, embarrassed.

". . . my troubles?" I finished the sentence for him. "It very well might."

"Excellent, then! I'll notify the Duke's solicitors. And, in answer to your question, I have absolutely no idea why he wrote to me on a recipe card. I've known him since he was a lad, but normally one expects the solicitors to arrange a matter like this."

I left him puzzling over the little card and went to look at the file on Dair Manor.

◦   ◦   ◦

19

"No, Thaniel isn't even slightly bonkers," Rick told me, when I mentioned the recipe card. I was belting my trench coat and trying to peer through the rainy darkness at the brilliantly spotlighted shape on the horizon that was fast growing into the great cathedral of Dairminster.

"He's simply the most unpretentious fellow who ever sat in the House of Lords. Unlike his wife, who has a coronet embossed on her toothbrush."

For a moment I wondered how Alaric Meade knew that. Then, deciding it was absolutely none of my business, I concentrated on the onrushing silhouette of the great cathedral which had towered above the banks of the River Dair since about the same time the first Knight of Cavage had ridden off to war. Dairminster Cathedral lived up to all its advance notices. Riveted against the night sky by its lighting, it shivered with life. It is a plain structure, compared to Canterbury or York, but there is a power about it which they do not possess.

I had never seen Dairminster before that stormy evening. But I remember it was so close, as the train squealed to a stop that I could count the stained-glass petals in the great lily window below the central spire. Rain poured from the mouths of the seven-hundred-year-old gargoyles that crouched along its roofline, fell in great swirling pools on the huge paving stones that led from the cathedral's door to the river's edge, glistened, sparkled, rushed to the river in a shining stream.

"Rick!" I must have gasped. "I don't believe it!"

For answer, a shock of red hair came between me and my view of Dairminster. A shoulder clad in rough, sweet-smelling tweed grazed my cheek. Lips light and cool as a butterfly made a surprise landing on my forehead. Rick laughed very softly.

"There will be so many things you don't believe, Milady Deborah. But all of them are true."

A chilly mist of Shropshire air invaded our railway carriage. The train had stopped and someone had opened the door from the station platform.

"Are you the lady from Singleton's?" a voice demanded.

"Yes," I replied, startled to see the figure in the carriage doorway: an expressionless half-grown boy in a very wet, very yellow slicker with a striped golfing umbrella held open behind him. "Who are you?"

"My title is Viscount Mabry," the child replied, gathering up the document case with its Singleton's imprint, "but my real name is Whitwell Cavage. Will you please follow me?"

"Hello, Whit," said Alaric Meade. The boy nodded.

"I would invite you to drive back with us, too, Mr. Meade," he said, "but my mother came after you in another car. She's waiting just outside."

Clutching the satchel that held my jeans, sweaters and tape recorder, I followed the young viscount out into the teeming night. He was barely tall enough to hold his umbrella over my head for the few steps we took, but he spoke like an adult.

"Get in the car quickly, please," he said, swinging open a large, square maroon car door with its window framed in black.

Glancing over my shoulder, I saw a long, light green Jaguar gleaming in the reflected light of the cathedral. Rick had thrown his bags into the boot and was climbing in beside the driver: a woman whose hair glinted bright yellow in the lavishly illuminated early dark.

"Please get in the car," Lord Mabry repeated quietly.

"Yes, milord," I replied, stepping from a wide running board into the back seat. He followed, shutting the great square door before sinking into the curving, velvet-cushioned corner at my right.

The car had gargoyles of its own. Three Welsh corgis stood in a row, glaring at me, their white forepaws firmly planted on the back of the driver's seat like half a dozen rabbit's feet, their aristocratic red fur faces shocked to see a stranger, their pointed red ears on the alert. Two of them barked in cadence; the third carried the melody, baying *"Hal-looooo, hal-loooooo"* until the chauffeur who sat beside them rolled up a dividing window that left the passenger compartment suddenly, completely, quiet. Somewhere a powerful motor started without a sound.

A small, flat light over my head made the compartment a cube of gold that glowed as we sped silently through the night. Inside its golden radiance all the interior walls were paved with microscopically carved ivory. My sodden shoes rested on a quite remarkable silk rug from Isfahan. And on the shimmering expanse of velvet upholstery between the boy and me lay an envelope bearing my name.

II

As I picked up the envelope, my companion spoke.

"This car was built for the last Czar of Russia, but never delivered," he remarked, staring straight ahead to the glass partition where the dogs still stood at attention. Then, speaking into a carved ivory chrysanthemum which hung at his side in a gleaming silver wall bracket: "Please turn off the lights back here, Mr. Grove."

Reluctantly I placed the letter in my briefcase as Grove touched a switch that plunged us into darkness.

"Thank you," I heard the boy tell the chrysanthemum.

"What lovely carving," I said, fighting the velvet silence.

"Mr. Grove says it was all done in China before the First World War. But, as the car wasn't finished until after the war, my great-grandfather got it instead of the Czar."

"Was your great-grandfather also Viscount Mabry?"

"He must have been. If your father is Duke of Dair and you're to become the next Duke, you have to be Viscount Mabry first."

23

"I see," I murmured. I had been met at the station by the heir apparent of Kendra and Thaniel Cavage, who were listed in *Burke's Peerage* as seventh Duke and Duchess of Dair, described in *Nobility* as Ken and Than, and occasionally referred to at Singleton Abbs as His Grace and Her Disgrace. This was Old Billy Cavage's great-grandson.

"How old are you, milord?" I inquired.

"Eleven," he said. "And would you please call me Whitwell? Or Whit?"

"Is it wrong to say milord?"

"My father won't allow it."

Outside, a shining light green fish flashed past us with a splash that sent great fountains playing over all the windows on our right. But inside the passenger compartment constructed for the Czar, we heard only each other's voices.

"That was my mother," my escort observed, "and that's quite a good car, too. It's twice as fast as this one, but it only seats two."

We were slowing down. We were turning sharply to the right. Outside in the torrent someone with a torch opened a tall iron gate and beckoned us to drive through.

The tidal waves Kendra and her passenger, Alaric Meade, had unleashed against our windows had ebbed away. Now, through the rain-dappled glass, I saw a row of great golden lanterns begin to pass in review on both sides of us.

"Is this Dair Manor?" I asked.

"No. It's the way to Esty Hall. Haven't you ever been in this part of England before?"

"Afraid not."

For the first time, Whitwell turned to face me. In the faint lantern light I saw that he was smiling.

"Oh, well, then," he said, "I'll have to tell you what the tour guide says when he brings the people here." His voice changed to a reedy singsong. " 'This A-venoo of Lights, folks, has three hundred brass lanterns, gift of the Sultan of El Vora to the Earl of Esty. This A-venoo of Lights runs from the banks of the River Dair to Esty Hall, home of the Gafford family since the thirteenth century!' "

I laughed, marveling at the lanterns as they seemed to swim past our streaming windows.

"Very good!" I applauded Whitwell. "But aren't we supposed to be going to Dair, home of the Cavage family?"

"This is a shortcut," he assured me. "I'm afraid it's haunted part of the way, but it does save rather a lot of time."

"Whatever makes you say it's haunted?"

"After we get to the last lantern, it's all forest. The man with no hands walks there."

"What man with no hands?"

"They say his name was Crinsley."

"Have you ever seen him?"

"No. We Cavages never see him. By the way, would you please tell me what you would like me to call you?"

"My name is Deborah Guest."

"Then should I say Miss Guest?"

"Just call me Deborah," I sighed.

"Oh." I had embarrassed him. "I do appreciate that, but my father won't allow it."

"Why ever not, if I will?"

"He says when you're eleven you must address everybody with great respect. Especially if they're over twenty-one."

I must look very old, I thought. *And how gauche of me to tell this exceedingly well-brought-up little boy to call me by my first name.*

"Your father is quite right. I'm Mrs. Guest," I said. *Only I'm not anymore,* I added silently.

Other children I have met would have inquired immediately about Mr. Guest, and I braced myself. But Whitwell asked me nothing. I realized with relief that this, too, was something his father would not allow.

"Here's where we turn into the forest, Mrs. Guest. If you look out the back window, you'll see the lights go out."

He was kneeling now, facing backward, watching the great double line of lanterns narrow into a single blazing point of light in the distance. Then suddenly there was only blackness where they had been.

"Diana put them on in your honor," he said, settling back into his seat. "It's far too expensive to use them except on special occasions."

"It must be. But who is Diana? And why is this a special occasion?"

"Diana lives at the Hall. I'm teaching her about cars."

"Then she must have put the lights on in honor of this car."

"No, Mrs. Guest. It's because you're from Singleton's."

"Why should that rate a salute?"

"Well, my father told Diana she could burn all the Sultan's lanterns at his expense the first time an auctioneer was invited inside Dair Manor."

"Oh."

"He swore it would never happen. Mrs. Guest, are you really going to take everything away?"

"I'm only going to make a list of things you don't want anymore."

"Well, my mother doesn't want anything anymore. But my father still wants everything."

"There must be many remarkable things at Dair," I said hastily, embarrassed by the child's candor.

"There are," he replied. "I'll show you."

But young Lord Mabry and I were destined never to reach Dair that stormy night. Perhaps Crinsley arranged it; I would almost believe that now. But no one could possibly have persuaded me of it then. Instead, as we drove through the rainswept forest beyond Esty Hall, I watched the big square window at my side as idly as if it were a television screen. I noted the soundless raindrops coursing the glass like tears, the wet oak leaf that blew against the pane and clung like a shriveled hand. Within arm's length, I saw young trees bent double, their boughs shuddering wildly, strangely silent in what must have been a screaming wind.

Then jagged spears of lightning streaked out of the sky. Suddenly something dealt the ground beneath us a blow so savage it rocked our massive old car over on its two left wheels. There it teetered, like a saucer about to smash, until the wind slammed it back on all fours again.

Bombs, I decided, sprawled on the floor in a thick cocoon of rug, letting the aftershocks die away before I dared to move. *They're bombing the Welsh border. Women and children first.*

"Are you all right, Mrs. Guest?" Whitwell inquired from the cushioned corner exactly opposite the one where he had been sitting.

Climbing back into my seat, I assured him that I was.

"And you?"

"Fine, thank you. But look at Mr. Grove."

Through the glass partition, where Grove's head and shoulders had been silhouetted, I saw only a flurry of frantic white paws scrabbling to rouse a shape slumped over the steering wheel.

Just beyond Grove's inanimate body, in the narrow tunnel of light our headlamps created, lay something monstrous: a tree so big its trunk bulked higher than our roof. It had just fallen. It had just missed us. It was still more alive than dead. Twigs from its outer branches clawed at our windscreen like desperate, drowning fingers.

Whitwell slid to his knees in the deep shadow behind the driver's seat. "They say Crinsley is strong enough to uproot trees," he told me.

I tried the door beside me. The latch retracted smoothly. But leaning against it with all my weight, I could open it only an inch or two before the wind forced it shut again.

"Is there some way to open that glass partition from our side?" I asked.

27

"Yes, that's what I'm trying to find. There's a crank hidden under two shields in this carving."

Instantly I was beside the boy in the darkness, running my hands across the ivory surface of the half-wall out of which rose the glass dividing passenger from chauffeur. My fingers brushed over a bewilderment of small, sharp bas-reliefs. Carved eagles. Imperial crowns. Crenelated towers. Swords. Shields.

Shields. Two of them, side by side. Did they slide apart? Were they hinged? Could I . . .? Yes! They opened like a French door and there was something metallic there that moved at my touch. I knew the partition must be coming down, because I heard a dog baying *"Hal-looo, hal-loooooooo!"*

I reached over the back of the driver's seat to take Grove's pulse, but as I lifted his wrist my own was taken prisoner inside a mouth lined with needles. One of the dogs, holding my arm and hand as if they were a bunch of celery, growled an unmistakable order from the back of its throat: "Don't move."

Is this how Crinsley lost his hands? I wondered. *It's an easy way.*

"Ruffles!" Whitwell shouted from beside me. "No!"

The growling stopped, but the mouth remained firmly clamped shut.

"Let go this minute!" Whitwell was climbing over the back of the seat now. Ruffles opened her mouth and withdrew into the darkness. Where her jaws had been, I was surprised to find, my wrist was not even damp.

"I want to take Mr. Grove's pulse if Ruffles will let me," I told Whitwell.

"Please wait," he said, "until I put all three of them in back." He bent into the corner where Ruffles had vanished, picked her up and deposited her on the floor of the passenger compartment, saying "Stay!"

"Woodbine," he said next, "come here."

In the darkness, a compact little body roused itself from the leather seat beside Grove and pattered over to the child. Instructions were issued, and I felt something fur-covered leap by and land with a joyous swoosh on the velvet seat cushions.

"Stratford!" Whitwell called. A small fur paw placed itself on my motionless hand and stayed there.

"Stratford!" Whitwell repeated sharply.

The paw resting on my hand became two paws.

"He was born in Buck House, so he thinks he's special," Whitwell murmured. "All right, Stratford. Jump!"

A sandpaper tongue licked my thumb. Moving my other hand cautiously, I decided to risk touching Grove's wrist again. Just below his watch, his pulse was steady.

Whitwell lifted the owner of the paws and tongue from my hand and tossed him into the darkness in the rear. "Please climb over now, Mrs. Guest," he said. "Then I'll close this partition again and the corgis won't bother us."

I clambered over a sharp ridge of metal and seated myself on the chauffeur's hard bench.

"How is Mr. Grove?" Whitwell asked, cranking up the glass partition.

"Alive but unconscious. And I'm afraid he has hurt his face."

Leaning across me, the boy bent close to Grove. "I don't think he's bleeding very much," he said matter-of-factly, "but shouldn't we get some help?"

"Indeed we should. But first we must pull him away from the wheel."

Whitwell and I somehow eased the unconscious Grove out of the driver's seat, and I took his place. The engine was still running. The headlamps were still on. We were no more than ten minutes from the Avenue of Lights. But when I looked over my shoulder, the oval rear window seemed no bigger than a cough lozenge. The rearview mirror mounted just outside the chauffeur's door was a black void, streaked with rain. And the gearshift lever I found at my side was a tall brass rod, rooted in invisible mysteries under the floorboards. How was I to back this mammoth piece of machinery out of this stormswept wilderness?

Until that moment, my only experience of cars had been the frisky little MG Gavin and I had bought on our first anniversary and taken three years to pay for. In London and the provinces, I had dutifully driven it to the stage entrance of every theater Gavin ever played in before the conclusion of every performance Gavin ever gave. But in the past few months I hadn't touched it, because—in every sense of the word—Gavin had flown. To Switzerland, then Morocco, then Peru, then Guam. To make his first film. With Cindy Sanders.

Stop crying and shift into reverse! I commanded myself and stepped on the Czar's stately clutch pedal, but not hard enough. I bore down on it, and it yielded slightly. But not until my leg muscles were quivering with strain could I force the pedal to the floor. Uncertain how long I could keep it there, I seized the handle on the gearshift lever, trying to pull it toward me. It wouldn't budge.

"Let me hold the clutch pedal down for you," Whitwell said, slipping to the floor. "Then push the gear lever away from you."

"Whitwell, I think you've got it just backwards."

"Mrs. Guest, on this car it *is* just backwards," he told me from the darkness under the steering wheel, where he was holding the pedal down with one hand on either side of my foot. I pushed the gear lever as he directed. It resisted me every inch of the way, but it moved.

"That's enough," the boy said. "You're in neutral."

The Czar's compartment had been soundproof; the chauffeur's was not. All around us I heard ancient trees groaning in the merciless wind. Were they mourning for their fallen comrade and vowing to join him in death? I had to get away from this place. I lacked the strength, but I had to get away at once.

30

"Now what?" I asked Whitwell.

"Take the gear lever to your right," the boy said. "Then push it as far forward as it will go. I'd do it myself, Mrs. Guest, but I still can't quite reach the pedals when I'm in the seat."

If Crinsley is strong enough to push trees over, I thought, *maybe I ought to ask him to lend a hand with this.* I was starting to giggle at the thought that a hand was exactly what Crinsley couldn't lend me when I remembered that the only time in my life I'd ever been hysterical had begun with giggles I couldn't stop at words I didn't find the least bit funny. I could still hear them; maybe I always would: "For a long time, Deborah, I've wanted to start life over . . ."

The brass stick was stubborn, but it was advancing toward the dashboard. After about twelve inches it stopped.

"I think that looks about right," Whitwell said from the floor. "Shall I operate the petrol and the brake for you?"

"Just the brake, please," I said, returning from London, leaving the anguished laughter there in my empty flat.

"All right." And he guided my right foot to another pedal. "When you're ready to back the car, step on this. When you want to stop, say so and I'll work the brake. And Mrs. Guest, I think you'd better go slow."

I nodded, and we began to creep backward into the stormy darkness. Bits of gravel flicked up, playing a nasty little pizzicato against the old car's sides as we ground cautiously, blindly back from the fresh-killed tree.

"My father will be very cross about all this," Whitwell told me, still crouched on the floorboards in his shiny slicker. "He didn't know I was going to ride to meet you with Mr. Grove. And he didn't say we could take this car. And he didn't realize we'd come this route so Diana could burn the Sultan's lanterns. And he'll wonder where we are, won't he?"

"I'm sure he won't think of anything except that Mr. Grove has hurt himself."

"If the car's scratched, he won't like that, either."

If another tree blows over and stoves in the roof, he'll

31

probably be downright peeved, I reflected, my neck aching from the strain of trying to see what lay behind us. *He'll also be minus one son, one chauffeur and three dogs who think Buckingham Palace is a lying-in hospital. As well as the ex-wife of the actor about whom an American film critic recently said: "Guest's good looks are almost as tedious as his awareness of them."*

Gavin's reaction to that description had more than prepared me for anything Whitwell's father, the seventh Duke of Dair, might be able to offer in the way of mindless rage. Or so I thought as I continued inching the limousine back to the beginning of the path.

o   o   o

The gravel suddenly ended, and our rear wheels rolled into a sickening thickness of mud.

Telling Whitwell to brake, I quickly put one arm in front of Grove to keep him from pitching forward. The stop was surprisingly smooth. What made me jump so suddenly was a voice I had never heard before. It was a man's voice, deep enough to sing Boris Godunov, and it was right beside me.

"Thank you very much, miss," it said.

"How are you, Mr. Grove?" Whitwell inquired from his post beside the brake pedal. "Do you think you broke your nose again?"

"Just a bit headachey, lad. A dent in the forehead is all."

"Did you see Crinsley?"

"Now you haven't been telling the young lady about Crinsley, I hope. That's a foolish story the old people believe, and you're not supposed to know a thing about it. Tell me, was I blacked out for long?"

"Quite a while, yes. Mrs. Guest backed the car all the way here from the tree, but now we've run the back wheels off the path."

"I'll have a look," Grove boomed, opening the door beside him as easily as if there were no wind. He stepped outside,

32

circled the car quickly and appeared at the door just at my elbow. There was a dark smear on his face, and I looked away.

Opening the door, he said, "This is the end of the bridle path. If you'll just move over, miss, I'll swing us around on to the Avenue of Lights straightaway."

❀   ❀   ❀

I shall never forget my first sight of Esty Hall.

The Czar's limousine roared through a surrealist landscape, past shuddering trees and deserted stables, across the narrow drawbridge over a moat, into a narrow courtyard with shining wet cobblestones, on to giant double doors set into the base of a huge round tower.

Could anyone hear our horn in this howling gale?

Someone could. The great doors swung open for us, and Grove drove through them into a firelit room that seemed vast beyond imagining. Rembrandt might have painted the scene: intense light reaching out from a high, hooded fireplace to probe the depths of an enormous cavern. The paneled walls looked almost black as we glided across the worn stone floor, stopping when at last we reached a massive flight of steps half lost in shadow.

"This can't be the garage," I breathed.

"No, not exactly," Whitwell told me. "However, when they still kept horses here, the Earl of Esty used to ride right up these steps to his bedroom door."

A woman with a round, red face and severely overpermanented white hair hurried down the steps to meet us. As we straggled out of the limousine, three people all very much the worse for wear, she dealt with us in strict order of rank and precedence. A glance sufficed for Grove and the streak of dried blood that ran from his forehead to his jaw.

"Excuse me," he muttered, stalking into the shadows. "I must ring up Dair at once."

She did not answer. Instead, placing a solicitous palm on

33

Whitwell's forehead, she cooed, "Oh, milord, you're frozen."

"I'm fine, thank you, Mrs. Travis," Whitwell said. "Is Diana about?"

"Watching the telly, most likely." Mrs. Travis sniffed. "Sit here by the fire, milord."

Whitwell stood his ground. "Mrs. Guest, this is Mrs. Travis," he said. "And please, Mrs. Travis, won't you call me Whitwell? Or Whit?"

"Yes, milord."

"Then why don't you do it, Travis?" a fluting young voice inquired. "Stop calling him milord."

I have never seen a little girl so beautiful. There is a Gainsborough drawing of Lady Hamilton that I have always admired; in another five or six years this child would resemble it. Now she was perhaps ten, a water sprite with a tangle of dark curls, who stood just at the edge of the firelight in a long, checkered dressing gown. Was this Diana?

"Come here, Whit," Grove called from an open door cut into the dark paneling. "Your father wants a word with you."

The boy darted away and the door swung shut behind him.

"Good evening," the water sprite said to me. "Are you the auctioneer?"

"I work for him," I told her. "Thank you for turning on the Avenue of Lights for Whitwell and Mr. Grove and me."

"Whitwell?" The eyes that tried to stare me down were large as a cat's, but of a clear, unchanging gray. "Do you mean Lord Mabry?"

I replied rather too slowly, as if I were reading aloud from an unfamiliar script to help Gavin learn his lines. "Lord Mabry has asked me, as he has just asked Mrs. Travis, to call him by his first name," I enunciated.

"That is very different from *referring* to him by his first name, isn't it?" the water sprite replied.

Whoever Diana was, she had apparently learned etiquette from the same teacher who had trained Marie Antoinette.

"Mrs. Travis," I heard myself saying in the low, controlled tones of an actress, "where is the ladies' room?"

34

* * *

The tourists' lounge in the cellar of Esty Hall compared favorably with its counterparts at Heathrow Airport, but was somewhat larger. Emerging from the ladies' room, I took a moment to look around. I was in an immense empty cafeteria where a sign reading SOUVENIRS AND POSTAL CARDS SOLD HERE confronted me under the single globe Mrs. Travis had lighted.

The sign hung on a wall of formidable Norman stonework that climbed some twenty feet, then curved into a fine barrel-vaulted ceiling. Eleventh century, I felt certain, built to fortify the wild Welsh border by order of the Conqueror himself. Thus, if Whitwell's imitation of the tour guide had been accurate, Esty Hall had been standing for almost two hundred years before the Gafford family took possession of it.

"Would you like a sweet?" A small voice interrupted the mental arithmetic I had been doing. "I know how to open the vending machine."

Her dressing gown was out at the elbows, but it would unquestionably require Gainsborough to do justice to her face,

"I think not, thank you," I replied.

"Oh, you're angry. I really shouldn't have corrected you in my own home."

"Nor in anyone else's."

She removed two small chocolate bars from the machine, slammed it shut and, stowing one of her stolen sweets in a dressing gown pocket, fell to unwrapping the other. "The thing is," she told me, "I'm never sure what's rude until after I've made someone cross."

"Indeed. How do we get upstairs from here?" I asked her.

"This way." She led me into a vaulted passageway built on a steep incline centuries before by men who had needed to roll endless kegs of provisions into the old hall's storerooms against the endless threat of siege and starvation. "You see,

35

Whit's father always tells him exactly what he should say, but Whit's grandmother always tells me it's not the right thing at all."

Following her up the cold stone ramp, I saw that she was barefoot. "What do your parents say is right?" I inquired.

"I haven't any parents. Didn't you know?"

"No, I didn't. I'm very sorry."

"Can't be helped." She shrugged.

I knew no answer to that. I waited for her to say more.

"You haven't had supper, have you?" The silvery little voice was kind.

"No," I admitted, suddenly feeling like a child myself.

"It's supper time now," she said. "We're going to have cake."

"You ought to have carpet slippers."

"Oh, do stop talking like a blasted nanny!"

"You also ought to have a nanny."

"I would if they had any smart ones."

"Are you sure the smart ones would bother with you?"

We had reached an enormous oaken door. It swung open like silk as Diana touched it. She turned to me with a graceful wave of one chocolate-smeared hand and the faintest inclination of her head.

"Please come in," she said.

I preceded her into a low, raftered room that had been old when the first Elizabeth was young. A rosy fire crackled on a Delft-tiled hearth, and a round, damask-covered table was set before it. Whitwell leaped to his feet as we entered.

Alaric Meade was already standing, carving a joint of beef as imperturbably as if he were the Earl of Esty.

"It's Mr. Meade!" Diana squealed, rushing to his side. "I told Whit you'd come back this weekend! And you did, you did!" She was jumping up and down with delight.

Rick put down the carving things, gathered her up with a swoop and held her tight. His face wore an expression I had never seen there before: infinitely tender, inexpressibly sad. And as easy to read as a neon sign.

36

He's her father, I read. *Why does she think she doesn't have one?*

"Certainly I did," he bantered. "I've never seen a real moat overflow, and tonight looked like my big chance."

He set her down as gently as if she were a bit of Sèvres, and she slipped into the chair at his right without ever taking her eyes off him.

"Where is Mrs. Guest to sit tonight?" he prompted her.

"Oh, over there," she said airily. "Please do be seated, Mrs. Guest."

The empty chair between Rick and Whitwell was burl walnut, Queen Anne, and the tenth of a set Mr. Singleton had been trying for years to assemble. I took it as a good omen that Diana offered it to me.

"We meet again." I smiled at Rick. He still wore the sweet-smelling tweed jacket. "What a pleasant surprise."

"You've had quite a detour." He smiled back, resuming his carving.

"How true. The biggest oak tree I've ever seen decided to fall in our path rather suddenly."

"They drove right into the Barons' Hall," Diana bubbled, reclaiming his attention. "Sounding the horn, *beep, beep, beep!* Right through the carriage doors! You should have seen them, Mr. Meade! It was grand."

Rick handed me a serving of meat on a dinner plate such as Stoke-on-Trent produces every day for hospitals and hotels: grayish crockery with a single dull green line. "Then I take it the road back to Dair Manor is blocked," he said, with perceptible lack of regret. "And I've borrowed the Duchess's car while she dresses for dinner. Of course, that won't be served until eleven, but perhaps I'd better ring up now and tell them I can't get back. Excuse me for a moment."

He slipped out the doorway before I could say a word about the shortcut through the forest beyond the Avenue of Lights.

"We weren't on the road, were we, Whitwell?" I asked.

37

I was seeing the boy for the first time now without his slicker and sou'wester hat. Blue-black hair, skin like milk, a proud little profile. And absolutely no visible clue to his thoughts.

"No," he acknowledged. "We were in Crinsley's Wood."

"What's that?" Diana asked.

"Oh, nothing." I saw him glance at her quickly. Then his gaze returned to his plate.

"You said somebody's wood."

"Mmmmm. It's just what some of the old people call the forest where your bridle path used to be."

"Why?"

"I'm not sure."

He's not supposed to know about Crinsley, I remembered. *And she actually doesn't know. Good thing, too; it's such nonsense.*

I changed the subject.

"Have you spoken to your father?" I asked him.

Under his cable-stitched blue sweater, he squirmed, but his face remained closed. "Yes. He said you and Mr. Grove and I are to stay here tonight."

"Your mother said much the same thing to me just now," Rick announced, resuming his place between Diana and me. "In no uncertain terms."

"What fun!" Diana exulted. "I love it when people come to spend the night. I've never done it, you know," she informed me.

"Done what?"

"Spent the night anywhere but here. Whit, sometime may I stay overnight at Dair?"

For one electric moment, terror sat at our dinner table, a dark presence in Alaric Meade's gray eyes.

"I suppose you could," Whitwell answered.

"When?"

Rick spoke as if the matter were all in jest. "Diana, surely you realize that no unchaperoned lady ever stays under a

38

gentleman's roof overnight. It's out of the question until you have a governess again."

The jest was lost on Diana. "I don't want a governess!" she said. "I want to spend the night at Dair!"

"And so you shall," Rick assured her, sensing a tantrum in the making, speaking swiftly to head it off. "But it can't possibly be tonight, now can it? The road to Dair is blocked."

Something, I may never know what, told me not to set him straight about that. Was it because, like Whitwell, I did not want to reopen the subject of Crinsley's Wood? Or because, like Diana, I wanted Rick to remain at Esty Hall? Or was I just worn out from my travels?

Whatever my reasons were, I said nothing.

All of our futures might have been different if I had.

◦   ◦   ◦

Food, wine and firelight had gone to my head. My words had acquired what Gavin always called "an ominously educational tone." I knew it. Still, I chattered on.

"You'd be surprised," I was saying, "how names can get twisted up as the centuries go by. I'm reminded of the Elephant and Castle."

"What's that?" Diana asked, her mouth full of cake.

"An inn. In London."

"Why does it have such a funny name?"

"People could never pronounce its real one."

"What was its real one?"

"The Infanta of Castile."

"Why don't we go into the library now?" Rick suggested, rising from his chair.

"Good," said Diana. "I'll race you there." She sped from the room with Whitwell right behind her. I put my gigantic damask napkin on the table, noticing for the first time the elaborate crest embroidered on one frayed corner.

39

"How did you get away from the big bash at Dair with such blinding speed?" I asked Rick.

"Frankly, I fled. I always do. Kendra briefed me on the guest list in the car, and as usual she's invited the riffraff of the world. Of course, in my line of work one gets used to riffraff. What I can't get used to are those damned dinners at eleven. I come over here in the evenings because they give me a square meal at a civilized hour."

With your daughter, I thought. *Am I the only one who realizes that little girl is your daughter?*

"How do you explain it to the Duke and Duchess?"

"My dear," Rick laughed, "Thaniel is the sort who doesn't ask for explanations, and Kendra is the sort who doesn't believe them, so I've never said much of anything at all. Now come along to the library."

Rick took my arm and we strolled into a magnificently paneled passageway.

The first face I saw there stunned me into silence. It had been painted on a square of wood some seven hundred years earlier, but its dark eyes still blazed with undiminished arrogance and its elegant long neck had never bent under the weight of five strands of pearls. I read the engraved metal plaque set into the frame and shivered. It said:

ELEANORA REGINA
1254-1290

"Speak of the devil, Deb." Rick was amused.

"Yes, this really is spooky. Here I've just given my celebrated lecture on how the Elephant and Castle got its name, and the first painting I see is Eleanor of Castile herself."

"The thirteenth century isn't entirely over around here," Rick replied.

"So I see. Wasn't Eleanor of Castile the wife of that king you were telling me about on the train this afternoon?"

"Edward the First. That's right," Rick said, leading me on toward the library wing. "Depend on him to marry a rich woman."

"But why would her portrait hang here?" I asked.

"I daresay she was a good friend of the Gafford family. The first Earl of Esty—a chap named Rufus Gafford—was always a particular crony of her husband's. Made it pay, too."

"Didn't he, though!" I marveled, as we passed a long, gleaming honor guard of armored figures seated astride their armored mounts. In the distance a clatter of running feet on oaken floors heralded the return of Whitwell and Diana.

"Yes," Rick continued, as Whitwell flashed by, "they rode off to the Crusades together before Edward became king. When he succeeded to the throne, he made Gafford an earl and gave him this castle and God only knows what else. It's all documented in their library if you're really interested."

"Tonight," Diana announced, arriving at Rick's side breathless, "I want Mrs. Guest to sleep in our Spanish Bedroom."

"I'd be overjoyed to sleep anywhere," I told her. "And soon."

"Then come with me."

Rick stopped her. "Diana, please ring for somebody first. You don't know which bedrooms they got ready."

Diana stared at him coolly. "Why, Mr. Meade," she said, "I am going to *tell* them to get the Spanish Bedroom ready."

"Then you'll have to ring, won't you?" Rick replied. "And when you do, I'd like to beg a bed for myself."

"Of course!" Diana said grandly, tugging at a petitpoint bellpull. To do the magnificence of her gesture justice, a footman in livery and a powdered wig should have arrived instantly. Instead, we waited for Augusta. She was plump, cross, distinctly slatternly and carrying a battery-powered camper's lantern, when she appeared at last.

"Augusta—" Diana began.

"—will you please show Mrs. Guest to her room?" Rick finished. "Good night, Deb." Behind his smile, I saw he was as tired as I.

I left him with Diana and Whit and let Augusta and her

41

piercing lantern lead me up a steep wooden staircase to a spacious landing where two more of Mr. Singleton's long-sought Queen Anne chairs flanked a mullioned window.

Then I followed Augusta along a corridor where tapestries depicting the Beowulf legend hung silently side by side for what seemed like five miles. At last we reached a tall, arching door, and she shone the lantern into a maze of gilt and mirrors, damask and marble, bronze goddesses and velvet banquettes. This was emphatically not the Spanish Bedroom. Some earlier Esty had brought this decor home from the Paris of Offenbach and Degas, where demi-mondaines frolicked at Maxim's. *Who ever heard of a bordello surrounded by a moat?* I wondered, as I followed Augusta inside.

"I'd of lit the fire," she whined, "but how was I to know you'd go to bed straight from the dinner table? Nobody knows what's what here anymore."

She busied herself with matches and kindling, and I looked inside a huge armoire. There, looking absurdly small, hung my trench coat. I put it on gratefully.

Despite the thickness of its carpets, the room was bitterly damp and cold.

If I were at Dair, I'd have two ghosts to worry about, I thought wryly. *Rick didn't mention any here at Esty Hall.*

"...what comes of having children inheriting a great house like this one," Augusta's lament continued as she rose from the hearth and proceeded to light the lamps. "If you'd of told me when I first come here thirty years ago that I'd be cleaning up after tourists twice a week, and most of them foreigners at that . . . ."

A stray reflection, lamplight multiplied by mirrors many times, bounced off something on the floor of the armoire. My document case.

"Thank you, Augusta," I interrupted, carrying the case to a tufted armchair by the fire.

"And who'm I working for now? They laugh when I tell 'em the Countess of Esty."

I thanked Augusta again and unfastened the case.

"It's no fault of hers she's only ten years old," Augusta continued. "She wouldn't be Countess if her parents had of lived, now would she?"

"No," I said, truly surprised. Tired as I was, I had not understood that Diana, who had no slippers, no governess and no parents that she knew of, bore a title almost as old as the eleventh-century fortress that was sheltering me tonight. Diana, Countess of Esty. Age ten. How very strange. How very sad.

"Dead and gone, both of them. Before she cut her first tooth," Augusta told me, turning down the covers on a mammoth gilded bed. "And very strange it was on both occasions."

She was about to tell me how Diana's parents had died, and I knew I didn't want to hear. Not with the storm still rattling the windows. Not when I had to face the rest of the night alone.

"Please don't tell me any more, Augusta. Please. Not tonight."

She picked up her lantern, swung angrily around and marched out, leaving the door not quite closed behind her.

Cursing her silently, I grabbed a lamp and, holding it high, walked some thirty feet into shadow to shut the door. I had my hand outstretched to touch it when I realized it was moving. Someone in the corridor was cautiously pushing it open. Only there was no hand on the doorknob and no face confronting mine. I watched it slowly open wider and wider. Then I was sure. There was absolutely nothing between me and the empty corridor except thin air.

I really should scream now, I thought, as something touched my foot. Instead, with the crazy calm of the doomed, I looked down. Looking back at me from somewhere well below knee level, eyes shining in the lamplight like a pair of marquise diamonds, stood a resolute little corgi. The thing resting on my foot, I realized, was a small paw.

"Stratford?" I whispered.

The dog continued to gaze up at me intently, his expression strongly suggesting that he could have answered me but considered it beneath his dignity to do so. In spite of everything, I had to laugh.

"Let's shut this wretched door," I told him, slamming it, "and I'll race you back to the fire."

He won, but graciously made room for me in the tufted chair. Settling myself beside him, I placed the lamp on a little marble-topped table at my elbow and took one exhausted moment to remind myself that tonight I must not think of Gavin.

But how could Gavin find me if he needed me? I was supposed to be at Dair, not Esty Hall.

Desperate to escape from the numbing knowledge that Gavin no longer needed me for anything at all, I reached inside my document case and pulled out the letter that had been waiting for me since I first stepped inside the limousine built for the Czar.

III

Inside the envelope I found a single sheet of paper that unfolded silently as snow, revealing a few jagged lines of the bold handwriting I had last seen on the little recipe card in Mr. Singleton's office.

Ms. Guest,

For the moment, please assume that everything in Dair Manor is to be sold.

This includes the contents of the gatehouses, harper's cottage, etc. The cars in the former carriage house will also be auctioned, but I think Singleton's had best send an automotive expert to discuss those with me. However, you are welcome to look at them if you wish.

I must ask you not to enter Castle Cavage, the old building on top of the crag, for any reason. It is unsafe.

I trust it will be possible for us to meet at some point during your stay.

T. CAVAGE

I would have to forward this to Mr. Singleton by the very next post, I thought, as I sank into the feathery depths of the vast Second Empire bed and felt the little dog land lightly on the comforter at my feet. True, I had badgered Mr. Singleton into giving me this assignment. But how could one person even begin to inventory all the household goods of the Dukes of Dair? What on earth was a harper's cottage? And why was Castle Cavage "unsafe"?

Hoping these questions would answer themselves in time, I fell asleep.

o   o   o

Someone had washed Diana's hair, starched her organdy dress to the crispness of a potato chip and prevailed on her to wear white shoes. She stood in a pool of sunshine on the landing as I came downstairs.

"How splendid you look this morning!" I greeted her.

"It's just because I have to be glimpsed."

"Have to be what?"

"Glimpsed. If you march round with Hookham and the tourists today, you'll catch sight of me. Of course, I'm not supposed to know anyone's looking."

"I'm afraid I haven't time for the tour, Diana. I should have been at Dair last night."

"Oh, but you do have time, Mrs. Guest! Whitwell and Grove drove back to Dair very early, but Mr. Meade's still here. When he wakes up, I'm sure he'll drive you there. Maybe I can come with you, if you don't mind my sitting in your lap. We haven't a car to spare here today. Travis just went to the hairdresser."

I hadn't realized they were that strapped at Esty Hall. Only one car. No more horses. Cafeteria crockery on the table. And the little countess pressed into performing twice a week for an audience that paid a quarter-pound a head to

46

take a guided tour of her home. Exploiting an orphan, that's what it was.

"Tell me, Diana, do you mind being—glimpsed?"

"Not really. Hookham gives me chocolates when I do it, and filthy old Travis gives me hell when I don't."

"What do you do?"

Gainsborough would have known how to capture the amusement that welled up in the child's eyes. "You'll see," she told me, and darted away.

And so, having nothing else to do until Rick got up, I walked down the incline into the barrel-vaulted cellar where the tourists stood yawning over empty cups of breakfast tea.

Tough audience today, I decided immediately. *Especially for someone aged ten.* I took my place between a trio of Oriental schoolboys and two massive women in rumpled saris. Behind me, an American voice drawled, "Joe Bob, go get my sweater off the bus. It's cold here. All this stone." Just ahead of me, two bearded young men in khaki shirts and lederhosen studied a guidebook printed in German.

"Why did a sultan give this house so great a gift?" I heard one ask the other. The other shrugged, then referred the question to a little bantam cock of a man in a checked waistcoat and tweed hacking jacket, who stood leaning against the souvenir stand.

"Why was the Avenue of Lights given here, if you please, Mr. Hookham?"

The little man came to life as if he had just been plugged into an electrical socket. "Ah, you haven't read your history of the Malay States, have you?" he parried, batting his eyelashes and flashing his dimples. "The little Countess of Esty's great-grandfather was out there many a time. Quite a hero he was. Handsome. Dashing. All the ladies loved him. And he was quite a horseman, too. They say the Sultan traded him the lanterns for a certain Irish hunter."

That must have been the Lord Esty who rode horses

47

upstairs to his bedroom door, I reflected. *I wish they had some coffee here.*

"I should have told you to bring more flashbulbs, too," the voice behind me said to the returning Joe Bob.

"Hey, let's get this show on the road," Joe Bob replied.

"Right you are, sir!" said our tweedy little guide, his fists moving happily through the motions of shadow-boxing, his smile the indestructible smile of the song-and-dance man.

Off we went.

One of the suits of armor dated from the last battle of the Crusades. "When was that?" asked one of the lederhosens.

"The year of Our Lord twelve-ninety-one Anno Domineye!" Mr. Hookham sang out, disappearing around a corner in the paneled passageway. Before any of us could follow him, he was back: face registering intense excitement, hands motioning us all to stand still and keep quiet.

"Something very unusual has happened," he whispered to us. "You're going to see the little Countess herself!"

"Ooooh, Joe Bob!"

"Hush!" Mr. Hookham commanded sternly, waiting for silence. Then very slowly, he mouthed these portentous words for us: "She has left the doors to the morning room ajar!"

Holding a finger to his lips with one hand, beckoning us on with the other, he tiptoed around the corner. The floors creaked as we tiptoed after him.

Diana sat at a piano about sixty feet away, showing us her right profile and her musicianship. The notes were Papa Haydn's simplest for beginners; the dying-swan hands were Diana's own. A flashbulb exploded behind me. One of the Oriental boys turned in surprise, then elbowed the boy beside him. They both went into a fit of silent laughter. Thereafter, Mrs. Joe Bob's camera held its fire.

I ached for the tour party to move on, but Hookham kept us standing there, staring at the sideshow.

"Most sweet," murmured one of the saris.

While not the worst director I could think of, Mr. Hookham was sadly predictable. Diana concluded her musical interlude exactly as I had feared. Rising from the piano bench, she strolled dreamily to the windows, pausing only to remove a daffodil from a vase. Holding the flower to her cheek, she stood staring into the distance, oblivious to our presence as Hookham signaled us all to follow him away on tiptoe over the creaking floor.

Round the first corner, Hookham turned and grinned. "You're very, very lucky people, you are, to catch that glimpse of the little Countess. Only saw her myself once before, and I've been here twice a week for the past ten years. Well, you can thank me, Jack Hookham, for letting you look. I'd lose this job if they knew I'd let you watch her—let alone take her picture, ma'am. I didn't know you'd do that, ma'am. I oughta take the film away from you, ma'am."

"You give him some money, Joe Bob," the voice behind me said. "This is a very rare picture, and I want it."

"Don't worry, honey," Joe Bob answered.

"And now let's see the famous Archer's Tower," Hookham said.

o   o   o

Kendra's green flying-fish of a car raced along the banks of the River Dair. Perched in my lap, Diana discussed the difficulties of the Haydn piano repertoire with Rick. I watched the great central spire of Dairminster Cathedral reflect the noon sunshine like a jeweled dagger thrust into the sky.

Far ahead, an enormous ax hung silhouetted over the river's swift current, as if awaiting orders to attack the opposite bank. The handle was stout and knobby. The blade faced up, a black monolith threatening the fleecy clouds.

"That's Castle Cavage," Rick told me. "All you see from

49

here is the rock spur and the castle at the tip of it, but when we get a bit closer you'll see Crag Cavage itself."

The crag jutted up from the river's edge to a startling height, but there was a gray seam running all the way up: a thin trail dodging between the boulders, finally disappearing into a small, graceless doorway cut into the wall of the hulking fortress at the end of the rocky ax handle.

I was glad I'd been forbidden to go inside.

"Now you know what they mean when they say Stone Age," Rick remarked, signaling that he meant to turn.

"Is it that old?"

"Easily. I suspect Cavages lived up there when they were still apes. But now, Milady Deborah, prepare to enter something a bit more civilized." And hand-over-handing the steering wheel, he turned into a narrow lane in the dense forests at the base of the crag and stopped in front of an ancient stone cottage.

"This is not," he continued, taking out his billfold, "the birthplace of the Brothers Grimm, though it looks that way. This is the west gatehouse of the Duke of Dair, and the gatekeeper—ah, here he is!"

A man in a duck-billed çotton cap had come to my side of the car. His eyes were in shadow, but I felt them on me.

"Morning, Your Ladyship," he said.

Where had Diana learned that regal method of lowering her eyelids instead of her head, holding her eyes shut just long enough to say "How do you do?," then opening them already directed to what the next moment would bring? This was the sort of virtuoso receiving-line technique I thought had died with the Dowager Queen Mary.

"We expected you last night, Mr. Meade," the gatekeeper said.

"Yes. But then that tree fell across the road. I see they've removed it now. Quick work."

The gatekeeper was silent, but I felt his eyes on me again.

Rick handed me a folded slip of paper. "This lady was also detained at Esty Hall last night," he said. "Give him that

50

piece of paper, please, Deb. It's your ticket of admission. Grove was to have given it to you last night."

I handed over the paper. The gatekeeper unfolded it, and I saw T. Cavage's jagged handwriting again, this time upside down.

"Pleased to meet you, Miz Guest," the gatekeeper said. "That'll be all right then, Mr. Meade, thank you." And he strode away out of sight behind the neat rustic cottage. The car crept around the corner after him, completing its turn just as he flung open a pair of iron gates so fantastically intricate they must have been copied from a length of black lace. We glided through them, and there was no more forest. This was a broad driveway lined on either side with trees so old their branches mingled overhead, creating astonishing patterns of sunlight and shadow below. Between the precisely spaced tree trunks on either side, I saw an infinity of green lawn sparkling in the noon glare. A herd of deer darted for cover as we passed. A marble nymph on a pedestal ignored us and continued gazing at her reflection in a pool blue as the sky. Then the driveway began to twist and turn, making a slow descent in a series of graceful curves. We plunged beyond the trees into open sunlight, and the white radiance of Dair took us in its arms.

From pictures in my guidebook, I had expected the great house to look at its visitors for a long time from a great distance before making them welcome, but Dair Manor hides till the last possible instant. There is no time to think about what makes it so beautiful, only a moment when its beauty bursts upon you. Then its curving colonnades surround you in an embrace from which only a few ever escape.

I know.

o   o   o

"And this is my room," Whitwell said, leading me between a pair of Ionic pilasters that one of his ancestors had caused to be dredged from the bed of the Tiber River and

51

installed in the west wing at Dair. *How much more splendor can I handle today?* I asked myself, stepping through immense double doors to see what priceless objects had been chosen from Dair's seemingly inexhaustible supply for the future Duke's use and enjoyment.

Against the wall at my left, I saw a brass bed, a small bookcase painted blue and a battered Victorian chest of drawers. On my right, two chintz-covered chairs faced each other across the hearth. Straight ahead, a metal bridge table held a gooseneck lamp beneath two framed documents hanging side by side on the wall.

Under this table was a wicker basket containing an old bath towel and a red rubber bone.

There was nothing else, except what Robert Adam had put there over two hundred years before: the perfect proportions, the tall windows built to catch every last ray of north light, the white wedding cake of a chimney piece, the sandalwood inlay in the ebony floor.

"I see you're noticing that I have no telly." Whitwell sighed. "Well, I did have, but my father says I can't have it back until I get through Caesar's *Commentaries.*"

"I never studied Latin, I'm sorry to say," I told him.

"You didn't miss much."

"Are these written in Latin?" I asked, bending over the metal table to look at the two framed documents.

"Yes," he said, proudly coming over to read them to me. "Can you guess what they are?"

"Well, let's see. All I can read are the people's names. They're not Latin. Jaymes Cavage . . ."

"He was the first Cavage to be knighted, Dr. Darsey says."

"Who is Dr. Darsey?"

"My grandmother's doctor. You're sure to see him. He comes here almost every day. A very fat gentleman with white hair."

"And who is Anne Gafford?" I read from the old document hanging on the left.

"A girl Jaymes Cavage didn't marry. At least, it doesn't look that way. You see, Mrs. Guest, these are both marriage contracts. The girl's family wrote down everything they'd give the boy if he'd marry the girl. In this one, they offer him three cows and a sheep and some lambs. But I guess that wasn't enough. Because down here at the bottom, somebody named Gafford signed it. But nobody named Cavage signed it."

"Isn't this a signature here?" I asked, pointing to the very bottom of the document. "It seems to say Cordel."

"Yes, he signed both of them, of course."

"Who did?"

"Saint Charles de Cordel. He was the Archbishop of Dair then."

"When?"

Whitwell did Hookham's singsong superbly. "The year of Our Lord twelve-hundred and ninety Anno Domin-eye," he replied.

"Well, Mr. Hookham," I said, "sometimes I can read Roman numerals myself. This one's—one thousand, two hundred and—"

"—ninety-four Anno Domin-eye!"

"But it says Gwyneth Gafford, not Anne."

"Yes, and it offers a good bit more. Twenty gold pieces and four cows and four sheep and—whatever this word means. But it still wasn't enough. Jaymes Cavage didn't sign it."

"Some men are very hard to please. I'm sure you have some studying to do now, Whitwell, so let me be on my way. And thank you for showing me so much of the west wing. It is even more beautiful than I had been told."

"Can you find your way back to your own room?"

"I think so," I said, opening the double doors. "By the way, you didn't tell me who Sir Jaymes Cavage finally did marry."

"That's because nobody knows."

It seemed a trifling oddity at the time. I closed Whitwell's double doors blissfully unaware that I had pried into one of the secrets of the lords of Dair.

o o o

I had been wandering for at least half an hour in search of my room when I heard a man singing. The voice seemed to come from the domed rotunda in the center of Dair Manor, and I stood in one of the four west-wing corridors that led away from it, uncertain which of the highly polished paneled doors was mine and afraid to find out via trial-and-error.

I walked quickly toward the great circular open space, where late-afternoon light poured in like honey through a ring of windows at the base of the dome. I found myself on the third of four stories that looked down into an oval arena where classical statuary stared blindly from arching niches recessed into the violet marble walls. Strolling across this arena, strumming a sort of squared-off lyre, was a blonde young man dressed for the role of Merlin.

"*Che gelida manina,*" he sang to an angry Neptune, whose grip on his trident had not relaxed since the Romans ruled the waves.

"Hal-looo," caroled his companion, staring up at me.

"Oh, shut up, Woodbine. Everybody's in the screening room, and you know it," Merlin snapped at the dog.

"I'm afraid I'm lost," I called down.

Merlin looked up, startled. *He's very handsome,* I thought. *I wonder if he's in costume or just crazy.*

"Why don't you take the lift down, ma'am, so I can see you? I can't wear my glasses in this rig."

"Where's the lift?"

"You open a door just to the left of the El Greco."

"Which El Greco? I've seen three up here."

"Near the head of the stairs," he called back.

I found the lift, a pretty white telephone booth with four

54

black pushbuttons set in its daintily molded walls. It stopped with a little bump, and Merlin opened the outer door for me.

"The screening room is at the very end of the east wing, which is that way," he told me, pointing with one spangled sleeve. "Are you in the film?"

"Goodness, no! I'm Deborah Guest from Singleton Abbs, and I've forgotten where my bedroom is, and I haven't seen anyone upstairs to ask. I thought there'd be so many servants in a great house like Dair."

"You have to ring for everybody but me."

"What do you mean?"

"Well, I hope you don't think I'm dressed like this for fun. I work here."

"As what?"

"Allow me to introduce myself, miss. Harold Clewys, at your service. I'm the harper. That is, my father's the harper here. I'm filling in for him while he's in hospital."

Now I knew what the harper's cottage was.

"What an unusual harp you play," I said.

"Just the usual Welsh harp," he told me. "Though this is a nice one. My father claims it's a thousand years old. Okay, Woodbine, I'll stop dallying if you'll stop pushing. Woodbine's the number-one house dog here and he sort of nudges me through my route every night. He's been my father's accompanist for many a year."

"What is your route?"

"It's all sort of a blur without glasses, but I think we serenade all the State Apartments whether there's anybody in them or not. Would you care to come along?"

I fell into step with him as he began a lively melody in a language I dimly recognized as Welsh. We passed an empty drawing room, strolled the length of an empty orangery, entered a deserted dining room. The song ended as we reached the windows. Straight ahead of us, pitch black against the fiery sunset, the ax with the upturned blade still hung across the river, menacing the skies.

"I didn't realize it was this close to Dair," I said, surprised to find that I wanted very much to turn my back on the landscape outside.

"The Old Place? Oh, yes. That's still the Duke's spiritual home, though nobody knows just why. But don't you go near it, you hear?"

"You're the second person who's told me that."

"I won't be the last. Look, I'm as sensible as anybody, even if I am wearing this sequined dress and singing about elves. I'm a piano salesman in Birmingham. But I was brought up in the harper's cottage here like my father before me, so I know some things you probably won't believe."

I don't believe in ghosts, I repeated to myself, *so Mr. Clewys can spare himself the trouble of telling me about Crinsley.*

He never mentioned Crinsley.

"A Lady haunts the place," he told me, as we turned away from the sunset and strolled through one glorious unoccupied room after another. "The eldest son here—by the way, the family name is Cavage—the eldest son is supposed to meet the lady once during his boyhood. And then, forever after, if someone is trying to kill him, they say she shows up and saves his life."

"That's nice," I said.

Strumming his harp lightly, Clewys said, "Look, I'd consider it tommyrot, too, except for one small detail."

In the distance, approaching us rapidly, I saw someone in a black dress and white apron. *She'll know which room is mine!* I thought with relief. *If this good-looking fool will just stop his ghost story.*

"Oh, really?" I said. "Someone's coming this way." It was wicked of me, but I couldn't resist adding, "It's a lady."

"What's she wearing?"

"Black with a white apron."

"Wrong girl. The one I've heard about always wears blue."

*   *   *

The maid led me to my door. This time I took some landmarks. Left at the Murillo, right at the Van Dyck, then two doors down the passageway behind the black door.

A friend had already found it, I was pleased to note. Stratford lay sleeping in a green wing chair.

IV

It was too dark to be morning, but two pairs of eyes were fixed on me, imploring me to wake up. One pair, iridescent and compelling, belonged to Stratford, who stood on his hind legs at my bedside, punching my pillow at intervals with one forepaw. The other pair of eyes, which I saw for only a moment before they vanished behind a thick fringe of lashes, were gentle and brown and had a lilting voice to go with them.

"Here's tea, mum. You'll want to be up early today."

"Not this early," I protested, just conscious enough to see that the china on the tea tray was too rare to put within reach of a playful dog. "Please. Just put that on the table."

"But, mum, Whitwell told me to make sure you were up early. He wants you to meet him in the gardens before full sun."

"Are you certain?" I sighed, struggling up on one elbow, finding the shy little face on a line with my own. *She's scarcely taller than Stratford,* I thought. *She must be on her*

58

knees. Is that what the Duchess of Dair requires of the servants?

"Yes, he's waiting for you now, mum. So if you'll please take your tray, I'll let your dog out."

A pink glow was forming in the sky I saw through the open windows, and a curious sound had begun to float into the room. The strumming must be Clewys's harp or one just like it. But what was the strange chant that rose and fell and seemed to be coming steadily nearer?

"What's going on out there?" I demanded.

The brown eyes ventured a peek through their curtain of lashes.

"Oh, mum, it's May Day! Do please go and watch!"

She was in a passion of haste, so I didn't detain her further, but took the tea tray and waited for her to stand up. She didn't. She simply turned and bustled to the door, saying as she reached up to turn the handle, "Come along, fellow. Come with Dwain."

Stratford pattered out of the room behind her, suddenly looking as big as a collie, while I sat staring sleepily, asking myself, *What's the matter with you? Haven't you ever seen a dwarf before?* and realizing that, face to face, I really hadn't.

The chant was closer now, and there was a distinct line of yellow slashing across the sky. I touched the exquisite little teapot Dwain had brought me. Just as I'd expected, it was eggshell-thin and scalding. So I set the entire tray on the nightstand, kicked about to find my slippers, then padded over to the windows. What I saw put every thought of sleep out of my mind.

About a hundred masked men with antlers strapped to their backs were dancing slowly through the eighteenth-century formal gardens of Dair.

o   o   o

"It's quite the oldest folk dance still performed in the west of England," Dr. Darsey boomed. "The dancers are all local chaps who inherit their places in the procession."

"There's Mr. Grove," Whitwell added quietly as a husky figure passed us, crouched under the weight of the antlers on his back, yet executing the two-steps-forward-one-step-back dance with the utmost care and concentration. He took no notice of us, though he passed within arm's length. He was singing something.

"What are they chanting?" I whispered to Whitwell.

His reply astonished me. "Rain, rain, go away. Come again some other day."

I looked up at Dr. Darsey for confirmation of this intelligence. Whitwell had been kind to describe the doctor as very fat. He was also very tall, and all his features were overscale. I was quite sure an entire slice of bread would fit inside his mouth with room to spare.

"It's true, Mrs. Guest," he assured me. "You must understand that very old ceremonies like this are really a ragbag of trimmings picked up here and there through the years. The song simply helps them keep the rhythm of the steps. The shirts and trousers all match, because the Dowager Duchess has new ones made for the men every year. The original dancers probably wore animal skins and kept absolutely quiet. Safer that way."

"Are the antlers a recent addition?" I asked.

"Oh, no. They're reindeer antlers, you know. I've never found any reference to reindeer in these forests, even in the earliest written records I've looked at."

"They're very heavy," Whitwell said. "It takes two men all day to hang them back up again."

"Where do they hang them?" I inquired.

The unreadable little face turned away from me ever so slightly. *He's pretending not to hear me,* I thought.

The three of us stood on the marble base of a giant equestrian statue, because the emerald lawn was still drenched with dew. There were surprisingly few other spectators.

Twenty or thirty women with young children watched attentively from stone benches, the curbs of two great fountains and the bases of other statues along the line of march. Off to one side, on the terrace that gave on Dair's huge North Courtyard, I saw Rick's red hair above a dark dressing gown. The intensely blonde hair I knew to be Kendra's flashed in and out of sight among a group of four or five people, all apparently taller than she. *Which one of them is the Duke?* I wondered.

But I had clearly asked questions enough already, so I stared straight ahead over the bobbing thicket of antlers, watching them advance on a dense stand of trees. Above the trees, Crag Cavage showed a silhouette I had not seen before: a crude up-ended slab wearing a pointed crown. There was no ax handle in sight; we stood directly facing it, so it had foreshortened into invisibility. For the first time, my impression of Castle Cavage was not entirely one of dread and aversion. From the angle the May Day dancers chose for their approach, the great rock and the ancient fortress on top of it had a look of almost overpowering primitive majesty.

It was full day now, and the last of the dancers was going by, but right behind him was a covey of schoolgirls. Some wore their school skirts and blazers, some wore jeans, a handful of others wore ruffly white dotted Swiss dresses. But all of them carried identical baskets crammed with lily of the valley, and all of them giggled.

They made no attempt to keep in step, but simply followed the dancers to the edge of the trees ahead. There, everything stopped: the dancing, the strumming of the harp, the chant, even the girlish laughter.

My eye traveled upward from the treetops, up the sheer stone side of Crag Cavage, up to the highest tower of the castle, looming colorless and cold against the blue May sky. There, somehow exacting dead silence from us all, stood a man in a shirt as white as the nearest cloud. Wasting no time, taking no notice of any of us gathered below, he strode

61

across the battlements until he reached a point exactly centered on the statue where Dr. Darsey, Whitwell and I stood. Something glittered in his hand. Something gold.

"Watch!" Dr. Darsey whispered.

I could not have done otherwise.

The man on the battlements held a golden sword. Not as I had ever seen a sword held before, but far back over his shoulder, as if it were a javelin. A sudden gust of wind slapped the white shirt flat against his ribs and swept his black hair into turmoil. He waited, motionless, for the air to calm. Then, with a mighty thrust, he hurled the sword into the sky.

It traversed a comet's glittering path before it fell back to earth somewhere in the midst of the trees.

Now everyone was roaring and cheering. The children were dashing for the woods where the sword had fallen, Whitwell running as fast as any of them. A dozen jubilant young men marched past us, bearing aloft a tree trunk decked with more flowers and ribbons than a Watteau queen playing shepherdess. The Maypole.

But the towers of Castle Cavage were deserted. The man who had thrown the sword had disappeared.

"Well, Mrs. Guest, what did you think?" Dr. Darsey asked, helping me down from the stone pedestal.

"I'm glad to have seen an authentic Maypole, Doctor. I rather thought they'd gone the way of the Yule log."

"Not here. The Dowager Duchess insists on all the old traditions. They'll actually dance around the Maypole as soon as they put it up."

We were strolling across the gardens toward the terrace from which Rick and Kendra and their coterie had watched the proceedings. It was empty now.

"I'd like to see that. Where will it be?"

"That's what everyone's scrambling to find out back there in the trees. The Maypole is supposed to go wherever the golden sword lands."

"Oh?" I said, staring up at him blankly. "Is it really gold?"

"No. It's survived from the Bronze Age, but Old Billy Cavage—the present Duke's grandfather—was rather a scamp in his Oxford days. One day, so the story goes, he sent Wilva to Asprey's and had it gold-plated."

"Wilva?"

"Yes. That's the sword's name."

"What does it mean?"

"God only knows. I'm sure you realize that much of what we've seen this morning is of prehistoric origin. I know a bit about it, because I see so many of the older people professionally, and I ask them about this and that. But there are things they either don't know or don't care to tell an outsider. The meaning of Wilva is one of those things."

"It's certainly a dramatic way to choose a site for a Maypole."

"I daresay it started out being considerably more dramatic."

"How do you mean, Doctor?"

"This is pure speculation, of course, But, in one of the anthropological journals I subscribe to, I happened to come across an article about a similar May Day ritual on a rather remote estate in Germany. Instead of a sword, those people throw a sacred rock and put the Maypole wherever it lands. But the implications seem the same to me."

"I'm afraid you've lost me, Doctor. What implications?"

"I don't mean to sound like *The News of the World*, Mrs. Guest, but I think there are certain grounds for believing this was originally a sacrificial ceremony."

We had crossed the North Courtyard and climbed the wide white steps of the balustraded terrace, but the good doctor's thoughts were still in Germany.

"When they take the Maypole down, they roast an ox on the spot where it stood. Exactly what they do here. But the fact that seems significant to me is this. The man who throws the rock is also required to choose the ox from a herd and to stun the ox with the rock before it is slaughtered."

"How gruesome. Surely they don't do that here."

"They did. Until Old Billy Cavage's time, the same hand that hurled Wilva from the tower used Wilva to cut the ox's throat."

Despite the lily of the valley, the intensely blue sky and the May sunshine sparkling on Dair's glistening windows, I shuddered as if I were in a cave.

"Well, I'm glad they've become more civilized, Doctor," I finally said. Then, to change the subject, I called upon my well-developed actor's-wife reflexes. "By the way, who played the knife-thrower just now? I thought he had extraordinary stage presence."

Dr. Darsey could hardly have looked more startled had a skylark flown by and said, "Good morning!"

"My dear lady," he said, "Wilva has probably been tossed from the top of that crag every May Day since the glaciers began their retreat to the Arctic Circle. But the same person has done the job every time. The head of the House of Cavage."

"Do you mean that was—"

"—Thaniel Cavage."

"The Duke of Dair," I mumbled weakly. Somehow I had been sure the Duke had been here on the terrace with his duchess and their guests. What was it Clewys had said last night? "The Old Place is still the Duke's spiritual home."

I turned to look back at the castle on the crag. From the terrace, it looked like an ax again. But now a solitary figure in a white shirt was striding down the rocky path that marked the crag like a crooked gray seam. For him, at least, there was nothing unsafe about Castle Cavage.

And I never posted his note of instructions to Mr. Singleton!

"Doctor," I said, remembering this, "thank you for all you've told me. I must post a letter now, but I hope we can talk again. This has been fascinating."

"Most enjoyable for me, too, I assure you." Dr. Darsey smiled. "Now may I ask you a question?"

64

"Of course."

"Have you any idea what you've gotten yourself into?"

"I don't know what you mean."

"Then I strongly suggest that before this day is over you make it your business to find out."

So saying, Dr. Darsey wheeled his great bulk around with the lightfooted grace only the overweight ever seem to possess, and stepped inside the great house to pay his daily visit to the Dowager Duchess.

I located the little lift in the violet marble rotunda, rode up, followed my landmarks and found my room without difficulty. Stratford had preceded me there and briefly opened one watchful eye to acknowledge my entrance.

Then he snuggled deeper into the green wing chair, while I searched for my document case. Someone, possibly little Dwain, had unpacked for me. I found my trench coat, my black velvet jeans, pink cashmere pullover, plaid dressing gown and the T shirt Gavin had brought me from the Cannes Film Festival all hanging side by side on padded satin hangers in a handsome mahogany wardrobe chest. The canvas satchel I had brought them in lay on an upper shelf, but the document case and my tape recorder were not beside it.

Dwain's sense of where things belonged was apparently different from Augusta's. *Look who's comparing maids!* I chided myself, remembering that I'd never had so much as a once-weekly char during the ten years of my marriage, and had always considered the servant problem a conversational topic as exhausting as it was inexhaustible.

The tape recorder turned up behind the tambour door of the nightstand. My underthings were folded and stacked inside the top drawer of a nice old mahogany chest of drawers. The document case must be in the desk.

I approached the desk with some interest: a Regency piece, meaning buyers would insist it was early nineteenth century while sellers would maintain it was late eighteenth.

This was a beauty, with a fine brass gallery rail around the top, a single long drawer in the apron and a wealth of satinwood stringing and inlay across its surface and down its slender long legs. Someone born too soon for the era of ballpoint pens had obliterated one of the inlaid urns on the center top with a truly massive splash of India ink. Otherwise, the desk was something of a treasure.

I opened its single long drawer. There was my document case, and yes, its contents were all present and accounted for. In fact, it contained more than I had put inside it.

There could be no question about that. Before leaving I had made it a point to ask if anyone at Singleton's had a floor plan of Dair Manor. No one had, and I was sure I had left London without one. Yet here was a sharp photostatic copy of what must have been Robert Adam's own diagram of the interior arrangement.

Someone was trying to expedite my labors.

      o   o   o

"Almost certainly Rembrandt," I sighed into my tape recorder late that afternoon, standing footsore in the west wing corridor that led to the Tiber River pilasters marking Whitwell's doorway. "Pen and bister sketch of a fat man sitting on a step. Looks very like the one Sir Joshua Reynolds gave to Thomas Lawrence that is now in the collection of—"

"—you lousy little limey!" somebody screamed. "Nobody's telling me who to invite to my house, and that includes you!"

The double doors to Whitwell's room had opened. I heard his reply: "Mother, he was very rude to Dwain."

A tiny blonde woman in white jeans and a light green satin shirt stormed through the doors and whirled to deliver her exit line. "I'll decide who's rude around here," she shouted. "Not you, you good-for-nothing little prig!"

Prig was not the only four-letter word she knew. As I turned my back and began inching away, she reeled off a

66

tirade that would have impressed even certain stagehands I have met. Then she banged the doors shut and clattered away over the marble floors with furious, staccato steps.

"If you caught any of that," I said into the little microphone after the angry footsteps had faded, "I'm sorry."

I took another few steps away from Whitwell's door, wondering if I should invent some excuse to go back and knock on it and deciding I could not presume to come between a child, however fiercely he had been scolded, and his mother, however unmaternal I believed her to be.

So that is the Duchess of Dair! I thought grimly. *Her son must be in shock right now. But it would only make matters worse if he knew I'd overheard.*

"At the left of the probable Rembrandt," I continued, "we find a framed photograph of Sir Winston Churchill in his robes as a Knight of the Garter. The photograph, which is in color, measures ten by fourteen inches and is inscribed in the lower left-hand corner: 'To Merle and Fred with the compliments of a friend.' "

"Mrs. Guest!" Whitwell's voice echoed down the corridor. "Is that you?"

I left Sir Winston and Rembrandt's fat man to commiserate with each other about the solitude of old age, switched off my tape recorder and sauntered in the direction of the voice as casually as if nothing at all had happened.

It was as if nothing had. I found Whitwell calm and composed, with not the slightest trace of a tremor or a tear shed, his face white and unreadable as ever.

I'd almost rather he were having hysterics, I thought. *He's actually used to this. She must do this to him all the time.*

"If you have a moment free," he said, "my grandmother wants very much to meet you."

"I'd be delighted! But how can I meet your grandmother when I'm wearing clothes like these?"

"What's wrong with them?" he asked, leading me along the gold-and-iron railing that kept us from plunging into the violet marble abyss one story below.

I wore the same blue denim pants and jacket I'd dived into at dawn after seeing the men with reindeer's antlers from my bedroom window.

"Nothing in particular," I answered, aware that a Gainsborough lady in powdered ringlets and coral satin panniers was staring down at me from her gold leaf frame in total disagreement. We left her, and the entire west wing, behind and entered a broad corridor that was *terra incognita* for me.

"Did you dance around the Maypole?" I inquired.

"Oh, no, Mrs. Guest. Certainly not. My father and I just watch."

"I understand there's an ox to be roasted."

"That's day after tomorrow. Today there's just a lot of hugging and kissing."

"That sounds rather nice."

He favored me with one of his rare direct glances. It conveyed scorn. I changed the subject.

"Has Diana been here?"

"No. Poor Diana always has to spend May Day in Dairminster, crowning the Queen of the May. They'll show it on the telly tonight."

"Mr. Hookham does keep Diana busy."

"He hasn't anything to do with this, Mrs. Guest. The Gaffords always crown the Queen of the May. Dr. Darsey says my family used to do it, but then the Gaffords took over."

Somehow I knew the answer before I asked the question, but I asked it anyway.

"When did that happen?" I asked.

"Year of Our Lord twelve hundred and something-or-other Anno—"

"—Domin-eye!" I chimed in.

The next moment, two tall green doors parted in front of us and we stepped into the exquisite, lost world of the Dowager Duchess.

Among their other glories, the great houses built by the Adam brothers possess the finest ornamental plasterwork in

68

England. Yet it is possible to single out the hand of one master artisan from among the hundreds who must have been employed to shape the infinity of swags and swirls and flutings on these stupendous walls and ceilings. Mr. Singleton once told me how.

"When it is so delicate you could swear it was made of soap bubbles, then you're looking at plasterwork by Joseph Rose," he had said.

Joseph Rose had unmistakably done the anteroom we were walking through now. We might have been crossing a bridge among the clouds. Over our heads, an army of cherubs trailed garlands and streamers that seemed to float, utterly weightless, out to the four corners of the universe. All the tricks of perspective were in play here. It was the most spacious room I have ever been in, though it took only four or five steps to cross.

Whitwell knocked on an inner door, and I remember expecting to be admitted to a throne room, to meet someone stern with snow white hair and a black velvet ribbon around her throat. Instead, the door swung open on a room blazing with the last of the afternoon sunlight, cluttered with books and magazines, cozy with chintz. I was aware that the walls were satinwood, golden and luminous from two centuries of polishing. But one glance at the personage who lay on the *chaise longue* in front of the tall windows and my attention strayed no more.

I knew this face. I had known it all my life.

It was a face of extraordinary fragility, and it wore a fleeting smile as it received Whitwell's kiss. Then I came forward.

The remarkable dark eyes acknowledged me, then vanished behind discreetly shadowed lids. A lovely, low voice said, "Do sit here across from me, Mrs. Guest."

Then the eyes opened, focused now on the chair she meant me to take.

So that's where Diana learned to do that, I thought, taking the chair obediently, unable to stop staring at the Dowager

Duchess's face. Her skin was as milk-white as Whitwell's; her hair was the color of smoke. She must have been unimaginably beautiful as a young woman, for she was beautiful still. And I had seen her as a young woman, I knew, but how could I have?

"Thank you for bringing Mrs. Guest here, Whitwell. Now she and I are going to talk for a while, so you had better run along."

Obviously I've seen a youthful portrait of her, I told myself as Whitwell departed. *But who painted it? Come on now, Deb, you don't forget things like that. Who painted it?*

"I understand you work for Walter Singleton," the low voice was saying, crisper now that the child had gone.

"Yes, that's true."

A light of intense irritation flickered across the magnificent face for a moment.

"Exactly what has he sent you here to do?"

The Duke's note of instructions, still unposted to Mr. Singleton, was in my jacket pocket. I handed it to her, saying nothing.

She tore it out of its envelope, took in its message with a single anguished glance and sank back against the bright chintz as abruptly as if someone had struck her.

"Oh, no," I heard her mutter. "She can't. She cannot do this!"

Dr. Darsey had asked me if I had any idea what I was getting into. Perhaps I was about to find out.

The Dowager's hands were trembling, preventing her from putting her son's note to me back into the envelope I had addressed to Mr. Singleton.

It was obviously no moment for me to look at any of the objects in the handsome old room, but I could not decently watch Whitwell's grandmother now, either. Accordingly, I began to study the landscape outside the windows as attentively as if I would have to paint it from memory that very night.

It was the first landscape I had seen since coming to Dair

that was not overshadowed by the old castle on its bleak crag. The Dowager's sitting room looked down on a rush of dark blue water, where the River Dair made its abrupt westward turn to the sea and flowed between intensely green banks into what was going to be a curiously pale, cold May sunset. On the horizon line, I saw the turrets of Esty Hall: a clump of chess pieces silhouetted against the light.

Had it not been for the light green sports car racing along the river road in the direction of those turrets, I might have been looking at a scene from the thirteenth century.

I wondered who was inside the car. Rick? Kendra? Or both of them? And why would they be going to Esty Hall if Diana were away crowning May Queens?

"Forgive me, Mrs. Guest," the Dowager Duchess of Dair was saying. "My son's instructions came as a surprise to me. Thank you for showing them to me, however."

She handed the envelope back to me, and her fine, long hand was completely steady.

"I am sure he realizes," she continued, "as clearly as you and I do that it will be quite impossible for you to carry out these instructions."

"I know it's more than one person could possibly do," I acknowledged.

"Oh, even if you brought a regiment of helpers, how would any of you know for certain whether I had held back some of my particular treasures?"

"We wouldn't," I admitted. *Where have I seen that face?*

The face changed. The dark eyes were trying to burn a hole in the satinwood paneling right beside me. The cords in the graceful, scarcely wrinkled neck stood out like knife blades. The voice, when at last she spoke, rasped with hatred.

"Yes, you would, Mrs. Guest. I could hide nothing from you."

"But, Your Grace, no one at Singleton Abbs has the slightest idea what you have in your possession."

"No one at Singleton Abbs, perhaps. Here at Dair it's a

71

different story. Long ago, when I was foolish and trusting, I shared a secret with someone—unspeakable."

She must have looked like Nefertiti, I thought, mentally trying the Egyptian princess's cylindrical headdress on this semi-reclining figure.

"Now, if I should try to conceal certain things I own from the auctioneers, she'll tell you. It would give her great pleasure to tell you. And who knows how many millions of pounds besides?"

"Please, Your Grace. I'm not here to confiscate anything. I simply—"

"She is here to confiscate everything."

I couldn't blame the Dowager for her anger. Who wouldn't rage at the prospect of seeing a Bronze Age sword offered on the auction block after several millennia in the same family? There must be other artifacts equally old, equally hallowed, valuable beyond the narrow confines of price to the matriarch of an ancient house. *Nefertiti's headdress was too vivid,* I decided. *The face I remember was surrounded by white.*

"Mrs. Guest, I think I have little to lose by speaking to you plainly. If you appreciate my position at all, perhaps I have a very great deal to gain. Will you please bear with me while I try to tell you what a wretched little cheapjack game is being played here?"

I have never listened to anyone more attentively in my life.

"Dair Manor consists of some forty thousand acres. There are probably fifty or sixty buildings on it, all told, this house among them. And, of course, the Old Place on the crag. Mostly, however, they are farmers' houses, barns, that sort of thing. I daresay you saw most of our farm families if you watched the Maypole ceremonies this morning."

I nodded.

"Well, all the land and all the buildings on it are entailed. I'm sure you know how strict the laws of entail are."

"I'm sorry, Your Grace. I know nothing about them."

"Very simply, Mrs. Guest, the laws of entail limit the inheritance of property in such a way that it must proceed in a specific order of descent. Our order of descent is from the eldest son to his eldest son to his eldest son, and on and on forever."

"I see."

"No, you don't, Mrs. Guest. Not yet."

"I'm sorry."

"Any other disposition of these lands and buildings would be illegal. My son must leave them, in their entirety, to my grandson."

The face was softer now. The eyes were far away. One long, slim hand toyed with a rope of phenomenally blue lapis lazuli beads knotted at the throat of her negligee.

"They are Whitwell's birthright," the low voice informed me. "They will be the birthright of Whitwell's firstborn son. They were my husband's birthright."

Her glance flitted about the room as desperately as a fly trying to escape the swatter.

"However," the voice sighed, "the contents of these buildings are not entailed. They can be emptied. To the bare walls. I know. I have asked my solicitors, and my greedy little slut of a daughter-in-law has asked hers."

And if they ever are emptied, the museums of the world will beggar their national treasuries, I thought, *to pay for just a fraction of what's here. It would be the auction of the century.*

"It must not happen," she whispered. "My son is desperate to divorce her, Mrs. Guest. He would give anything to have his freedom and custody of his child. But must he give everything? Of his, and the child's, and mine?"

I was afraid to speak, afraid any word might propel her over the edge of this emotional precipice. But I knew I must.

"I'm not here to spy, Your Grace, just to make a list of what I find. If anything's hidden, I won't find it, and what's more I won't know it's missing."

"Ah, but *she* will! She came here like a kitten, Mrs. Guest.

73

So tiny, so pretty, so young. And my son was so proud to have charmed her away from Hugh Gafford that he fairly glowed with the triumph of it all. I'd always wanted a daughter, and—I'm afraid I told her too much and showed her too much and gave her too much. She had a cunning little way of admiring things I wore. She'd admire them over and over again, until it seemed terribly hardhearted not to let the poor little girl have them. That's how my emeralds went. But she was always so fantastically grateful. She'd thank you a thousand times. That's all she did, really, the first year she lived here. She admired and admired, and thanked and thanked. And then my poor husband had his heart attack and died."

And she became the star, I added silently.

"I came home from burying him and found two men with yardsticks creeping around my dressing room on their hands and knees. They were glaziers, and they said they'd been sent to measure for mirrors. The Duchess of Dair intended to mirror the walls."

And the star gets the best dressing room, I sighed to myself.

"I thought my son would send her packing for that," the Dowager said softly. "But she is very shrewd. She always proceeds from a position of strength. At the time of my dear husband's heart attack, she was three months along with Whitwell. Long enough to be sure she was pregnant. Not long enough to have told my son. When he challenged her about driving me out of the rooms my husband and I had occupied, she told him, though."

And he gave in to her, I thought. This was not the first beastly-daughter-in-law story I had heard; they are standard fare in the theater, too. But how could I tell a noble lady who had led a sheltered life that there is no weapon like a baby?

I didn't have to.

"She has ruled him through their child ever since," the low voice said.

"I see." This time I did.

"Had Whitwell been a daughter, it might have been different, but the Dukes of Dair prize their sons beyond imagining."

"Don't you suppose most men do, Your Grace?"

"Perhaps. Have you a son?"

"No, Your Grace." *Gavin Guest would have no baby in the house except himself*, I found myself thinking, surprised at the anger I felt.

"Then you have missed a very special kind of loneliness."

For the first time, the old woman smiled, and I knew at last where I had seen her face before.

"When my son was born, I felt as if my husband and my husband's father took him into some sort of secret society with rules that I was not to know. Now Whitwell is also a member, I fear."

But you had your secrets, too, I thought.

"Perhaps I exaggerate, Mrs. Guest. Perhaps my husband and his father were no more secretive than any other men. They simply had their traditions. Hurling the sacred sword on May Day. Shearing the first sheep single-handed. The harper. The dwarf. And yet ..."

Curiosity gave me courage, and I pressed her. "And yet what, Your Grace?"

The almost-Nefertiti face turned to me, weary with the strain of remembering, and I heard her say, "After his father died, my husband would not spend a night away from Dair for any reason short of war. And he would never tell me why not."

What is so significant about spending the night at Dair? I wondered. *I've done it without incident. Yet a titled ten-year-old neighbor can't wangle the invitation. And now I learn this about the late Duke who must have been Old Billy's son.*

The slender hands toyed with the ecru lace of the negligee.

"I've wandered from the point most dreadfully, Mrs.

75

Guest. This is not what I intended to discuss with you at all."

"What had you meant to discuss, Your Grace?"

"Frederick Pennington," she replied, watching me like a frightened faun.

Good, I thought, careful not to bat an eye. *Tell me about Frederick Pennington. What became of him after you deserted him to marry your sheep-shearing, sword-throwing Duke? Why didn't he ever paint again after you modeled for his "Portrait of Isis"?*

But then the door leading from Joseph Rose's fantastic little bridge of clouds burst open, and the Duke of Dair looked in.

"Mother, quick! Think of six names beginning with X!"

Only his black-thatched head, one white-shirted shoulder and a hand with a heavy signet ring showed around the corner of the door. The face, which was pretending to smile, had been a handsome one before fatigue and anger had set their stamp on it. The tension of the jaw, the fine lines forced merriment was creating around the deadly serious dark eyes, the desperate grip with which the lean fingers clutched the satinwood door, all contrasted oddly with his absurd request. Six names beginning with X, indeed!

"Xenophon," said the Dowager. "Do come in, Thaniel. Xerxes. Xavier. You may come in, Thaniel."

The Duke had noticed me. He shook his head quickly.

"Actually, I can't, Mother. Forgive me. I didn't realize you had a visitor."

"If you come in, I will introduce you."

"I'd be honored, but I can't come in, because I'm holding a crate with six puppies in my other hand."

The Dowager's lapis lazuli necklace was suddenly swinging wildly back and forth just above the polished floor beside her chaise. Her hands were deadweight on the ecru lace. Her eyes were closed. *She's died!* I thought. *Just like that! Gone!* I realized I couldn't move.

The Duke of Dair moved like lightning. With what

76

seemed like a single motion, he leaped inside the room, tucked a cushion under his mother's feet, held a slim silver vial under her nostrils, and jabbed over and over again at the little white bellpush set into the wall beside her. All the while he was muttering to himself, "Mother, you have to stop this, you really do! It's been ten years now, and you've got to pull yourself together. I thought you'd gotten over all this long ago, otherwise I'd never ... "

A white-uniformed nurse had joined him. She took the Dowager's pulse, frowning slightly.

"It's all my fault, Mrs. Mackleroy," he said.

"Yes, Your Grace. I saw," was her answer.

The old woman's great eyes opened again, twin furies in the exquisite face.

"Take the dogs away!" she whispered.

"I think, if you don't mind ... " the nurse said to me. I was being dismissed.

"Yes, of course," I said, rising hastily.

"Mother ... " the Duke began. I saw Mrs. Mackleroy put a finger to her lips. Then I stepped back on the bridge of clouds. A crate in which six newborn red fur puppies squirmed slowly in their sleep forced me to stop immediately to avoid losing my balance. A strong hand took my arm just in time to steady me.

"Thank you," I said, appalled at the distress I saw on the face that had once been handsome.

"Would you mind ringing for somebody to take these damned dogs?" he replied, bending to pick up the crate. "The bell is just outside the green doors."

I hurried ahead, opened the doors for him, found the bell and held my finger on it.

A maid appeared at the end of the broad passageway, so far away that she looked like a black-and-white mechanical doll about an inch high, just wound up and moving fast.

"Where's Grove?" the Duke called to her. Grove's name ricocheted off every shivering prism of the crystal chandelier overhead, and sent jangles of cold coursing down my spine.

"It's May Day, and he's . . ."

"Oh, never mind, Ethel. Can you carry this?"

She could, easily.

"Ask Smithwright to dock their tails and get them back to their mother before she wakes up."

"Where is their mother, Your Grace?"

"Where she always is at times like these."

"Your boot cupboard."

"Exactly."

Ethel and the crate bobbled some sort of curtsy and went in search of Smithwright, whoever he might be.

I was alone with the seventh Duke of Dair.

"My name is Thaniel Cavage," he said, and I distinctly remember thinking, *He's not even trying, and his eyes feel just like black velvet. Watch out, old girl!*

But he was trying.

"I presume you're one of the film people my wife has invited for the weekend. However, I haven't seen a film all year, so you'll have to tell me your name."

His eyes had traveled down to the tips of my scruffy sneakers and back up again.

"You flatter me, Your Grace—"

"Why don't you call me Thaniel?"

"But, Your Grace—"

"You are very pretty, but it's you who are flattering me. Allow me to be Thaniel, please. Who are you?"

"Deborah Guest."

I might as well have said Typhoid Mary. The black velvet eyes went blank. The warmth clicked off between us.

"The auctioneer," he said. "No doubt the next pretty woman I meet will be an executioner."

"I'm really not an auctioneer. I just . . ."

". . . work for Singleton's. I know. Well, let's see you in action, eh? Come along, Miz Guest, whatever Miz means. Come with me!"

His hand was strong, and the signet ring hurt where it pressed on my knuckles, as he half-led, half-dragged me back to Dair's great central rotunda, past the El Greco that hung beside the little lift, to the top of the grand staircase. Then, suddenly, I was flying, my hair streaming out behind me, my feet barely touching the violet marble steps, using each as a springboard rather than a resting place, my hand held captive by a man whose supply of adrenalin was easily as remarkable as his collection of worldly goods.

We skimmed over the parquet floors like skaters with a stiff breeze at our backs, passing decapitated marble heads of state from Rome to Milan and points between, with a Venus or two for good measure. At one turning, I brushed against the figure of Clewys, but my greeting was drowned out by my captor's cry of "Woodbine! Follow me!"

From that moment on, there was a red dog at my heels.

Where are we going? I thought. *What did this madman mean by "Let's see you in action"?*

When we arrived inside the sheet-shrouded Red Room, I was too winded to speak.

"Quick test, Miz Guest!" the Duke cried, pulling a dust-cover off a chair as dramatically as a magician might have unveiled a birdcage filled with doves.

"Thanks!" I gasped, sitting down in it immediately.

"Very good, Miz Guest! Did you see that, Woodbine? Our auctioneer has correctly identified a chair! At this very moment, she is sitting in it! How shall we challenge her next? Ah, this may be just the thing!"

A bullfighter might have envied the grace with which he uncovered the little table, but I did not. Fighting for breath, I said, "That table—"

"Excellent!" he exclaimed. "It is indeed a table!"

"—is Hepplewhite."

"First rate, Miz Guest! Wouldn't you say that was first rate, Woodbine? It shows real scholarship. Hepplewhite is right!"

79

With that, he tore the sheets away from an object wrapped like a mummy case, tall and silent between two windows.

"And what do you call this, Miz Guest?"

"A very fine example," I inhaled deeply, "of a Joseph Davis tall-case clock," I inhaled again, "made about 1700 with the characteristic," I paused for breath, "seaweed marquetry—which suggests the clockmaker may have employed—a cabinetmaker from—"

"Stop right there, please."

I did, gladly.

"Where was the Davis workshop?"

"In his heyday, Wrapping Dock."

"You'll do," the Duke said. "Now I must leave you. Good night."

He strode out of the room as swiftly as he had entered it. He couldn't have taken more than six steps when he stopped and, with a single spin of his heel, turned and came back to me.

"I've been rude as a pig, haven't I?" he said.

There was only one answer. "Yes."

"I ask your pardon. Can you forgive me?"

"I suppose I shall have to."

"Thank you for your patience,"

Then he walked away again, the dog trotting briskly behind him. I stared after them, wondering why—for perhaps the first time in my life—I felt like a goddess.

o   o   o

Outside the windows, sunset had begun. I turned and watched the night close in as if it were a ceremony in my honor. A faint and curiously cheerless lavender light washed over the grim battlements of Castle Cavage. The last clouds hurried by its bleak towers as if determined to get as far away from them as possible before dark. And then, just as the last cold sunbeams struck the jagged face of the crag, I saw two figures walking quickly up the narrow path between the boulders: the Duke and his son and heir.

"I told you there was a Lady up there," Clewys said blithely, amused that his voice had made me jump with fright. "That's who they're going to visit now."

The man and boy had reached the summit of the crag. As we stood watching, they disappeared into the graceless, gaping hole that served as the old castle's entrance.

"Stop putting me on, Clewys."

"Only trying to acquaint you with the Duke's little ways, I assure you. But if you don't choose to believe me, you can always believe him instead."

"What does that mean?"

"He and the boy will vow they go there every night to fetch the evening's wine."

"Why do you doubt that? It sounds quite reasonable to me."

"Oh, it's the truth. It's just not the whole truth."

"Clewys, you're trying to tell me ghost stories. Stop it."

"I'll stop. But first I'll ask you this. If all they're doing is fetching wine, why don't they ever let anyone else do it for them? And why must they go after it every blessed night? Why not every other night? Or once a week? Oh, there's more than wine up there in the old castle, and everybody here knows it except you."

He was born and brought up here, and he really believes this, I thought.

"Clewys," I said, turning and staring straight into his clear blue eyes. "How can you tell what's going on over at the old castle? Last night you made me come all the way down from the third floor because you said you couldn't see a thing without your glasses."

"It's a good ploy with other girls. Pity you notice everything."

I had to laugh as he shuffled away, pretending to be

embarrassed, with his father's thousand-year-old harp strapped to his chest and the tireless corgi, Woodbine, policing his spangled hem as carefully as if he were a piece of prize livestock. Not until he was out of sight did I turn back to the window facing the Old Place. Darkness had engulfed it. There was no sign of life, although I knew there were two people inside.

Perhaps there are more than two flashed through my mind. For at that very moment, the Dowager's words came back to me: "After his father died, my husband would not spend a night away from Dair for any reason short of war. And he would never tell me why not."

Dear God, I thought, *maybe there really is a Lady there.*

o   o   o

My supper came on a wheeled tea-wagon with a white tablecloth. A maid I had not seen before whisked the pewter domes from a plate of lamb chops and a bowl of thick soup, and disappeared out my door without speaking.

"Room service is the same everywhere," I observed to Stratford, chasing him out of the green wing chair. "Although perhaps a bit tastier here," I added, sampling the soup.

Last night I sat here and thought about Gavin, I reflected. *Tonight I have so many other people to think about. Though I must say none of them went so far as to suggest eating with me.*

Hadn't Rick said Dair employed the best chef in Britain? Perhaps his fourth assistant had underdone my chops while his master, having instructed him to give me the last drops of the soup as a conciliatory gesture, gave his full attention to the meal he would serve Kendra and her guests at eleven. I doubted that the Dowager would be among those present to sample whatever he prepared, but I wasn't sure about the Duke. Did he and his "greedy little slut" still keep up appearances when there were guests? It was none of my business, I knew, and I was cross to find myself speculating on the subject. Tossing my napkin on the table, I stepped into the compact bathroom that must once have been a sort of vestibule between my room and another and began to prepare for bed.

When I came out again, I paused by the window, where only that morning I had watched as the men in reindeer's antlers danced. Now the gardens were deserted, and the fountains and statues gleamed cold and white under a moon that was almost full. Beyond them, almost suffocatingly black against the navy blue sky, stood the crag.

My eyes followed the ax handle out to the upturned blade, and saw what at first I thought was moonlight, reflected perhaps by a patch of stone worn to a shine by the rain of centuries.

But moonlight doesn't sway or flicker. This was a flame.

High on the thick black wall of Castle Cavage, deep inside one of the narrow slits that served as its windows, there seemed to be a lighted candle.

V

I wanted very much to share this discovery with someone,
but my bedroom had no telephone and I could hardly
venture out into the palatial corridors of Dair in my plaid
dressing gown. Even if I had felt energetic enough to get
dressed again, what had I to wear? I tried to envision the
banquet table where Kendra's guests would gather at eleven:
diamond necklaces alternating with dinner jackets for a
hundred yards each way, a liveried man in a powdered wig
behind each chair, a dazzle of candlelight and crystal and
Georgian silver, with Rick—would it be Rick?—at Kendra's
right, and the Duke, if he were there at all, seated facing
her.

No place for me.

I had no choice but to go to bed, and it felt as if I had
only just shut my eyes when there was Dwain again with the
eggshell-thin teapot on the pretty little tray.

"Did you enjoy the May Day, mum?"

"Very much indeed. Thank you for making me wake up and go to see it."

"It was a beautiful day, wasn't it? Today's stormy again." She was standing on a chair, closing my window.

It reminded me of what I'd seen the night before.

"Does something special happen on May Day night, as well?" I asked her as she jumped back to the floor.

"Well, mum, the courtships don't exactly stop at sundown."

That explained it, of course. I laughed.

"Castle Cavage must be a godsend for the young lovers around here," I remarked, taking my steaming teacup from the tray.

"No, mum. That's one place you won't find them."

She took the cover off the sugar bowl, put the sugar spoon in it and held it up to me.

"I think last night was an exception, Dwain," I said. "I'm almost certain I saw a lighted candle in one of the very high windows over there."

Dwain hid her brown eyes under their remarkable lashes, retired her smile, set the sugar bowl back on the tray a split-second too fast. Everything rattled.

"I'll take your dog now, mum." She was almost at the door.

"Have I said something to upset you, Dwain?"

There was no answer. She was gone, and Stratford with her.

◦　　◦　　◦

Two stories below my room, on the level where Whitwell, his grandmother and the contemptuous Gainsborough lady in coral satin made their headquarters, I stood before a gigantic pair of gilded white doors, saying into my tape recorder, "The contents of the Picture Gallery at Dair must be remarkable indeed, for its doors are both chained and

85

padlocked. I find this surprising only because three El Grecos are hung in the halls outside this Picture Gallery so casually that one might almost doubt their authenticity."

At that moment someone shot past me without a sound, halting barely half an inch from the padlocked doors, then turning to nod.

"Whitwell, you absolutely terrified me!" I said as the boy stepped off his bicycle. I was amused to see that he wore riding clothes: a camel's-hair jacket, tan whipcord jodhpurs, burnished brown boots.

His impassive young face allowed itself a twinkle of delight, then hastily suppressed it.

"Hurry, Mrs. Guest," he said, thrusting the handlebars into my unwilling hands. "You ride, and I'll run."

I hadn't been on a bicycle for fifteen years, and everything they say about that is untrue. You do forget.

"Whitwell!" I called after him, wobbling meanwhile between the gold-and-iron railing on my right and the life-size T'ang horse on my left. "Come back here and tell me where we're going! I can't ride this thing."

The child reclaimed his bike and pedaled away, calling back to me "Please hurry, or he'll be gone!"

I followed the bicycle into one of the State Apartments Clewys and I had serenaded on my first evening at Dair. Inside, I found Whitwell at the windows, watching a small silver plane rise into the stormy sky. The wind was giving it something of a bouncing about, and I didn't envy its pilot or passengers.

"Not the best flying weather, is it?" I said.

"Oh, my father's a very good pilot. It won't bother him. There, look at him bank and turn!"

"Where is he going?"

"London."

I was surprised to find that something in my throat tensed for an instant, preventing me from speaking. If I had said anything, it would have been, "I wish he had invited me."

"He goes to London most Saturdays," Whitwell continued. *Where some woman waits for him*, I decided, *in a flat filled with red roses and soft music and the scent of Vent Vert. She is beautiful and titled and nineteen years old.*

All I finally said was, "Will he be gone long?"

"No, he'll be back before night."

Whitwell's grandmother had said it of her husband. Apparently it was also true of her son. The Dukes of Dair never stayed away overnight for any reason short of war. And when they went to war they never died in battle.

The little plane disappeared into a sky so flat and gray it looked as if it had been paved during the night. Whit turned away from the window.

"Have you any idea how I might get the keys to the Picture Gallery?" I asked him.

"No, Mrs. Guest, I really haven't."

"Perhaps your butler would know. I probably should have introduced myself to him when I got here, but I didn't know where to find him."

"I don't think we have a butler this month. Mr. Gragg only stayed a week, and my mother just sent to Japan for a new one."

"Then I guess I can't see the Picture Gallery this morning. Although obviously there's something important inside."

"I don't know. I've never been inside. Are you sure you don't want my bicycle, Mrs. Guest?"

"Quite sure. But thank you, my dear."

Had this child never heard an endearment before? A rush of pink had climbed into the set, white face as I spoke. Well, I'd heard what his mother called him, and I'd seen his grandmother accept his kiss without returning it, then send him directly out of the room. *Poor little chap*, I thought.

"I'll leave it here in case you change your mind. Now if you'll excuse me, it's time for my riding lesson."

"Riding? But it's about to pour!"

"I know, but Mr. Smithwright says a good horseman must be able to manage his mount in any weather."

Alaric Meade strolled past the open door of the drawing room, saw us and stopped.

"Good morning!" he called.

"Good morning!" I replied.

"Excuse me, please, I'm late for my lesson," Whitwell mumbled quickly, ducking behind Rick and out and away.

"How's the spoon-counting, Deb?" Rick said, joining me on a handsome Chippendale sofa that faced the windows.

"Staggering! I can't even total up the Renaissance paintings, let alone the cutlery."

"I'm sorry not to have seen you yesterday. Kendra woke us all up before three to see the sword-slinging and then insisted that we all dance around the Maypole, sound asleep though we were. After that, five of us went into Dairminster to watch Diana crown the Queen of the May."

So, I thought, *it wasn't Rick who drove Kendra's car from Dair to Esty Hall yesterday.*

"Who else went along?" I inquired.

"Sir Arnold Williams and Mr. Monroe-Park."

"Who are they?"

"Two of the richest men who ever decided to spend their declining years investing in film production and, more importantly, pinching starlets. Each was accompanied by someone eminently pinchable."

While Kendra drove to Esty Hall, I said to myself, *for reasons best known to herself.*

"Rick, it sounds truly scintillating. How did Diana do?"

His gray eyes went all swimmy for a second.

"Very, very nicely. Unfortunately, however, the Queen of the May was almost six feet tall, so somebody had to lift Diana before she could put the damned crown on top of this local Amazon's head."

"Was it anybody I know?"

"The Queen of the May?"

"No. The Diana-lifter."

"Well, I just happened to be the one standing nearest her, so naturally— Oh, hell, Deborah! I assure you she isn't the first countess I ever picked up."

' "While we're title-dropping, let me put you in your well-earned place, Mr. Meade. Yesterday *I* hobnobbed with a viscount, a duke and a dowager duchess!"

"And what did you think?"

"Seriously?"

"Yes."

"They all puzzle me, Rick."

"Can I help you sort any of it out?"

"I'd be delighted if you'd try."

"Fire away."

I might have begun anywhere. I might have asked Rick if Kendra had ever shown Whitwell any affection that would balance out the hatred she had poured all over him in my hearing when she thought they were alone. I might have asked him what—or, more likely, who—impelled the Duke to fly to London most Saturdays. I might have asked cocktail party questions: When did you and the Duke first meet? Did you know that the Dowager was the model for Frederick Pennington's famous "Portrait of Isis"? Isn't it odd that there was a candle burning in one of the upper windows of Castle Cavage last night? Did you ever hear that the Duke had to win Kendra away from somebody named Hugh Gafford, whoever he is?

I asked none of these questions. The words that sprang to my lips were these:

"Why is the Duke's mother so terribly afraid of dogs?"

Rick's reaction frightened me badly. He stood up abruptly, marched over to Whitwell's bicycle and bent over it, examining the metal work carefully. When he looked up again, his face was shadowed with pain.

"Deborah," he said quietly, "you must have some god-damned kind of sixth sense."

"Mr. Singleton once said I did, but he was talking about cookery books," I said lamely, trying to save the situation.

"Any other woman would have asked me, one way or another, 'Is Thaniel still sleeping with Kendra or are you?' But not Milady Deborah. You put your finger on the real reason I keep coming here, have kept coming here, year after year after year."

Whatever else he was about to tell me was drowned out by a sudden uproar just outside the open door. I heard Grove's Boris Godunov basso roaring "Call Doctor Darsey!" over the rush of gasps and chatter. Then Grove entered the room where Rick and I sat. The limp little form that sagged in his arms wore a camel's-hair jacket and burnished brown boots.

"Strum wouldn't take the jump at the edge of the apple orchard," he said. "Threw Whit right over his head."

"I'll get Mrs. Mackleroy," Rick said, already halfway out the door.

Who was I to say what should be done next? Nevertheless, Grove seemed to be awaiting my instructions.

"Put him here on this sofa, Grove. I'll stay with him while you go after his mother."

Then Grove was gone and Dwain was with me, examining Whitwell's unconscious form with small, exquisitely gentle hands, whimpering "No, no, no, no, no ... " so softly that only I could hear.

"What happened, Dwain?" The boy's eyes opened at last.

"That Strum, that brainless wild animal they're letting you ride, stopped at the jump and let you take it all by yourself, that's what happened!"

"If you'll fetch some water, we can wash his face," Mrs. Mackleroy interrupted, white and starchy and calm. Dr. Darsey was only a few steps behind her. Dwain continued to denounce the horse, Strum, refusing to leave Whitwell's side until, at a swift, urgent glance from the doctor, I took her hand and led her out of the room.

"Where can we get some water?" I asked, bending over as if to speak to a four-year-old.

"They don't need water. They just wanted me away." Tears sprang up in the lovely brown eyes.

"You mustn't cry, Dwain. He's alive and conscious, and he's going to be quite all right. You don't want his mother to see you making a fuss, do you?"

"Not likely she will, mum, seeing as she and her fancy friends haven't yet come in from wherever they went last night after dinner."

"But it's ten o'clock in the morning, Dwain!"

"Quite true, mum. However, dinner cannot be served to the Duchess before eleven at night, and it's never finished until long after midnight. By then, everybody's drunk and they tear off in any cars they can find the keys to. Once they went to Birmingham and took a plane to Paris, France, mum."

"This must be a very trying job."

"I guess they all are, mum, if you can't quit."

Mrs. Mackleroy emerged from the drawing room. "Doctor thinks there's nothing broken, but the lad's to stay in bed for the rest of the day. Is his room ready, do you know, Dwain?"

Smiling for the first time, Dwain fled across the wide passageway and touched a section of the paneling. As it swung open, I saw steps painted a rather military shade of tan, a bucket and a ladder. Then Dwain pushed it shut from inside, and I saw nothing to indicate that a door was there. Robert Adam had wanted Dair to look as if it ran by magic. It had taken a very gifted carpenter to hide the way to the steps the servants used.

Whitwell came limping out to us. Dr. Darsey hung back, watching the boy's progress intently.

"I'm so very sorry to cause all this trouble," Whitwell said, sounding drained. "Please don't mention it to Grandmother,

Mrs. Mackleroy. No, I don't need any help, thanks." He shook off her hand. "It's just a few yards to my room. Besides," he fixed her with his disconcertingly direct stare, "I can bathe myself!"

The three of us stood watching him until he reached the Ionic columns that marked the entrance to his room.

"Nothing obviously broken," the doctor said. "But I'd like to X-ray his shoulder tomorrow if it's still twinging."

"Why is he limping?" I asked.

"Just a couple of bruises, I promise you. Who's in charge of him these days?"

"I'll ask Grove," Mrs. Mackleroy replied.

"It's going to take somebody Grove's size to keep that boy still all day. But I think it's important, so please do what you can, Mack."

"I've got my hands full with the old lady," Mrs. Mackleroy snarled at me, as she smiled a calm professional smile at the doctor's enormous departing back. "They ought to get the boy a servant of his own; he's old enough. And God knows they've got the money."

Mr. Singleton was not paying me to be a baby-sitter, but something made me say, "I can help keep an eye on him."

I have never been more disastrously mistaken.

o   o   o

I had not heard Dr. Darsey say anything about a sedative, but Mrs. Mackleroy gave Whitwell a white tablet shortly after lunch. Perhaps it was only aspirin; whatever it was, he slept deeply through the afternoon, quite undisturbed by my remarks to my tape recorder.

" ... twenty-six, twenty-seven, twenty-eight, twenty-nine, thirty—count 'em again, Deb—*thirty* solid-silver marrow spoons, each sixteen inches long, weight to be determined."

I clicked the little machine off and looked out the high Adam windows. The gray-pavement sky had cracked. Now the rain was blowing against the glass as if a careless gardener were turning his hose on us from time to time. Beyond the splattered windowpanes, however, the shape of the dark, upturned ax still threatened the heavens. I wondered if there would be a candle flame over there again tonight. If the weather kept up like this, would I be able to tell?

Back to work. Switching on my electric torch, I delved into the fifth of the velvet-lined silver chests Grove had brought me during the afternoon, and began to examine what appeared to be an iron for hair-curling.

They'll never believe this in High Holborn, I laughed to myself, thinking of the gleaming Silver Vaults and their proprietors—all of them regulars at Singleton's silver sales.

"One curling iron," I dictated in my best upper-class accent. "Solid silver, weight to be determined but very heavy, eleven inches long. Engraved on the handle with the Cavage family crest, the usual unembellished X on a shield. Embossed on the inside of the lower curling spindle with the name—are you ready?—of Paul Revere. I suggest this be authenticated very carefully."

I stopped the little machine, switched on the torch so as to replace the alleged Paul Revere curling iron in the proper velvet tray, and sat back to rest my eyes from the close work of deciphering hallmarks. My gaze strayed to the thirteenth-century marriage contracts hanging over Whitwell's makeshift desk, and I marveled at the wonders time brings. Here I sat among a glittering wealth of silver: an infinitesimal part of the treasures acquired as the Knights of Cavage came up in the world and became the Dukes of Dair. Yet there lay the next Duke, sound asleep in his Spartan chamber, as ignorant of his thirteenth-century grandmother's name as I of mine. *And he probably never heard of Paul Revere, either,* I thought, pointing the torch back into the chest preparatory to removing the next precious object.

"What time is it, please?" Whitwell was awake.

93

"Four-fifteen. How do you feel?"

"Is my father back?"

"Not yet." *Neither is your mother,* I added silently.

"But it's four-fifteen, you're sure?"

"Four-sixteen, actually."

Whitwell was at the window in one bound, searching the skies. Mrs. Mackleroy entered at almost the same moment. Together, she and I put the boy back to bed.

"Now you're to stay there, you understand?" The nurse was smiling her professional smile. "Dwain will bring your tea. Then I'll be back to give you a little something that will make you more comfortable."

The door closed behind her.

"How's the shoulder?" I asked.

"Shoulder? Oh, my shoulder. Yes, it's just awful, Mrs. Guest. My shoulder does hurt quite a lot."

He was half out of bed, staring at the windows as he spoke.

"Don't get out of bed again. You know you mustn't."

"What time is it now?"

"Four twenty-two."

The boy was frantic. *Probably has to go to the bathroom and doesn't want to say so,* I thought.

"I'm sure it's all right for you to go to the bathroom, if you get right back into bed afterwards."

"Isn't there any sign of the plane?"

"I'll look again."

I walked to the windows. The small plane, looking like a desperate sparrow, was bobbing up and down in the distance, helpless against the swirling air currents.

"Here he is, Whitwell!" I sounded as over-jovial as an amateur master of ceremonies who has been in doubt that the evening's guest of honor would appear.

The child was beside me again, his face expressionless as always, his fists clenched. "Oh, Mrs. Guest, he can't land!"

94

"Of course he can," my jovial voice chattered on. "Just sit here and watch him."

As I pulled over a chair for the boy, I saw him glance at my wristwatch. Four thirty-five.

"Thank you," he said, sitting down. The little plane had decided to circle and approach the landing strip again. "My shoulder really is bothering me, Mrs. Guest. Do you suppose I could trouble you for some aspirin and a glass of water?"

"Why, of course, my dear."

I crossed the room and stepped inside his bathroom. This, too, had been an antechamber of some sort: round, windowless, with an intricate round mandala design in the marble floor and plumbing fixtures ranged along the far wall where once a door with a Grecian pediment had been. The pediment remained. I took a moment to admire it while the water ran from lukewarm to icy. In the mirror just under the pediment, I saw a flash of white. Someone had gone past the bathroom's open door, running hard.

"Whitwell?" I stepped out of the bathroom, leaving the running water, empty glass and aspirin bottle behind me.

Not a sign of him.

I ran to the doors between the Ionic columns. One of them was ajar. Peering around it, I saw Whitwell disappear into the paneled wall where I knew the tan steps were.

"Come back here; you're *hurt!*" I shouted, sprinting after him. "Where do you have to press this paneling to make the door open?" I demanded of the completely deserted corridor. *Where the fingermarks are, you fool,* I answered myself. I had the door open in time to see one white pajama leg ending in a small bare foot scooting out of sight on the landing below me.

Everything after that was a nightmare. I ran through a mile of narrow tan pantries, dodged around an enormous table where an old woman stood serenely ironing a man's black sock, hurdled stacks of old newspapers, pickling crocks, sacks of potatoes, baskets of beans, always just fast enough to keep a flash of Whitwell's white pajamas in sight. *Where is he going?* I kept thinking. *What is so desperately urgent?*

When I found myself outdoors in the drenching rain, I began to understand what the destination was. Whitwell had left by the door nearest Crag Cavage and was racing toward the immense dark rock without a trace of the limp he had had only that morning.

And I was following, using I know not what for breath.

He's going to have pneumonia in addition to whatever else he's got, I thought, stopping in consternation. *Maybe the fall did something to his head.*

Sodden pajamas plastered to his thin body, Whitwell was still pumping his arms and legs valiantly and getting closer and closer to the trees at the base of the crag.

Can't anyone see us? I thought, swiveling to look at the great shining windows of Dair. *Isn't anyone going to help?*

Nobody was going to help.

"Rick!" I screamed. "Rick, help me!"

Rain continued to blow against the glorious old windows, but I saw no one stir inside. I'd caught my breath again, and I remember saying, "Here's where the auctioneer's assistant really puts her foot in it." But I had, after all, offered to keep an eye on Whitwell, and—viscount or not—he was only eleven years old.

I put my head down and ran toward Crag Cavage for dear life.

o   o   o

It smelled old. Old and cold and empty. I didn't want to go inside the castle; just standing on its graceless threshold made me want to turn and run. But I'd followed my charge this far, up a treacherous rock path so narrow I'd skinned my elbows, so bumpy I'd fallen down twice; I had better follow him through this hideous doorway, too.

It was impossible to guess when this doorway might have been built. Before the Cavages had heard of proportion, certainly. It was a narrow door; two dray horses would have a squeeze going through at the same time. And it was a low door. Had I reached up I could have touched the stone in its roof.

But it was cut like a tunnel into a monumentally thick wall. *Advance carrying a spear,* I thought, *and you'd have a five-minute walk before you could so much as scratch anybody.*

All I carried was the electric torch I'd put in my pocket when I went to fetch Whitwell the aspirin and water he'd said he needed. Now I flicked it on and let its thin white beam lead me inside the darkness of Castle Cavage. For a moment, that thin white beam was all I saw, and it crossed my mind that Gavin might have to be told I'd entered this forbidden building ("Not even a duke could tell Deborah anything," Gavin would say with a yawn) and been found face-down on the slimy rock floor with bats in my hair ("How very untidy," he'd sigh. "Don't you agree, Cindy darling?"). Then the tunnel ended and the space in which I found myself seemed infinitely high and wide. I swung the torch around to my left. The beam stretched as far as it could, but the room I was in went on forever. I brought the torch cautiously to the right, dead certain that something was inside this ancient rockpile besides Whitwell and me. Something that might jump into sight in the very next split-second. Certain as I was, it was all I could do to keep the torch in my hand and the scream in my throat when the beam of light picked out the first glistening bit of bone.

It was far ahead, seemingly in midair, a curve of polished ivory with an ugly sharp point. I made myself walk toward it: one step over the lumpy rocks, two steps, three. *Somebody's woven a web of bones,* I thought for an instant. Then I realized what they were. The reindeer antlers the May Day dancers had worn.

I walked between the high walls where they hung, challenging each other from a distance of barely six feet. Fifty sets of them on my left, fifty on my right. Whitwell had said it took two men to hang them back in place, and now I knew where. As I neared the end of the double file of antlers it occurred to me that the two men, whoever they were, might not yet be finished with their task. They might, in fact, be waiting for me just beyond the range of my torch.

But there was only a heap of rocks ahead, stacked one on top of the other like packing cases: crude stone steps going up as abruptly as a ladder.

I had read about steps like these. Swordsmen's steps, the old books called them. Built so that an invader would find his sword arm banging into the stone wall on his right if he tried to climb the stairway, while at his left not even a rope railing interfered with his opponent's swordplay—or the sheer drop that awaited the loser of the duel. Over the centuries many heroic men had probably hesitated to mount this deadly stairway. I didn't hesitate at all, for just as I reached the bottom step I heard someone cry out high overhead and I knew the voice was Whitwell's.

I have no clear memory of going up that stack of stone blocks, but I will never forget the sight my torch picked out at the first turn they made.

Whitwell lay sprawled on his back, his left hand clutching his right shoulder, his mud-splattered bare feet dangling over the unguarded side of the steps fifty feet above the stone floor I had just crossed. His voice was somewhere between a summons and a sob, rising and falling in a slow, racking rhythm.

"It's all right, Whitwell. I'm here," I called to him, rounding the pie-shaped step that marked the turn. There was no answer, only the steady rise and fall of the unhappy little voice.

Poor child, I remember thinking. *He's really hurt that shoulder badly now and he's calling me to hurry up and help.*

Then I reached his side and knelt on the cold rock slab, pointing my torch toward the wall. Enough light reflected back for me to see Whitwell's face plainly, as I bent over him.

He took no notice of me whatsoever. His pain-filled eyes were focused grimly on a point somewhere to the right of my right ear, and his voice continued to deliver its message to the darkness.

Young Lord Mabry was speaking to someone I could not see in a language I had never heard before.

VI

Calm. I must keep calm.

"Whitwell, let's go home now."

His recitation continued as if I had not spoken.

"Come along, my dear. It's freezing in here, and—"

And then I thought I heard a footstep.

My voice died. A second footstep sounded. Now there could be no question about it. There was someone else in Castle Cavage, and whoever it was was climbing the stone steps.

Hide!

I tried to. I put out the torch with one hand and clamped the other tight across Whitwell's mouth. There was a blessed instant of silence and total darkness. Then Whitwell tore my hand away and screamed as I have never heard any human scream before or since. Over and over, till the ancient stones rang with the sound of it, he screamed the single word "FATHER!"

Someone rounded the turning of the steps. A match flared not eight inches from my chin. The hand that held it wore a signet ring. Then a slick wet raincoat swept between the hysterical child and me, and the screams subsided into a muffled wail.

"There, there," I heard a man's voice saying. "Here I am, son. Here I am. Hush now."

Thank God, I breathed. *It's not the Lady. It's only the Duke.*

My relief was distinctly premature.

"Miz Guest," the same low voice continued, so low I remember only the hissing sibilance of it. "Leave this place at once."

"But the child—"

"At once!"

"Whitwell is—"

"You will say no more, Miz Guest. You will leave this place. Now!"

I had no choice, so I stood up, lighted my torch and started down the steps. Just before their turning, however, I swiveled the beam suddenly and saw the hand with the signet ring fly to shield the Duke's eyes from the light. It gave me the minute I needed.

"Your son," I called up to him, "was thrown from his horse today and put to bed. But nothing could keep him from coming here. I think he fell just now, going up these steps. I also think he is delirious, because I found him babbling absolute mumbo-jumbo."

The storm broke with a roar as I continued down.

"Why don't you say what you mean?" the Duke shouted after me. "Call us barbarians! Call us savages! But leave us in peace to speak whatever mumbo-jumbo we must! Now get out, get out, get out!"

I was stumbling down the steps, running away from his voice as fast as I could, but I was still on the rocky stairway when I heard Whitwell's voice rise again.

"She heard me, Father. She followed me here and she heard. She . . ."

Somewhere a heavy door slammed, and I heard no more.

Then I was back in the corridor where the antlers hung, facing each other high above my head. I ran the full length of that strange, silent hall. I have never wanted anything more than I wanted to leave Castle Cavage behind me.

○　　○　　○

Within half an hour I had packed. I could have done it faster, but things kept falling out of my hands. I remember being very careful not to look out of the window. I didn't want to see the Old Place again.

Finally I was out of my room, standing beside the gold-and-iron railing, thinking *This is the end of me at Singleton's* and waiting for the little lift. There was sudden noise and confusion on one of the lower floors, but I kept my back to the railing, deliberately distancing myself from whatever had happened.

I did not quite succeed in shutting out Dr. Darsey's voice, booming, "The boy will be perfectly fine tomorrow. If he hasn't caught a chill." But I never took my eyes from the small glass window cut into the lift door.

At last a light appeared there, rising slowly till it filled the entire pane. I reached to open the door but it was flung open from within, and the Duke came lunging out of it. He was still in his shiny raincoat, and he held two dusty bottles of wine.

"You mustn't go," he began.

Mr. Singleton should have told me this man is mad, I thought.

"I really must," I said, smiling an ingenue smile.

"I had to send you out of there just now. There was no time to explain, but you had to leave. Do you understand?"

"Of course I do," I lied.

102

"I had plainly told you never to go there. Do you remember?"

He had taken me by the arm. He was leading me away from the lift.

"Where are you taking me?" I whispered, too frightened to speak aloud.

"To dinner," he whispered back.

    o o o

Flames shot to the ceiling from the copper pan of crepes suzette which Grove had just placed on the table, drenched with cognac and touched with a long match.

"I see you have nerves of steel, Miz Guest," the Duke said as the conflagration subsided. "That didn't make you bat an eye."

That's because I'm numb, I thought, smiling.

"We'll have coffee in the study, Grove," he continued. "In just a little while."

Grove was the first non-actor I had ever seen back away from a table to a doorway, bowing at the beginning and the end of his walk, without stumbling over anything. I watched the door close after him with some trepidation. Now, for the first time in well over an hour, I was again alone with the Duke of Dair.

We sat at a window that overlooked the river, in the sort of glistening little kitchen one sees in American architectural magazines: all spotlights and steel. I had been playing the one role at which any actor's wife must excel—the role of audience. My smile never left my face. I laughed on cue. I alternated the phrases "How interesting!" and "Oh, really?", speaking both with over-vivacious brightness. A casual observer would probably have thought the Duke and I were getting along famously. Actually, I had my hands twisted up in the damask napkin in my lap, because they had begun to tremble badly the moment Grove shut the door.

For at that moment, my host had dropped the urbane, charming mask he had probably worn in public all his life. Now his dark eyes were unmistakably troubled.

"Earlier today," he said, "you were kind enough to take quite a risk for Whitwell, and you had your head handed to you in return. By me."

I wanted a cigarette, but Gavin and I had given them up five years earlier, so I continued smiling. The Duke went on.

"As you probably noticed, I have a loud voice and a wretched temper. I would like to apologize for both of them, if I may."

I expected him to switch on the seductive black-velvet eyes then, but he didn't.

"Please taste these crepes, Miz Guest. You barely touched your dinner, though you're very good at pushing the pieces about. I know Grove isn't the world's best cook, but he really can't help that. The recipes are usually mine."

He reached into his jacket pocket and brought out a sheaf of the familiar little cards imprinted with the word "Recipe." Obediently, I speared a forkful of crepe suzette, begged my hand to stop shaking and got the food inside my mouth.

"I always take recipe cards along. You never know when you may chance on something rather special."

A *demented duke, for instance,* I thought, still smiling as he removed one card from the batch and read it attentively.

"We'll have this tomorrow night," he informed me.

"How interesting."

"Yes. By then I hope you won't be quite so afraid of me. Though I really can't blame you, considering the tantrum I had."

"Nothing at all," I mumbled, distressed that he had sensed my fear.

"It wasn't nothing. The fact is I'm not sure how much I said to you. I only know I said too much."

I wondered what Mr. Singleton would think if he could see us: the Duke in the rumpled gray suit he'd put on to fly

104

himself to London, me in the Cannes Festival T shirt I'd pulled on over jeans and sneakers to explore the padlocked Picture Gallery. *Mr. Singleton would think of his commissions, old girl,* my common sense promptly told me. *And they would be astronomical even if nothing but the dishes on this table ever reached Singleton's auction block. So pull yourself together and tell this poor fellow whatever it is he wants to hear.*

"There is no need to apologize," I assured the Duke.

"I assure you I'm not trying just to apologize. The matter is more serious than that. I am trying to find out exactly what I told you earlier this evening. In the home of my ancestors."

He must have been quite uncommonly handsome, I thought, keeping my vivacious smile securely in place. "Really nothing that made the slightest sense to me," I told him.

"Then repeat it to me, if you please."

I very much wanted some of the wine in my glass, but I knew my hands were shaking too badly to bring the glass to my lips.

He was waiting and there was no evading those dark eyes.

"You simply said I shouldn't have come there—which was absolutely true, since I still have your note of instructions here in my pocket. I was going to post it on to Mr. Singleton, but I guess I never found out how to post a letter from here."

I was so terrified I was starting to cry.

"I'll have it posted," he said, taking it from me. "Please go on."

"I would never have gone there except that Whitwell—"

"I know. You meant well. But you aren't telling me what I said to you."

"I didn't understand it."

"Do you remember it?"

I will never forget it, I sighed to myself, nodding to him.

105

"Just say it for me. Please."

Thinking they might well be the last words I ever spoke on earth, I said, " 'Why don't you say what you mean? Call us savages or barbarians, but leave us in peace and get out of here.' "

"Tell me what I said about the mumbo-jumbo."

"I don't remember."

"Please try."

"You didn't say anything about mumbo-jumbo."

"Yes, I did. I told you it wasn't mumbo-jumbo."

I have always asked too many questions. This might easily have been my last, but I was too strung up to suppress it. "If it isn't mumbo-jumbo," I whispered, "what is it?"

"God only knows," he replied. "Some sort of survival from antiquity. My family has lived here literally forever, so I suppose at one time we got into the habit of— Ah, well, I won't speculate. Let me get to the point."

His eyes were quite unreadable now, but I saw his hand tighten around the stem of his wine glass as he spoke.

"Apart from my grandfather, my father and my son, you are the only person with whom I have ever had any conversation at all about these matters. I will not insult you by suggesting that you might deliberately pass the information on, say to—the press. I feel sure you would think twice before you did a thing like that. No, I must implore you to exercise the greatest care never to reveal it—unintentionally. To anyone."

"I have already forgotten all about it," I told him.

"I'm glad you have. You see, Whitwell's life depends on it."

*　　*　　*

Her dress was a flutter of chiffon, yellow as her hair. Drunk though she was, she was surprisingly pretty and even tinier than I had thought. From one hand she dangled a bottle of champagne, with a certain wanton elegance that probably dated back to Zelda Fitzgerald. Her other hand clutched the arm of Alaric Meade.

"Look!" she squealed at us across the iron-and-gold railings of the rotunda. "There goes the mysterious Duke of Dair with tonight's mystery guest!"

Rick bent quickly and said something to her which we could not hear. The Duke ignored them both and continued propelling me from the little kitchen where we had had dinner to the room where Grove had our coffee waiting. Kendra, however, twitched her arm away from Rick and came lurching toward us. She succeeded in reaching my side before we could enter one of the narrow passageways leading away from the rotunda.

"Boo!" she cooed to me roguishly. "I'm ever so glad to see you!" Then she dimpled up and laughed a little silver bell of a laugh, delighted with her own rhyme. There was no way for the Duke and me to pass her by without knocking her down. Something told me the Duke was considering that alternative. Fortunately, Rick caught up with her immediately.

"Kendra, fair moon of my delight," he said, folding her free hand into the crook of his elbow, "it is my honor to present to you the incomparable Deborah Guest."

"Howdy," she said, beaming at me. Her eyes were exactly the color of pea soup.

"Good evening," I said.

"We haven't much time," the Duke said to, I was surprised to notice, me. "Can you—?"

But there was no getting past Kendra just then.

"Mystery guest, Deborah Guest, Singleton says that you're the best." She giggled, swaying like a yellow tulip at my elbow. "Welcome to Dair, honey! If you can count what's in it, it's all yours!"

The Duke's hand had tightened on my elbow to the point of pain.

"Delighted to meet Your Grace," I said. "So nice to see you, too, Rick. Now if we could just—"

"Can't a poor, struggling editor get any dinner from you bloody aristocrats?" Rick interceded, leading Kendra away. "It's almost eleven now, isn't it? I happen to be starving."

"The night is young!" cried Kendra, stumbling across the marble floor beside him, swinging her champagne bottle by its neck. Suddenly she pivoted and fixed the Duke and me with a green-eyed glance.

"You be sure to look in the Picture Gallery, honey," she crooned. "Nighty-night now."

Although the way ahead was clear, the Duke did not move forward. I looked at him, wondering why the delay. He stood motionless, eyes shut, face drained of color, one hand clenched into a white-knuckled fist, the other still gripping my elbow.

He's gone into a trance, I thought. Then his lips moved.

"Four hundred and ninety," he muttered. "Four hundred and ninety-five. Five hundred." The dark eyes opened, blazing. "And now, Miz Guest, perhaps we will be permitted to have our coffee."

❈ ❈ ❈

The Duke's study was one of those rooms in which I can never decide where to sit or what to look at: a treasure house of books and paintings, paneling, porcelains, trophies, scale models of cars with very long bonnets, photos of dogs, horses and improbably large sheep. I stood just inside the door, watching my host make his sure-footed way through the luxurious confusion toward a satinwood console table where Grove had left a gleaming coffee service on an enormous silver tray. En route, he passed between a small Japanese television set and two corgis who were watching attentively as masked men galloped across its lighted screen.

"Sorry, fellows," he said to them, switching the telly off.

108

"If you don't clear out, the lady's going to put you up for auction."

The dogs looked at me with unmistakable resentment, then jumped down from the chair where they had been sitting and slowly pattered out of sight through a paneled door at the far end of the room.

That will be his bedroom, I said to myself. *I must make this a very quick cup of coffee.*

Yet half an hour later I found myself accepting a snifter of brandy and regretting that I had chosen to sit in a solitary armchair instead of on the companionable sofa where my host sat.

Perhaps I could rectify that. I rose and began to examine the study's far-reaching bookcases: Bernard Shaw's letters to Ellen Terry, some American admiral's recollections of the Battle of Midway, then an exquisite bit of velvet lying in a heap. Moving slowly toward my prey, I picked it up idly and said, "This looks like one of those caps the Venetian doges wore."

"Yes. Lord Byron once left it here, I'm told. How much do you think it will bring?"

I said what I always say, "A small fortune," and stopped in front of a snapshot of two men in white flannels. The older held a tennis racquet; the younger held a baby. All three were laughing.

"My father's the one holding me. Old Billy's the tennis player."

"Your grandfather?"

"Technically. He was also my best friend. Taught me everything I know, but it wasn't half of what he knew."

"Did you call him Old Billy?"

"Certainly. Everyone in the British Empire called him Old Billy. You should have seen him."

The little drawing was no bigger than a postcard, and someone had purchased its frame at Woolworth's. It was propped against a fat, calf-bound volume with a Latin title I couldn't understand. There was something compelling about it, so I picked it up and studied it. It was a swift, exquisite pencil sketch of a young woman with a swirl of long black hair. Her dress fitted her as closely as a sweater from the collarbone to well below the knee. From there, a clump of pleats fell to the ground. The sleeves interested me. Although the young woman's arms were raised as if to stop traffic, the sleeves were cut so full they hung down almost to her toes.

Must be an illustration for something by Chaucer, I thought. Then, true to my Singleton's training, I squinted to read the signature in the corner. It was not, however, a signature. The scrawled words read "Dunkirk 1940."

"This," I said, "is a perfectly beautiful drawing."

"Do you really like it?"

"I really do. Whose work is it?"

There was a moment's hesitation, then the answer came.

"A chap named Frederick Pennington."

An explosion of thoughts occurred inside my head.

Every art book, even the tabloid newspapers, will tell you that Frederick Pennington painted only one picture: the "Portrait of Isis" that now hangs in the Louvre. He painted it in 1920 and disappeared. Yet here's a sketch he made in 1940. Where did he spend the twenty years in between?

"Wherever did you get it?" I inquired, hoping I sounded casual.

"It belonged to Old Billy," he said crisply. "I'm going to see you back to your room now, Deborah."

How abrupt, I thought. *I've said something terribly wrong.*

"I can find my own way, thank you."

"Harold Clewys and Ethel say otherwise. Come along."

He took my hand and led me out into the chilly marble hall. His hand was warm. I realized that I was very pleased to be hand-in-hand with him. We strolled past the doors of the Picture Gallery.

"Here's where my day began," I told him.

"You mean Mother gave you the keys to the Picture Gallery?" His voice was strained with disbelief.

"No, but I'm glad to know where they are. I'm looking forward to seeing what's in there, all locked up, when your El Grecos and Gainsboroughs and such are just hanging out in the halls where anyone can look at them."

"Oh, Jesus," he whispered to himself.

"What's wrong?"

"Well, my mother won't let you go in there, and my lady wife won't rest until you do, and I anticipate a real brawl."

"Thaniel, why? What's locked up in there?"

He walked along silently for a moment, then he looked at me and I saw he was frowning.

"I haven't the slightest idea, Deborah. I've never been inside."

We climbed one flight of the grand staircase, turned left at the Murillo and right at the Van Dyck. Then we were facing the black door.

"Go through here," he said. "You're the second door on the left."

He's not even going to try to come in with me, I thought, surprised at how disappointed I was.

"Tomorrow," he said, "I'll show you Dairminster Cathedral if you'd care to look. If not, promise you'll have dinner with me again."

I couldn't speak. I simply looked at the dark eyes in the white face and nodded.

"Good. We'll drive Whit to school, or to Dr. Darsey— depending on how he feels when he wakes up. Then we'll look at the Cathedral. Good night, Deborah."

For a moment I thought he would not even kiss me, but he did. Too briefly, and only once, but with consummate tenderness. In spite of all that has happened since, I have never forgotten that kiss.

111

VII

The yellow tulip had wilted during the night. Kendra, Duchess of Dair, lay sprawled at the foot of the violet marble steps, looking—from where I stood at the railing on the third floor—not unlike a wad of discarded yellow cleansing tissue.

My first thought was *He's killed her!* My second was *He should have done it years ago!* Fortunately, my third was *Easy, old girl. Just because a man's asked you to visit a cathedral, don't start thinking about marching down the aisle.*

So I was not utterly crushed when Kendra began to sing.

"Love is a simple thing . . ." she trilled as I went down the steps in my silent sneakers ". . . love is a silver ring . . ."

"Good morning!" I saluted her, careful not to stop.

"It's still night!"

"No, really, it's after seven."

"Come back here. I have news for you."

She waited while I retraced my steps.

"What news is that?"

"I am the law west of the Pecos."

"I see."

"I am the law east of the River Dair."

"Mmmm-hmmmm."

"It's true-oo."

"Of course."

"Only I never have my own way about anything."

"Oh?"

"But I will. You wait and see. I married him. I had his lousy baby. And now he's going to do exactly as I say."

"Fine."

"So stop telling me it's morning."

"OK."

I turned away from her and saw Whitwell approaching from the direction of the lift. He wasn't limping. I turned back.

"Your son's coming down the passageway. Do you want him to see you like this?"

"I'm waiting for him, thank you very much. Whitwell? Ugly, ugly name. You do hear me, Whitwell? You have an ugly, ugly name."

"Good morning, Mother," he said, giving her the briefest possible peck on the forehead.

"His father named him, not me. I never have my own way."

The boy shifted his bookbag from one shoulder to the other without a flicker of expression on his face or, I was pleased to notice, any apparent discomfort.

"What did you want my name to be?" he asked.

"Gafford," his mother snarled back.

⚬　⚬　⚬

Morning sunshine poured through the gigantic lily window of Dairminster Cathedral, and it looked as if a very good electrician had used every colored gel in the spectrum to

113

light the soaring Gothic interior. Thaniel and I followed a path of dancing blues and purples to an archway cut into the wall near the river entrance.

"I'm glad there aren't any tourists today," Thaniel said. "When Esty Hall is open, they swarm all over this place, too."

"I don't wonder. It's magnificent."

"Selfish of me, I know. But I think how terribly my grandfather would resent having his eternal rest disturbed by strangers. Hi, Billy, old fellow," he said, tapping a bronze plaque as amiably as he might have slapped a friend on the back. "Keeping an eye on things for us?"

Mad, I thought. *Handsome, probably harmless, but unquestionably bonkers.*

"Forgive me, Deborah. Part of the May Day drill around here is visiting the tombs of my ancestors, and here they are. I can't seem to get used to the idea that Old Billy's gone for good, so I don't say prayers for him. Somehow I'm not sure he needs any. Now, my father is another matter."

We had moved on to another plaque.

"As far as I'm concerned, my father was never really alive. He simply had no time for me and left it to Billy to bring me up. So I don't say prayers for him, either. And as for the rest of them—"

We had descended a shallow flight of stone steps.

"—I never met any of them, so I think a nod and a smile will suffice."

"I wonder that you come here at all, Thaniel."

"Billy always did it. He'd notice if I didn't, wherever he is. So, here I am. Now let's go leave a check for the poor and—"

"Wait a minute. Please."

I have no enthusiasm for crypts, but this was a small medieval masterpiece. A banner floated from the ceiling: white with a pale blue X stretching to all four corners.

"Our crest," Thaniel said. "I think we're entitled to a bit of gold on it now, but that old rag still has considerable wear left in it."

114

I had moved on to a wood carving which commanded the center of the stone floor: a man-sized angel with mighty wings, wielding a sword triumphantly. I followed the figure from head to foot and recoiled hastily. One foot rested on a decapitated head.

"It's only the Archangel Michael, stamping out evil." Thaniel laughed. "Here he is again."

I had seen the tapestry a thousand times before. Its design is strong; its colors have faded to a lovely glow; it is a staple illustration in needlework books and frequently turns up on greeting cards.

"I hadn't realized this was here, Thaniel."

"It's here and it's going to stay here. That fellow there with the black hair is supposed to be the first Knight of Cavage."

The tapestry is very dramatic. An archbishop in full regalia and a black-haired man in tunic and hose, holding a shield with the pale blue X on the white field, stand on either side of the statue of the Archangel Michael. Behind them there is a cathedral shape with a central spire like Dairminster's. It is seen only in silhouette. Behind it flames rise to the sky.

"You know, I've always wondered about the flames. Did they have a fire when they were building the Cathedral?"

"Not that I know of. Probably represents hellfire or something thirteenth-century like that."

"Probably. Oh, look!"

"I was waiting for you to notice that. It's what brings the tourists down here."

Medieval noblemen's tombs all look alike. The deceased's likeness is carved full-length on top of a stone sarcophagus. The pose never varies. They lie on their backs in their very finest clothes with their hands in an eternal attitude of prayer and a hopeful look on their faces.

This one's effigy was exquisitely painted. The hair that peeped out of his coif was black with a wing of gray on one side. The gold dagging on his tunic was fresh as it had been seven hundred years before. And the dog stretched out at his feet might perfectly well have been Stratford: an orange-red corgi with one white hindpaw and only a stub for a tail.

"The dog is perfection!"

"His master apparently thought so, too. They tell me this is the only tomb in England with a dog on it. Old Billy brought me here to see it when I lost my first dog. I was about four years old, and I guess I was making a dreadful fuss. Then Billy showed me this and told me it was proof that corgis go to heaven. Fortunately none of the clergy overheard."

"Maybe it's true. Is this the First Knight of Cavage's tomb?"

"Yes. Sir Jaymes. The one in the tapestry. Born just plain Jemmy Cavage in the thirteenth century. Then Edward the First knighted him and he went to the Crusades."

"Whitwell showed me some marriage contracts he never signed."

"We have no idea who Sir Jaymes married. All we know is that every other Crusader came back loaded down with gold. Jemmy came back with a little boy in front of him on his saddle, introduced him as his son and never told anybody who his mother was. Not that it makes any difference, but I understand the tour guides make quite a mystery story of it when they bring people here."

I admired the carved Latin inscription on the sides of the stone sarcophagus. "As tombs go, it's really very beautiful," I said. We moved to the next praying nobleman's tomb.

"This is Jemmy's motherless son. He grew up to be Sir Michael Cavage."

"Well," I said. "That is impressive."

"We still have his manuscripts somewhere. At least, we did."

The original manuscript of the life of Saint Charles de Cordel, the Archbishop of Dair, by Sir Michael Cavage might bring considerably more at auction than a Gutenberg Bible, I reflected. *It's earlier, and there's only one.*

116

"Sir Michael seems to have married," I said.

"Yes. All the others are buried in pairs. Jemmy's the only loner in the lot. But he has his dog."

"It's not quite the same."

Thaniel shrugged. We were now facing a glass case with a bit of hand-inscribed parchment inside it.

"This is a letter Sir Michael once wrote to Cordel," Thaniel said.

"I can't read any Latin except Roman numerals," I apologized. "What does it say?"

"Oh, it's just a thank-you-for-your-kind-expression-of-sympathy sort of thing."

"The date looks like 1308 to me. Who died in 1308?"

"Sir Jaymes. The First Knight of Cavage. The one with the dog."

I fixed Thaniel with a stern frown. "Please remember, Milord Duke," I said, "that I am the lady from Singleton's. Look at Sir Jaymes's tomb again. He died in 1310."

"Hmmmm. So he did. Well, I'll try to explain that in my next lecture. Meanwhile, let's get some lunch."

◦　◦　◦

"I know, I know." Thaniel smiled at me sadly across the checkered tablecloth at the Red Dragon Inn. "We marry people because we think we'll die if we can't have them. Then we spend a long, long time wishing we were dead."

"I never really regretted marrying Gavin. I still think there must be some mistake, that he'll phone or something."

The hand with the signet ring touched mine for a fraction of a second.

"Why on earth would you want to hear from him?"

"I'm used to hearing from him."

"This is a very, very fresh divorce, isn't it?"

"Six days."

"You have no idea how lucky you are. I hope he never

117

phones you. But the way things like this work out for me, he's probably trying your number right now."

"I doubt it."

"I only said it because you seemed to need a ray of hope."

"Am I that forlorn-looking?"

"No, you're damned pretty. How long were you married to him?"

"Ten years."

"Then you are at a disadvantage, aren't you?"

"Disadvantage?"

"Forgive me, but it's obvious you've never so much as looked at another man during those ten years. You seem not to know that you're ten years older than you were at the time of your marriage."

"This is beginning to sound like a scolding."

"Well, you certainly kept me at arm's length last night."

"You certainly stayed there."

His dark eyes were positively dancing. Was it mischief? Spite? Amusement? Desire? I didn't know him well enough to tell.

"Deborah," he said, "have you any idea what goes on at the Cannes Film Festival?"

"Only in a general way. Gavin never took me there."

"I don't wonder. Yet last night, in your souvenir shirt from that annual orgy, you sat primly in an armchair talking about paintings, for God's sake! I was almost afraid to kiss you goodnight. And a lot of good it did me!"

I felt that I must be blushing terribly.

"We are in a public place," I whispered.

"Nobody's paying the slightest attention to us. But even if someone were, would your reputation be—tarnished?"

"No, but you seem to think I should have fallen into your arms and begged you to do with me as you pleased."

"That sort of thing has happened to me from time to time."

"I congratulate you. It will not happen this time."

118

"Good! It's extremely tiresome."

He was actually laughing.

"You know, Deborah, it's the women I can't have who are my downfall."

"You don't sound as if there have been very many of them."

"How do you think Kendra got her claws into me?"

"I've wondered."

"She let me think she was mad about Hugh Gafford."

"Diana's father?"

"Yes. Dead at twenty-eight, poor devil, and I've missed him more than I would ever have imagined. We were rivals in all things, from nursery days. He played tennis better than I did, so I used to practice off a wall in desperate secrecy hour after hour. I could handle a car better than he could, so I daresay he did his share of brush-up driving all alone in the wee hours. As for trophies from horse shows and dog shows, we were fairly evenly matched. Then Hugh found Kendra. You can't imagine what a pretty little thing Kendra used to be."

"I'm surprised that he let you meet her."

"Went out of his way to introduce us. When you've got a really dependable rival, it's downright addictive, you know. You hunger for the competition. I guess he couldn't wait to bring Kendra to my attention. At any rate, he told me they were getting married in the spring. I instantly thought to myself 'We'll see about that!' and set to work. I followed the two of them around all winter and made rather a fool of myself."

"How?"

"Kendra was getting a great deal of press attention at the time. You know the sort of thing. The beautiful American heiress who is sweeping all the blue ribbons in all the dog shows with her fancy little Pekingese. You add the future Earl of Esty and the future Duke of Dair, plus their pet pups, to that."

"Every truck driver must have been placing bets on the result. Odd that I don't remember anything about it."

"It was fifteen years ago. I'm sure you weren't allowed to read the tabloids then. But I assure you the three of us were smeared all over them, because we entered every damned dog show from Monaco to the Midlands. By March, Hugh was no longer speaking to me. By Easter, Kendra had come home with me to meet Old Billy."

"What did he think of her?"

Thaniel grinned. "I can't repeat what he said; there are ladies present. Anyway, I didn't listen. I was sure the sun rose and set on this rare and perfect little creature from Oklahoma. And so we were married. That was the same summer Old Billy passed away."

I watched the grin disappear.

"It was years before I would admit it, even to myself, but I knew on our wedding day that I'd made a bad choice. How bad I had yet to find out, but I was terribly troubled by Kendra's behavior right after the ceremony."

I waited, but he had signaled the innkeeper to bring our bill.

"She was just giving me an intimation of what I could expect in the years ahead. Greed. Cruelty. And a dazzling ability to disguise them both as adorable little-girl mistakes. Shall we be on our way now? We've got an ox-roasting to go through before dinner."

"I should have thought the roast ox would be dinner," I said, following him into the sunlit parking lot outside.

"Custom prohibits my partaking of any of it, I'm happy to tell you. However, I have to carve."

"May I watch that?"

"I insist!"

We had reached the automobile Thaniel had chosen for the expedition: a 1948 Humber Hawk, he had told me. Now he hunted for its doorkey and I watched what appeared to be a white hearse pull out of a parking place just opposite ours. As it swung about, I caught a glimpse of the driver's face.

"Thaniel," I said, "what kind of car is that?"

He turned and whistled appreciatively. "A stretched Eldorado," he said. "Looks like some oil man's idea of heaven."

I got into the Humber Hawk beside him. "Actually, I recognized the driver," I told him.

"One of the Rockefellers?" he inquired wryly.

"No. It was Mr. Hookham, the man who guides the tours at Esty Hall."

◊ ◊ ◊

Never having been to an ox-roast before, and not having any wardrobe to draw on in any case, I wore the pink cashmere pullover and black velvet jeans. If you check last June's issue of *Nobility*, you'll see them, I'm afraid. Alaric Meade had three photographers blazing away, and one of them seemed to be assigned to me.

"Rick, what are you trying to do to me?" I protested, as a bibulous gentleman in sheik's clothing topped by a ten-gallon hat deposited me in Rick's lap after a wild dance across the marble terrace. "Who on earth was that, and why did you want my picture with him?"

"Milady Deborah," Rick replied with a rather too-straight face, "that was one of the North Sea oil people Kendra has been cultivating. And you are the best-looking woman here. Please try to accept the fact that you're a celebrity."

"Please be serious. I'm an auctioneer's assistant in sneakers."

"I'm doing a story about you called 'The Eyes of Singleton Abbs.' And very lovely eyes they are, by the way."

"Mr. Singleton will sack me if you do a thing like that!"

"Nonsense. He'll double your pay and buy a lot more advertising from me. Now let's go watch Thaniel do the star turn."

We threaded our way through an exuberant crowd. Some could only have been Kendra's guests: nymphets with diamond bracelets and hand-stitched boots, chubby men in regrettably snug denims and wristwatches that could clock a racehorse under water, my erstwhile dancing partner in his sartorial salute to oil-producing regions everywhere. Others were clearly Dair Manor people in their partygoing best: dark suits for the men, print dresses for the women, hair ribbons for the girls, neckties for the boys.

Not ten yards from the woods at the base of Crag Cavage, the ox was turning on the spit, attended by two men in splattered aprons. The fire beneath it cast its light on a dozen long picnic tables covered with bright cloths and big bunches of spring flowers.

"I don't see Thaniel," I said to Rick.

"Thaniel, is it? Didn't you say you were just an auctioneer's assistant?"

I probably blushed.

"You aren't going to put that in your story, are you?" I said.

"Put what in my story?"

"The Duke."

"Certainly not. Unless, of course, you happen to be photographed with him, in which case my conscience as a reporter would hardly allow me to—"

Suddenly the dance orchestra broke off.

"What happened, Rick? That's my favorite song."

"Hush," he whispered. "The serious part starts now. Look!"

I looked. Two lighted matches were standing upright in the low doorway of Castle Cavage. Then they began to move forward and one fell behind the other. It was almost five minutes before I realized that the lighted matches were flaming torches, that Whitwell held his with both hands and never took his eyes off it, and that behind him Thaniel held a torch in his left hand and the great sword Wilva in his right.

They made the descent of the crag as if there were no one

else within five miles of them and approached the ox without acknowledging anyone's presence by so much as a glance. Then the spit was stopped. Thaniel stepped forward, handed his torch to one of the aproned men and lifted the great sword to his lips.

Nobody breathed, I'm sure. I know I didn't. I watched transfixed as Thaniel raised Wilva high over his head, then brought it down and drew it lightly across the full length of the roast ox. Then he thrust the blade into the fire.

The second aproned man, who had been hovering near Whitwell, now stepped forward and took his torch. Thaniel withdrew the sword from the flame, turned away from the fire, the spit, the ox, all of it, and, holding the sword aloft, ran as if he were a boy of sixteen across the moonlit gardens into the glittering drawing rooms of Dair. Whitwell was right behind him.

Grove had appeared with carving implements and a queue of Kendra's friends began to form around the ox.

"Will you allow me to get a plate for you?" a voice boomed. It was Dr. Darsey, towering over even Rick, who's tall.

"Mrs. Guest is with me, Doctor," Rick said cheerily. "But we'd be delighted if you'd join us."

I felt a flashbulb explode a bit too near my left cheek as I stood between my would-be dinner partners.

"Thank you both," I said. "I've got to get back to—"

"Thaniel?" Rick smiled the question. I thought there was a touch more peppermint than sunshine in his smile.

On the green lawn beyond the tables, I caught a flash of spangles and saw people milling about.

"Oh, no, Rick," I began. I never finished that sentence, because a hand touched my arm. I knew whose it was without looking.

"Allow me," Thaniel said, and with a bow even Marie Antoinette might have considered extravagantly low, he led me to the moonlit lawn where I had seen the spangles.

Clewys stood waiting, harp in hand, at the head of a long

123

double line of dark suits and print dresses. We took our places at the far end and the harp began. Perhaps the music lasted half an hour, perhaps no more than ten minutes. I couldn't say. I know only that Thaniel led me through the intricate figures of a country dance so rhythmic I was conscious of nothing but its beat.

The long double line of onlookers turned into a circle before our dance was done, everyone clapping hands in time with the music, nobody uttering another sound. And Rick's man with the flashbulbs was among those present.

Sometimes I look at the pictures in last June's *Nobility* and marvel at details I didn't notice at the time. The faces in the background, for example. Whitwell's. Kendra's. Dr. Darsey's. Rick's.

VIII

"Her Grace, the Dowager will take lunch downstairs today," Ethel informed me as I entered the vast White Dining Room. "At noon sharp. Will you be finished here by then, miss?"

"I'll duck out in time, then come back."

"Very good, miss," she said, doubt written all over her wide, rosy face, and—or was I just imagining things after last night?—disapproval, too. She gave the buttercups in the cut-crystal bowl a final tweak and bustled away.

"The central portrait, facing the entrance ..." I began telling my tape recorder. Then I turned it off. Thomas Chippendale at the top of his form can lure me away from even Sir Joshua Reynolds, and if the japanned cabinet-on-chest in Dair's White Dining Room is not the top of his form, I cannot think what is.

I went to it as if drawn by magnets, and spoke to it as if it were alive.

"I hope no one with central heating ever gets hold of you," I said. "You're too beautiful."

The measurements were odd. The cabinet was forty inches wide on the outside, but with its interior drawers removed half an inch of interior space remained unaccounted for.

"Up to your old tricks, eh, Mr. Chippendale?" I said, pressing the roof of the cabinet's interior tentatively.

Mr. Singleton has often said I'm quite good at finding secret compartments, and I think he attributes it to ESP or witchcraft or what he likes to call "that special sense my father had."

The plain fact is the eighteenth-century cabinetmakers repeated themselves oftener than their patrons suspected. Even Chippendale. Even at his best.

So I was far from astonished when the little secret drawer shot forward, just missing a collision with my chin. What surprised me was that there was a piece of folded paper inside.

In the Goods Received rooms at Singleton's, we constantly find secret compartments in old furniture which has been sent to us to sell. Usually they are empty; people who own old furniture give it a very thorough going-over for possible hidden treasure before letting the auctioneer have it.

Was this hidden treasure I had just unearthed? I stared at the folded paper for a long time before I could bring myself to look inside. Clearly, the paper was of modern manufacture. That ruled out anything belonging to the early lords of Dair. Still, someone had valued it enough to put it inside a drawer the average person would never have located, let alone opened.

I'm only human. I couldn't put it back unread. So I said to myself, "Whatever this turns out to be, I'll hand it over to Thaniel immediately," and only then did I allow myself to unfold and read it.

I was, frankly, disappointed when I read the date: "Somewhere in France, May 1916," but then I read on.

Dear Father,

So it is true.

No rational man of the twentieth century would believe it, which is why I have scoffed, but I now know that it is true. What happened to you at Mafeking in 1900 has now happened to me. I would be dead now were it otherwise.

She leaped between me and a nasty-looking Mauser in the hands of a Hun who had crawled to within 20 feet of our dugout. She shouted something at him, and he shot at her instead of at me.

It gave me an extra second—all I needed. He is now one of our prisoners.

Like you, I could not understand what she shouted. I cannot even quite remember what she looked like, because she vanished as suddenly as she appeared.

Long black hair, long blue dress. Tiny little woman. But she saved my life in battle.

You always said she would.

W.

Where had I seen that W before?

Of course! It was in my document case at the bottom of a 1919 letter to Mr. Singleton's father. It was the first letter of William Cavage's signature.

I had vowed to show it to Thaniel, whatever it was, perhaps just because I wanted an excuse to see Thaniel again before the evening. So I tapped the little drawer shut again and proceeded to close the cabinet's magnificent lacquered doors. Then, with the unfolded letter in my hand, I turned to leave the White Dining Room, and found myself staring straight at a green paisley necktie knotted over a pale gray shirt.

"Is it anything really juicy?" Rick inquired.

"I didn't hear you come in here."

"Thick rugs."

"Why didn't you speak?"

"I was about to. Sorry if I've startled you, Deb."

"That's all right. This is an interesting piece of furniture here."

I hesitated to try to walk past him. Although he was smiling, he hadn't moved out of my way and I realized he was close enough to take the piece of paper away from me simply by reaching out for it.

"Yes. I must admit I've always found secret compartments very interesting."

So he had been watching.

"I was about to turn the contents of this particular secret compartment over to its rightful owner," I said with a smile, deciding to venture a step toward the doorway.

Rick swung out of my way immediately, turned and began to walk to the doorway with me.

"Can't I just peek before you do this noble deed?"

I was genuinely troubled.

"Rick, I don't know. If we were at Singleton's, I'd gladly show it to you. But we're visitors here, and—"

"After last night, you're a bit more than a visitor, Milady Deborah. That's why I came looking for you the minute I got up."

A pulse began to pound in my throat and I stared at the familiar gray eyes, waiting to see a glint of the sunshine I usually found in them. There was no trace of it.

"Kendra was literally wild with rage last night," he continued, "and you must be very, very careful. This is—"

The door that led to the passageway burst open and a grimy little face looked in.

"Mr. Meade, Mr. Meade! Good morning! Oh, hello, Mrs. Guest."

"Diana! What a lovely surprise!" Rick lifted her up for a hug and kiss. "I was going to call on you in a little while."

"I didn't know that," she said, "so I came to visit instead."

"Did Mrs. Travis drive you?"

"No, I rode my bicycle," she told us proudly.

"Isn't that a terribly long ride?" I asked.

"I took the shortcut you and Whit told me about. It's super."

"What shortcut?" Rick asked.

"Whit said it used to be our bridle path. He called it Crinsley's Wood."

"Really?" Rick said, setting Diana down and walking over to ring for a servant. "Why did he call it that?"

"I asked him, but he didn't say."

Ethel answered Rick's ring, and he asked her to find Whitwell and take Diana there. Diana had certain objections to this.

"Can't I just stay here with the two of you?" she asked.

"Not just now," Rick said quickly. "I'll come after you when Mrs. Guest and I have finished talking."

Although obviously skeptical about this, Diana allowed Ethel to lead her away. Rick stood looking after her, struggling to keep the worry from surfacing on his face. He failed.

"That's not the first time I've heard the name Crinsley," he told me when Diana was out of earshot. "He's the reason Diana's mother would never come to Dair after sundown. It's something even Gaffords by marriage don't do. But I've never heard of Crinsley's Wood before. How do you happen to know about it?"

"Grove and Whitwell drove me through it the night I arrived. Whitwell said it was haunted by a man strong enough to uproot trees. Grove scolded him for telling me."

"I don't doubt it. The topic is totally taboo. I've never been able to get fact one about Crinsley from anybody around here. And when you can't even bribe people into telling you about their ghost, dear Deborah, they have an exceptionally dangerous ghost."

"Whitwell told me a great deal more than I cared to know."

129

"How true. You stepped off the London train and instantly became the world authority on the subject. Well, please share your erudition. Tell me where Crinsley's Wood is."

Why is this so important? I wondered.

"At the end of the Avenue of Lights, we turned left."

"There's nothing there but shrubs and trees."

"Well, I guess we must have nosed through some underbrush, but I assure you there's a gravel path. According to Whitwell, it leads directly to Dair, and it's much quicker than the river road. I couldn't swear to that, because we had to turn back before we got to the end."

"Because a tree went down. Uprooted by Crinsley, do you suppose?"

"Oh, Rick, please. A little boy told me some old wives' tales during a bad storm, and—"

And that same little boy speaks gibberish to someone invisible every night around sundown, I reminded myself. Three days at Dair and my disbelief in ghosts was fading fast.

"Did he tell you anything else? Did you see anything odd? Do you know anything more about Crinsley? Anything at all?"

"No, I don't."

Rick was on his feet again. "Bless you for telling me this much," he said. "And remember, watch your step with Kendra."

He was almost out the door when he remembered the other thing he had to tell me. I knew it must be important, because he stepped back inside the lovely old white room and closed the door behind him.

"By the way, Deb, I talked to my office in London last night. Gavin and Cindy are in the news again."

"Oh, Rick, he's not dead, is he?"

"Regrettably, no. He and Cindy just had a little lovers' quarrel in the presence of five hundred people in the lobby of the Drury Lane Theater."

"They've only been married three days."

"Time enough for even Gavin to realize that the only

thing he's got that Cindy's other men haven't got is grounds for divorce." Rick smiled at me. "I'll see you later."

Then I was alone again, with the curious letter Old Billy had written to his father still unfolded in my hand.

*   *   *

I couldn't find Thaniel.

I sped through the lofty splendors of Dair's principal floor: the violet marble statuary hall with arched niches that was at its heart, the seeming infinity of broad passageway that radiated out of it like spokes from a wheel, without hearing a sound except my own footsteps or seeing anyone at all.

Clewys had said one had to ring for the servants. I was too bashful to do that. What if the person who answered questioned my right to ring? Worse still, what if I stammered as I inquired—in my most offhand way—where the Duke might be?

After last night, you're a bit more than a visitor, Rick had told me. *Kendra was in a wild rage,* he had said.

All of a sudden the whole message sank in. *I'm the talk of the county this morning because Thaniel picked me to dance with last night!*

I headed straight back to the White Dining Room, opened Mr. Chippendale's not-so-secret drawer and replaced the letter where I'd found it.

"The central portrait, facing the entrance," my tape recorder played back to me, "is a fine example of Sir Joshua Reynolds' later portraiture," I continued, approaching the canvas, "and shows a family group seated in a garden."

"The Italian Garden," someone behind me said.

I whirled to find the Dowager Duchess in the doorway, and began to apologize for remaining in the room when I'd been told to clear out.

"I'm delighted that you stayed," she told me. "Please join me for lunch."

She was, I had thought at first, in a wheelchair, but as she

131

glided into the room I saw it was a sort of miniature automobile, painted silver. She guided it to the head of her long, gleaming banquet table, where she rang a tiny bell that appeared to be made of gold.

A man I had not seen before was at her side instantly, bowing.

"Have Ethel set another place at my right, please," she instructed him. "Come sit here, Mrs. Guest." She smiled at me, adding, "I do hope you like Scotch salmon."

I do. It was a sumptuous luncheon, and my hostess's mood was sunny as the day.

"I think I may have found the right governess for my young neighbor, Lady Esty," she confided to me. "A Miss Harmon, very highly recommended for the post by a friend whose daughter will go to boarding school for the first time this fall. If Miss Harmon could contend with that little girl, she's the woman I've been searching for. Have you met little Diana, Mrs. Guest?"

I told her the circumstances of our meeting.

"Then you're aware the poor child has no family at all."

That's what you think, I observed silently, nodding an assent.

The Dowager laid her napkin on the tabletop and lifted one languid hand above it. No further signal was necessary; the manservant materialized from behind a closed door that must have had a peephole.

"We'll have coffee—where would you like to have it, Mrs. Guest?"

"Is it warm enough to go outdoors?"

The exquisite face changed slightly. "I haven't left this house for years," the lovely, low voice said softly. "Would the conservatory suit you?"

"Of course, Your Grace."

"Then come along."

I followed her small silver car into the south wing of Dair, and into a glorious tall room where sunlight streamed through windows two stories high to warm the tangle of palm fronds basking below. We made our way to the windows and looked out at a field of rosebushes coming into leaf. The manservant placed a chair for me, and Ethel appeared with a butler's tray-table which she set up.

I sensed the change in the Dowager's mood almost before I had taken my first sip of coffee. The novelty of having a luncheon companion had given her a distinct lift at first. Now, perhaps she was tired from the unaccustomed strain of playing hostess. I was beginning to wonder if she should go back to her own rooms, when she said, "I'm so thankful the dogs kept out of our way just now."

I said nothing.

"You must think I carry this feeling about dogs to extremes," she continued, stirring her creamy coffee very slowly, avoiding my eye.

"Many people share your feeling."

"I used to adore them. Then something happened to make me hate and fear them all. I had to have—I had to have psychiatric attention for quite some time afterwards."

And I thought that nurse was on hand because this beautiful old woman can't walk! I told myself, smiling politely.

"But apparently I'm not over it, after all. I'm so very sorry to have fainted yesterday, Mrs. Guest."

"You may simply have been overtired, Your Grace. In fact, I am afraid I'm overtiring you again."

She lifted one fine, long-fingered hand to silence me.

"Not so, Mrs. Guest. What do you think of the prospects for roses next month?"

There were rosebushes as far as I could see, to the very banks of the shining river that glinted like a satin ribbon far below us.

"I think it will be beautiful even if none of them bloom."

"It's showy for a month," she conceded. "But ah, you should have seen it years ago. I'm forgetting! You were looking at it when I came into the dining room."

"Was this the Italian Garden Your Grace spoke of?"

"It was. I had it destroyed."

"You did?"

"Yes. You see, the previous Lady Esty—poor little Diana's mother—was killed there. And no one saw what happened but Diana and me."

I wondered if I should ring for someone, but I didn't see a bell. I wondered if Ethel or the manservant might have stayed inside the manicured wilderness of the conservatory with us. I hoped the Dowager Duchess and I were not alone.

"Lacey was an angelic girl. I often wished that she had married Thaniel instead of Hugh. I think she might have felt the same way, though she never said so. She'd had no mother, you know, so she came to call on me a good deal oftener than one's younger neighbors usually do. I became very fond of her. I was keenly disappointed that I couldn't visit her in hospital when Diana was born, but the Dairminster Lying-In simply has too many steps to climb."

Perhaps I could change the subject.

"So many public buildings are so badly designed," I observed.

"I couldn't visit Lacey, so as soon as she came home she came to visit me. And she brought Diana with her, all wrapped up in a pink bunting and sound asleep. It was a lovely summer's afternoon. I was sitting right over there where the pergola used to be. You couldn't have seen me from these windows, though, because the hedges had been allowed to grow too high."

Why doesn't somebody come here? I thought. *She's getting upset. Where's that nurse of hers?*

"That must have made the conservatory very dark," I said. "Don't you agree flowers need sun?"

She didn't hear me.

"Lacey came into the garden, wearing the most beautiful pink silk dress, and she walked over to me and put the baby in my arms. 'Here she is at last!' she said to me. 'Allow me to present my daughter!' Then she sat down no farther away from me than you are, and—"

134

The old woman suddenly raised both of her magnificent long hands to her throat. Now her eyes were wild.

"My dog, Oma, lay sleeping at my feet. She was a sweet, good poodle, and I had picked her out of the litter myself and raised her by hand. But all of a sudden—I have thought about this for ten years, but I still cannot believe it—Oma went for that poor girl's throat!"

The Dowager was screaming. I clutched both her shoulders and shook her, but she didn't know I was there. I prayed for someone to come, and quickly.

"Nobody heard me!" she screamed. "Nobody came to help!"

"Stop this!" I said. "Hush! Don't remember any more!"

"When Dwain got there, it was much too late. Lacey was dead. Her throat was just a big hole with blood gushing out of it. And Oma had the strangest expression on her face. As if she expected me to praise her. Oh, my God, that dog was proud of what she had done! Proud! Proud!"

Someone wearing white wrestled her way between us.

"Troublemaker!" Mrs. Mackleroy roared at me. "How did you upset her like this?"

Then she plunged a hypodermic syringe into the Dowager's tensed and trembling arm.

° ° °

I must have taken ten wrong turnings, but I found my way back to the White Dining Room at last.

I went directly to the Reynolds portrait opposite the doorway and looked at the garden in the background. There, indeed, was a pergola, dripping palest blue wisteria. Here, indeed, were dark green hedges destined to grow much higher as the years slipped by. And facing a fine bronze statue of Mercury there were two handsome stone benches.

If the Dowager sat on this one, holding Diana, I thought, *Diana's mother must have sat on that one. Or was that whole ghastly story only madness? Is the poor old woman insane?*

135

A rousing tenor voice was singing "Men of Harlech" outside in the passageway. Clewys, closely supervised as always by Woodbine, marched into the White Dining Room and kicked the door shut behind him.

"Now, Clewys—" I began, hoping he would not continue with his comic flirtation. I was in no mood for nonsense that afternoon.

His face was grave, however, and his hands never stopped strumming the fine old harp. He stopped singing only long enough to say, "Get the little girl home to Esty Hall before sundown. Cavage land is a dangerous place for a Gafford to be after dark."

IX

Diana drove a hard bargain.

She would, she finally assured Rick and me, return to Esty Hall if certain non-negotiable conditions were met: Rick must drive, and I must come along and spend the night. Had Diana known she was in a race with the gathering sunset, she might have demanded even more. I know I would have acceded to almost any demand she made; Clewys had made a profound impression on me with his unsmiling warning. Perhaps he had given Rick the identical warning. Someone had.

I had barely time to collect my trench coat and leave a scribbled note, which some instinct told me to address to Grove, about my destination. Then little Dwain said, "Hurry, mum. Mr. Meade and the little Countess are waiting for you in the North Courtyard, and they've got the engine running."

I gave her the note addressed to Grove, silently cursed the fate that was preventing me from having dinner with Thaniel for the third consecutive evening, and dived into the big

137

Land Rover that was idling just outside the door. It pulled away instantly.

"Let's take that shortcut of yours," Rick said. "I'd like to see it."

"If you like," Diana agreed grandly. Five queens couldn't have looked more on top of the world than she, seated between us in the front seat, her muddy bicycle up-ended in the cargo space behind us.

"Far be it from me to interfere with anyone else's itinerary," I ventured, "but has the fallen tree been cleared away?"

Diana looked at me with something verging on respect.

"No, it hasn't," she said. "I had to climb over it and pull my bike up after me. We can't go that way after all, Mr. Meade."

"Are you sure we can't drive around the tree?" Rick was annoyed.

"Quite. The woods are very thick there."

"But Diana, don't you have somebody who clears your bridle path?"

"Maybe I did. But there aren't any horses anymore. I think I've just got filthy old Travis and Augusta."

"There must be others."

"They all work for the gentlemen from London, Mr. Meade. They're to impress the tourists, Hookham always says."

"Hookham," Rick repeated. "Why is that name so familiar?"

"He guides the tours."

"No," Rick said. "I know that name in quite another connection."

"Margot Fonteyn's maiden name was Hookham," I said.

"Well, that's not the connection I mean," Rick replied. "Still, it gives him a lot to live up to."

❖   ❖   ❖

138

Mr. Hookham was certainly trying to live up to it. We had to dodge among vans from the BBC News to get off the river road and approach the bridge over the moat. Mr. Hookham stood valiantly on the bridge, beside an almost catatonically rigid Mrs. Travis. A chap I recognized stood beside them deferentially, a microphone in his palm. As we clambered out of the Land Rover, I heard Mr. Hookham say, "Only ten years old, but born to tragedy, she was! Like her mother and father before her."

"Do you think she has met with foul play?" someone shouted from the crowd of newspeople at the edge of the stone bridge.

Rick removed the muddy bicycle from the Land Rover, and I took Diana's hand firmly in my own.

"Is there a back entrance?" I asked her.

"Oh, let's get on the telly!" she replied. "If they want Mr. Hookham and filthy old Travis, you know they'd rather have us."

Gavin had acquainted me with that point of view on several occasions. Since I haven't a performing bone in my body, I have never understood the attitude, but I have still to find a way of preventing its exponents from rushing to meet their public. Thus I happened to appear with Diana, Countess of Esty, in front of her ancestral towers when she assured an anxious world via satellite that she had, in fact, not been kidnapped.

"Where have you been, my baby?" Mrs. Travis shrieked at the beginning of the take. She was, I thought, rather convincing.

"Don't cry, Travis," Diana replied. "I am perfectly all right."

To put it mildly, I thought, watching her play the scene. *You are so all right they are going to have you on the telly for the rest of your life. Make sure they pay you next time.*

Eventually, they let us go, and we trudged through the cobbled courtyard into the doors in the base of the tower.

"What was that circus all about?" Rick barked at Mr. Hookham. "Did you try looking for her or did you just send out the alarm?"

Mr. Hookham had the face of an innocent piglet with dimples.

"Well, now, Mr. Meade, sir, if you'd been expecting to find the little Countess practicing her piano lesson in the morning room, and there was nobody there, wouldn't you imagine the worst?" he replied in his vivacious singsong.

"Not necessarily," Rick said. "I'd have inquired of the neighbors first."

"Well, of course, you run with all the rich folk at Dair, so maybe you know things I don't know," Hookham slammed back. "Or maybe you just like to have the spotlight all to yourself, is that it?"

"I am staying for dinner, Mrs. Travis. Mrs. Guest will remain for the night. I hope that is quite convenient for you," Rick snapped as we entered the Barons' Hall. He took Diana by one hand and me by the other and led us into the fine, low room with the Delft tiles around the hearth.

"Good night, Hookham," Diana said with a smile. Then she flicked a finger and the oaken door swung shut behind her. Even Alec Guinness could have learned from her timing. Unfortunately, Rick was too angry to notice.

◦   ◦   ◦

Rick left Esty Hall at ten, saying he had just time to change for the Duchess of Dair's formal dinner at eleven and he thought Diana should be getting to bed.

"Bed?" said Diana. "I never go to bed this early, Mr. Meade. Haven't since I was quite a little girl."

"When you have a governess ..." Rick began, glancing at me.

"She'd better be a night owl," I said philosophically. "Can you send a car for me tomorrow morning?"

"I'll come for you myself. What time is best?"

"Nine? Nine-thirty?"

"Excellent! Now I must dash." Rick strode out of the raftered room, leaving Diana and me to watch the firelight die, from our seats at the round dining table. Diana was concentrating on ways to defer her bedtime. She thought of a good one.

"You know, Mrs. Guest," she leaned over and confided to me, "the gentlemen from London were here yesterday."

I bit.

"Who are these gentlemen from London that you keep mentioning?"

"The National Trust sends them. They're always looking at the bottoms of things."

"How do you mean?"

"They look at the bottoms of the dishes and the chairs and the flowerpots and the water pitchers. Then sometimes they lock them up in glass cases, and sometimes they take them away. Yesterday they took things away."

"What things?" I asked, hoping that none of Mr. Singleton's three burl-walnut Queen Anne chairs had been removed.

"A lot of things out of the library. They said they were highly important letters."

"No doubt they were."

"From the time of Edward the First."

"That's long ago."

"How long ago, Mrs. Guest?"

"Seven hundred years, at least. Surely you know the dates of Edward the First's reign."

"No, I thought maybe you did."

"He became king in 1272 and remained king until 1307," I told her. "Now please don't ask me anything hard, like George the Sixth, because I didn't have to memorize anybody after Victoria."

"I kept one."

"One of the letters?"

"Yes. It's scary. Would you like to see it?"

141

"I'm not sure." *Esty Hall is scary enough as it is,* I thought.

"It's in my room. I'll get it if you don't mind my leaving you alone."

I do mind, I realized. "Not at all," I said.

She darted out of the room, her black curls bobbing with excitement, leaving the oaken door open. I stared idly at the rectangle of golden light, then turned my attention to a painting on the wall behind me. When I turned back, a squat shape had filled the center of the rectangle.

"Who's that?" I said too sharply.

"It's me—Augusta. I need a word with you right away."

She stepped inside the room and pulled the door shut behind her.

"Don't let the little girl go into Crinsley's Wood again," she told me, breathless with anxiety. "It's the most dangerous place a Gafford can go."

"But, Augusta! She rode all the way through it this morning on her bicycle and came out on the other side, happy as a lark."

"Ah, but that was broad daylight. If you and the gentleman hadn't driven her home, she'd have been caught in the Wood after dark, and she'd be dead now. Stone dead."

"Why?"

"Because Crinsley would have killed her. They say he killed her father. Well, he'll kill her, too, if he gets the chance!"

"Augusta, who is Crinsley?"

Her teeth were chattering.

"He's a killer, that's who he is! Comes out at night to make sure none of the Gaffords sets foot on Cavage land."

"I've driven through Crinsley's Wood long, long after dark, and—"

"Oh, you wouldn't see Crinsley. You have to be a Gafford to see him. But if you see him, you don't live to tell the tale. So I beg you, keep Her Ladyship away from—"

142

"Away from what?" Diana's silvery little voice had an edge of cold steel.

"Away from sweets," I improvised. "Augusta and I were just commenting on how much cake you like to eat. It's not the best thing for the teeth, is it, Augusta?"

"No," Augusta growled, stacking the dinner dishes one on top of the other with a series of small crashes.

Come back and talk to me later, Augusta, I thought helplessly. *There is so much more I need to know.*

"My teeth are just fine, thank you very much," the water sprite said with self-possession worthy of a woman of thirty. Then she waited, smiling and silent, as the Dowager Duchess had undoubtedly trained her to wait, for Augusta to withdraw.

When the oaken door closed behind Augusta, Diana reached into her pocket, eyes bright as a conspirator's.

"Here it is," she said, handing me a torn paper so limp and old it felt like a large rose petal. "Read it."

There was no mistaking the first word. It surprised me so that I said it out loud.

"Jemmy."

The message was brief and painful and to the point. I spelled it out slowly and found that it said, "Jemmy doth ryde to JeruSalem nor taken Me to Wyfe. A Lady walkes, A Ghoast. I wode not tarry here wyth nawt but Crynsleigh."

I turned the old paper over and read the single word "Esty."

"That's not really so scary, is it?" I asked.

"The part about the ghost is pretty scary," Diana insisted. "In 1272, I suppose people believed in them."

"It's different now." I beamed at her. "And it's time we went to bed."

❖   ❖   ❖

Diana's bedroom had at one time been paneled in walnut.

She had superimposed a layer of glossy photographs of actors and actresses she had seen on television, including the left-profile shot of Gavin which I have never liked. I was not entirely displeased to find that she had fastened it to the wall with a wad of chewing gum.

She gave me a tour of this pantheon of performers before she permitted me to bid her goodnight and go in search of Augusta.

"She promised she'd fix up the Spanish Bedroom for you," Diana assured me. "So just pull that cord with the tassels, and she'll come. Are you sure you don't want me to take you there?"

"You stay here and get into bed, thank you, Diana. And if you'd like to drive back to Dair tomorrow—"

"Oh, I would!"

"Well, Mr. Meade will be here at nine or nine-thirty." *I wonder if Diana could tolerate being kissed goodnight,* I thought, as I turned to leave her. *Maybe,* I decided, *by Rick,* and closed her door behind me.

A few steps over the creaking floors brought me to the tasseled bellpull, and I gave it a couple of medium-strong yanks. Somewhere miles away, I suppose it sounded. I heard nothing. I stood and waited in the dim light, then decided I might as well continue my wait sitting down.

The very moment I was seated, something whizzed over my head and there was a strange, splintering noise, then silence. I had to squint to be sure what was there, and when I was sure, I could not believe it.

There, still quivering from its flight through the air, its point stuck in the paneling about where my heart had been seconds before, was a knife. A knife with a piece of white paper taped around its handle.

Someone had thrown a knife at me!

May Scotland Yard's fingerprint people forgive me, but that knife was out of the wall and clutched in my fist before I drew my next breath, and I was running away from the bellpull and the chair beside it as if another knife might fly at me any time. In all my life I had never felt so threatened, so helpless, so alone.

A shaft of moonlight pierced the dim, tapestry-hung passage far ahead of me, turning the twisting staircase bright as a set for Romeo and Juliet's balcony scene.

Stay in the dark! something warned me. *Don't be a target again!*

But what if someone were following me? Did I dare stand still in the darkness, waiting to be overtaken, seized, stabbed?

I'm armed, I reminded myself. *I have this knife. I can fight. If I keep moving, I'll be harder to shoot and harder to stop. I'm going down those stairs.*

But at the foot of the stairs all the electric lights went on and somebody pried the knife out of my clenched fingers, and it is just barely possible that I lost consciousness for a little while, although I am no fainter.

X

"What the hell is going on?" Thaniel was saying to me from several miles away.

What are you doing here? I thought, as rather faintly and in slow motion I tried to answer his question:

"Someone warned me that Diana should leave Dair before dark, so I promised to come back here with her and stay for the night."

"With this knife in your hand?"

The knife was in his hand now: slim, shiny, sharp as a razor. Its handle was no longer wrapped in paper.

"Thaniel, someone threw it at me just now."

"Yes. Someone had a message to give you that couldn't wait."

"A message?"

He handed me a bit of white paper, still bent from being taped around the knife handle. I took it and read these hastily scrawled words: NO GUESTS WANTED HERE.

I read them again and again, though their meaning could hardly have been plainer.

"Where were you when the knife was thrown?" Thaniel asked.

"A few steps from Diana's bedroom door. I was waiting there for the maid to answer the bell."

"Can you walk?"

"I'll try."

I was, I discovered, slumped on a cushioned window seat. Thaniel stood beside it, looking down at me, his black hair tumbled, his face pale. Now he held out the hand that wore the signet ring. I clasped it and let him pull me to my feet.

"If you can," he said, "I think we should both look in on Diana. I don't want to leave you here alone."

"No, please don't."

I found I could walk perfectly well, and I followed Thaniel back up the twisting steps into the darkness.

How well you know the way, I thought.

"You shouldn't have come here, Deborah. But then, of course, Diana shouldn't have left here."

"I think Esty Hall is terribly lonely for the child."

"Yes, she needs a nanny. But so do you."

"Now, really! I'm very well able to—"

"—get a knife in the heart. Yes, so I see."

Who threw the knife at me? I was screaming inside. *Was it you?*

"It was just about here that it happened," I said, stopping at the chair beside the bellpull. "Just as I sat down, the knife flew out of nowhere into the wall. Here. Right over my head."

I watched his hand slide into his jacket pocket. It came back into sight holding a packet of matches. He struck one and examined the freshly splintered paneling. Then he raised the knife. I stood frozen to the spot, unable to take my eyes off the glistening little instrument of death as its blade glided back into the place from which I'd wrenched it. It went in

147

deep and held fast. Then Thaniel removed his hand from it and I saw its handle for the first time.

It was an almost perfect example of medieval English metalwork.

"Fits, doesn't it?" Thaniel was saying.

"Of course. Did you think I was lying to you?"

But Thaniel had turned away from me. Now he stood, silent and wary, staring into the darkness from which the little knife had so suddenly come flying.

"Come along," he said at last. "We must see if Diana is all right." There was an instant then when I might have wrenched the knife free from the wall again, but fortunately I didn't touch it. For Thaniel took only a step or two toward Diana's door when he remembered, turned back and grabbed the knife with one hand and my arm with the other.

"I shouldn't have run away from her," I told him. "You don't think whoever it was—did anything to her, do you?"

For answer, Thaniel released my arm and opened Diana's door a fraction of an inch. Inside, a woman's voice was saying, "I cannot begin to thank by name the hundreds of people who put time and muscle into our spring festivities ..." The door opened wider. Someone who looked like the Spirit of Shropshire Garden Clubs was reading a prepared address to the TV audience.

That audience included one water sprite in a torn dressing gown who lay motionless at the foot of the bed.

Thaniel and I reached her in a dead heat. She was sound asleep.

"Thank God," I heard a voice say. It might have been mine.

Thaniel lifted Diana from the foot of the bed and put her under the covers.

How very gentle he is, I thought, and switched off the Garden Clubber.

Diana opened her eyes for a moment, most reluctantly.

148

"Thank you, Augusta," she sighed.

We stepped back into the passageway, shut the door and stepped into the shadows from which the knife had been thrown. I didn't want to go in that direction, but Thaniel said, "It's all right. Don't hang back. There's nothing here but the new stairway and the door to the box room."

"You seem to know the terrain very well."

"I should. Diana's father and I used to explore this place every time it rained."

"Oh," I remember saying, as we started down the new stairway, which might have been new in about 1893. "Then you must know all sorts of ways to let yourself in."

In spite of the darkness and the ugly knife that was still in his pocket, Thaniel laughed out loud, a great baritone boom of a laugh that made me wonder—not for the first time—if he were a madman after all.

"Deborah," he finally said, "I suppose I can't blame you. After all, I did turn up at almost the same moment as the knife thrower."

Yes, you did, I thought.

"I didn't mean anything like that," I said.

"Well, if you didn't, you should have. God knows I had a distinct brush with cardiac arrest when I found you running around in pitch darkness like Lady Macbeth."

"Did you think I had knifed somebody?"

"I had no idea what you'd done. All I knew was that you'd left Grove a note announcing that you were coming to Esty Hall. He was good enough to share it with me instead of following you here himself."

"He must have known I meant the note for you."

"He suspected as much. Thanks for confirming it."

You still haven't told me how you got into this house, I reflected, smiling, saying nothing.

We were now in the corridor where Rick and the two children and I had reviewed the procession of armored knights mounted on armored warhorses that stormy night when I arrived from London. Thaniel dodged among this motionless army as swiftly as if he bore news of victory. In his wake, a long line of lights went on. Suddenly, from one end of the vast procession to the other, everything within my eyesweep sparkled as only burnished and damascened steel ever does, and Thaniel emerged from a shining confusion of shields and spears to beckon me to his side.

"I will now return this nasty little item to its rightful place in history," he said, opening a small glass cabinet. I thought he delayed a beat too long about putting the knife inside, but at last he placed it on a sort of red velvet cushion and closed the glass door over it. Only then would I step forward to look at the knife more closely. The glass and the red velvet robbed it of reality for me, and I was glad. It was now just another neatly labeled curiosity in a museum.

The typed card at the base of the red velvet read: "Dagger belonging to Rufus Gafford, First Earl of Esty, A.D. 1250-1315."

Thaniel's voice pulled me away from the glass cabinet.

"Come along, Deborah. I want you out of here."

Aren't you going to tell the police? I asked him in total silence. *Aren't you going to stay and protect Diana? If you aren't, I most certainly am.*

"I'll have to get my coat and bag first," I said.

"Where are they?"

"Diana said the maid had promised to open up the Spanish Bedroom for me. If she did, then I suppose my things are there."

Thaniel's face was quite expressionless.

"Leave them there," he said, taking my arm. "We'll send for them in the morning."

I was going to have to say it.

"Shouldn't we tell the police?"

"Of course. I'll ring them up from Dair." By then he had propelled me out of the armory into a small entryway where a sign announced that smoking was prohibited. As he dealt with a row of bolts and chains that secured the outside door, I said, "We simply can't leave that little girl alone here with somebody who throws knives!"

I will never forget Thaniel's face when he replied, "Please, Deborah. Don't fight me. Trust me. The note said nothing about Diana. It specifically invited *you* to go away."

Much against my instinct, training and better judgment, I followed him through the open door into the chilly moonlight.

"My car's in the courtyard. Do you mind the walk?"

"No. In fact, I think Esty Hall is very beautiful by night."

"I've never thought of it as beautiful. Picturesque perhaps. But if you've grown up at Dair, it's hard to think of any other building as beautiful."

"Apples and oranges," I murmured.

"True. And both in the same leaky basket, which is fast sinking to the bottom." There was no missing the sadness in his voice.

"Maybe not. If there's enough oil under the North Sea—"

"—Scotland can afford to go it alone," he silenced me. "No, Deborah. This is almost all over and done with now." He stopped suddenly and gazed up thirty, forty, surely fifty feet to the Archer's Tower on top of the pale stone curtain wall encircling Diana's storybook castle. "Imagine. These stones were put in place almost a thousand years ago and nobody's knocked a hole in the wall yet. But walls can't keep the world out. Not even walls like these."

I've never told him about the letter Old Billy wrote from France in 1916, I thought.

"Now Esty Hall is a tourist attraction," Thaniel went on. "And I'm afraid Dair will be the next."

He turned abruptly and we resumed our walk toward the stone bridge that led into the courtyard. I could almost see the rage that was flaring up inside this lean, pale man.

"It didn't have to be this way. It didn't have to be this

way at all," he said, as if he were talking to himself. "With Esty Hall, I suppose it was God's will. Three deaths in the same year did more than just orphan poor Diana. They left her a pauper as well."

"Three deaths?"

"Yes." He sighed. "First, Hugh's father, Lord Esty. Then Hugh's wife, Lacey. Then Hugh himself. Diana's the last of the line. The death duties were so high that everything had to be sold up including the cups and saucers. The same thing you've been sent here to arrange for Dair."

We were trudging briskly over the courtyard's cobbles toward a silver automobile that looked almost as long as a banquet table opened to feed twenty-four.

"But when the contents of Dair go under the hammer, I shan't have the comfort of thinking God meant it to be."

Thaniel bent to open the door on the passenger side for me, and I saw the angry frown that cleft his forehead like a pointed arrow. Saying nothing, I stepped inside the car, felt the door clunk shut beside me and waited for him to cross to the driver's side.

Am I leaving you at the mercy of a killer, Diana? I thought, staring at the ancient walls, *Or am I about to drive away with him myself?*

"Allow me to drive you back to Dair," Thaniel said, climbing into the driver's seat, adjusting a lever, turning a key, "before it becomes an empty shell. This, by the way, since you seem to admire them, is a stretched Eldorado. Sorry I haven't a white one."

The car started up like silk and moved with a sort of languid fury, gathering speed and more speed until the trees blurred as we passed them. We were on the river road before Thaniel spoke again.

"Have you ever thought what hell must be like?" he inquired, as casually as if he were asking the right time.

"No, not really. Have you?"

152

"Yes. I imagine hell to be whatever one is least able to endure, drawn out ad infinitum. For you, it would probably be to love one man after another and have each and every one leave you flat."

Touché, I thought, wincing.

"For me," he continued, "hell would be to want freedom desperately, try over and over to get it and never, in all eternity, succeed."

"How do you know that?"

"Because that's exactly how I've had to live for the past ten years. In hell. Trying to buy my life back from a woman who will not rest until she tastes my blood. She refused a cash settlement in seven figures, so I offered one in eight. She refused that, too. I added one of the El Grecos, a lot of the Georgian plate, some Greek statuary, I no longer remember the whole wretched list. She refused those, too. Her answer is always the same. She says, 'It's going to take more than that, boy.' Well, now at last I know how much more. She's going to make me sell every last thing I've got."

Gavin had given me everything in our flat except his clothes, and I couldn't bear opening the wardrobe where they had hung because I missed seeing them there. How could I possibly comfort someone facing the loss of so much more?

"Maybe, considering the wealth tax . . ." I began.

"I can handle a wealth tax," he snapped. "Not forever, of course, but for a good long time. Her Majesty's Government won't take nearly what the Duchess of Dair is demanding. If I sell everything in my house and give her the money, she'll let me have my son and my divorce. Otherwise, she will take him away."

"Can she afford to do that?"

"Easily. Her father was in oil in Oklahoma. Kendra is very well off."

"Then why—?"

"Strip Dair? Impoverish me? Squander Whitwell's inheritance before he inherits it? Why, indeed? I can only think the pretty little thing I charmed away from Hugh Gafford is the supreme sadist of our time."

"Can't you just stall her along, Thaniel, until your son is old enough to—"

"What do you think I've been doing? No, Deborah, her solicitors won't permit any more of that. I've got a deadline now. I must sign an agreement next week, promising to auction the entire contents of Dair before the end of this year."

"What if you don't sign it?"

"The next day, she and the boy will be gone."

"But you know he'd come back the very first chance he got. He adores you, Thaniel."

"It might be a long, tough trip for a boy of eleven. She'd find people to watch him very carefully. So carefully that I could probably never even speak to him by phone. She'd find ways to divert him, too. I might not matter to him nearly so much when he turned twelve. Or thirteen. And I need him here. Even if the house is empty, there are fifty thousand different jobs he's got to know when he becomes Duke after me."

Like fetching the evening's wine, I thought.

"I'm afraid I've begun to think thoughts quite unbecoming to a peer of the realm," Thaniel said quietly, slowing the silver car. "At first, I thought I might kidnap Whitwell. Unfortunately, I couldn't figure out a way to do that and also keep him here with me, living as I want my son to live. Then I began to think how very nice it would be if his drunken little mother had the good grace to disappear."

I was right, I thought, aware that something in my throat was hardening into a lump of ice.

"Did you ever know, Deborah, that there are ways to arrange for someone to disappear?" He was looking away from the road now and I saw the anguish in his face.

154

"I've heard rumors," I faltered.

"They are more than rumors," he said, steering the big car off the road to a low building I did not recognize in the darkness, and stopping dead. "There have always been killers for hire. I suppose there always will be."

He had touched a button at his side, and I felt the window beside me sinking wide open. A head wearing a duck-billed cap leaned in. A torch no bigger than a fountain pen flared briefly.

"Evening, Your Grace," a voice said. "Mrs. Guest, is it?"

"Evening, Blanchard," Thaniel replied easily. "Are we the last ones in?"

"That you are, Your Grace, but not by much. I just this minute closed the gates behind the Duchess. It's a wonder you didn't see her just ahead of you on the road."

Thaniel smiled in the faint light but said nothing.

Blanchard darted away around the corner of the cottage Rick had assured me was not the birthplace of the Brothers Grimm. Thaniel touched the lever that closed the window beside me and steered the immensely long car slowly into position to go through the high iron gates Blanchard was busily swinging open.

"I'm sure I don't have to tell you," he remarked, "why hired killers are not a good idea."

Then the big car moved forward through the black-lace gates. Stunned as I was, I nevertheless nodded to Blanchard as I rode past him. Thaniel took no notice of him whatever. We glided slowly down the exact center of the broad, tree-lined allée, the car's silver bonnet reflecting an infinity of leaves fluttering in the May moonlight, the lump of ice growing in my throat, freezing my voice into stiff, cold silence.

"They can free you of someone," Thaniel observed judiciously, as if anxious to give the devil his due. "But then who is to free you of them? I mean, the fact is, Deborah, unless you want to be blackmailed for the rest of your life, which is

155

the sort of endless helplessness that I've had just about enough of, you're better off doing your own killing."

We were out of sight of the black-lace gates and Blanchard. We could not yet see the great colonnades of Dair. Yet Thaniel was stopping the silver car.

And if you can't face killing your wife, why not kill the auctioneer's assistant? It could buy you a bit of extra time, I thought, fumbling stealthily for the handle of the door beside me.

"For God's sake, stop trying to open your door," the quiet voice continued. "I really must tell this to someone."

Was he going to tell me he had thrown the knife?

I could not scream. My whole throat had turned to ice. But perhaps I could sound the horn. I lunged for it.

He was quicker than I and very much stronger. The hand with the signet ring closed around both my wrists effortlessly. The other hand slipped around my shoulders, almost as if Thaniel meant to caress me, and took a firm grip on my upper arm.

"Please listen to me," he said, as gently as if he were trying to propose. "Kendra was at Esty Hall tonight, too. I followed her. I don't know who opened the door for her, because I let myself in by a secret way, but she was alone when she went up the stairway that leads to Diana's room. I watched her, and I thought—God forgive me, Deborah—I thought, 'If I had a gun now, I could kill her.'"

I knew that actors cried once in a while, but I had not realized till then that dukes did.

"I want to kill her, Deborah. I have to kill her."

He was sobbing now, and the hand that had been clutching my arm was withdrawn to cover his streaming dark eyes.

"Next time, I *will* kill her!"

The hand that had been holding my wrists immobile relaxed its grip. I might have opened my door or sounded the horn then, easily, for both my hands were free. I used them, however, to caress the dark tousled head that sank into my lap at that moment.

I have no idea how long I sat there, stroking Thaniel's hair and whispering over and over again, "Don't cry. Don't cry. Don't cry, my darling."

        ◦   ◦   ◦

She found me in the music room next morning, a bit too early for either of us. Her eyes looked like green grapes on two rather dirty white saucers. They had no idea that her mouth was smiling.

"Is that old piano worth anything?" Her satin mules had once been white, I noticed, watching them slap across the parquet floor, past the huge rosewood grand at which I sat, to press the button that would summon a servant.

"A small fortune," I replied.

"How small?"

"Well, it was made by the Decker Brothers."

"Never heard of the Decker Brothers."

"Americans. In their day, a lot of people thought they made a better piano than Mason and Hamlin or Steinway. But they shut down at the beginning of the First World War, and they never reopened."

Dwain was standing in the doorway.

"You rang, Your Grace?"

"Yeah. I wanted a bottle of cold champagne. Since it's you, better make it a split." The tinkling laugh lasted until the door shut.

"What's that old book you're looking at?"

"It's some music, Duchess."

"I can see that! Is it worth much?"

"Only if it's authenticated."

"What does that mean?"

"Well, I can make a note that a piece of paper bears the signature of W. A. Mozart, but an expert would have to be called in to say that it really is Mozart's handwriting, and another expert would have to decide if it really is Mozart's music."

"Is that what that says? Mozart?" She slap-slapped to my side and peered at the book intently.

"That's what it says. Do you happen to know if he was ever a guest here?"

"What difference would it make?"

"This might be music he wrote here, left here and never had published. If so, it would cause an international sensation. "

Dwain was back, her face expressionless, bearing a magnum of champagne in a gleaming bucket of crushed ice. Behind her, Grove carried two champagne glasses on a small tray. Wordlessly, they set these refreshments down on a delicate tea table. Grove opened the bottle without a trace of pop or fizz, and turned to Kendra with exquisitely studied deference.

"Shall I pour, Your Grace?"

"You do that little thing," she replied.

One minute later a glass was pressed into my hand, and my hand was raised in acknowledgment of my hostess's toast.

"To small fortunes!" she cried.

I took an obligatory sip and set my glass down. It was nine o'clock in the morning.

The Duchess of Dair arranged herself comfortably in the curve of the fine old piano, one elbow resting on its polished surface, her jeweled fingers toying with the champagne glass, her green eyes fixed on me. Over her shoulder I watched the door close softly behind the servants, leaving Kendra and me alone.

"You really do your little schoolteacher act to a T," she observed. "Experts. Authentications. International sensations.

Anybody'd think you worked for a museum instead of an auctioneer."

"You asked me for information, Duchess."

"I asked you for prices. That's different. That's what auctioneers are supposed to know about. Prices. Money. Cash! But what do I hear about from you? The Decker Brothers, for Christ's sake!"

She was drunk before she sent for this champagne, I thought. *I wonder what time she started. I wonder if she's been building up to this all night, ever since she returned from Esty Hall.*

"Well, it's a cute little act," she went on, "and you can cut it right out right now. Because I know what old Singleton and my noble husband are trying to do."

The satin mules slap-slapped back to the tea table to refill the champagne glass, then made their slatternly way back to the bow of the piano.

"They're trying to stall," she announced. "That's why I put the plans of this house in your desk. To speed things up."

"I assure you that—"

"If they make everything something that might be an international sensation," Kendra enunciated carefully, "they could keep this place overrun with experts for the next hundred years. And never start the auction."

I wondered if the emeralds flashing on her fingers were the ones the Dowager had reluctantly surrendered to her years before.

"Well, that's way too slow for me," she said, suddenly smiling. "Although I'm sure you'd like it fine."

"On the contrary, Your Grace. If there's no auction, Singleton's gets no commissions."

"I imagine the Duke could give Mr. Singleton something to make it worth his while." I will never forget her next words. "I'm quite sure he's already giving you something."

I was on my feet as fast as if two bolts of lightning had

159

collided in front of me, and I do not know what I might have said if Kendra had not at that exact moment doubled up with laughter. She sank into a deep chair, shrieking with her own amusement, one emerald-laden hand slapping her knee, the other holding her brimming glass miraculously still and steady. I waited for her to quiet down. When the giggling subsided, I spoke.

"If you are suggesting that there is anything—"

"Suppose you just shut up and let me tell you what I'm suggesting."

The change in the green eyes was astonishing. I found myself retreating from them, taking refuge again on the bench behind the rosewood piano. Kendra's voice was different, too: almost sad.

"I'm suggesting that this whole auction thing is too damn slow, that's all. I'm suggesting that there's another way. I'm not sure, but you could check it out for me pretty fast. Interested?"

I nodded.

"Okay. Did you ever hear of Hugh Gafford? He was Diana's father, and he always swore there was Crusaders' treasure stashed away in the old castle on top of Crag Cavage. He once said, 'Everybody knows that old Jemmy, the first Knight of Cavage, came back from the Crusades with a fortune in gold and jewels, and not stolen either. Jemmy had a child by some sultan's daughter, and she died— but he kept the little boy and the dowry and brought them back to Castle Cavage and never took his eyes off them the rest of his life.' Well, Thaniel always denied the whole story, but I've always believed it. Because Thaniel never misses a night of going over to the Old Place, but he never lets other people go there. Although he says he's just going to pick out the evening's wine."

So that's what it's all about, I thought.

"Poor Hugh. He was the last Earl of Esty. Seven hundred

160

years' worth of 'em, and they handed that story about Castle Cavage and the sultan's treasure down from father to son."

I watched the green eyes in silence. They were focused on something far away. Something they feared.

"If there really is a treasure like that," Kendra mused, "we wouldn't need any experts. Gold is gold. Diamonds are diamonds. If you could find out if they're there, I could do the rest."

"The Duke has forbidden me to enter Castle Cavage for any reason," I told her.

"I could be gone from here tomorrow," she replied.

"It's impossible, Duchess."

"My husband could have his son and his ratty old furniture and all that crap that's locked up in the Picture Gallery."

"Do your own treasure-hunting!" I flung at her.

The green eyes just got greener.

"My husband could have his divorce very fast."

She seems to think I'd do anything for him, I told myself, feeling my heart clench inside me. *But would I? Would I?*

"It is something I'd have to think about," I snapped. "Possibly for years. And now, if you will excuse me—"

I left her in the music room, pouring more champagne, and went in search of Thaniel.

The rotunda's violet marble was skimming by under my feet before it struck me that Thaniel must never know of the offer Kendra had just made to drop her demand for an auction. Much as he loved Dair, much as he longed to preserve its contents intact for Whitwell and Cavages yet to come, he treated the Old Place on the crag as if it were somehow sacred. Was it possible that he prized whatever was hidden there more than all Dair's El Grecos and Grecian antiquities and Georgian plate put together? Was Kendra, in fact, offering to abandon a cruel plan to fleece Thaniel for one even crueler? And was I, Deborah Guest of Singleton Abbs, even thinking of helping her?

161

I turned and gazed at the blind stone face of the angry god Poseidon and knew the answer was yes.

I was going treasure-hunting inside the forbidden walls of Castle Cavage, because it might prevent the auction at Dair. It might or it might not. However, it was a chance I had to take for one overwhelming reason.

It might also keep Thaniel from murdering his wife.

XI

I couldn't visit the Old Place after dark; Thaniel would insist on knowing where I'd gone. No, I would have to go up the path between the boulders in the clear light of day and hope everyone inside Dair Manor had better things to do than watch me from the window. Lunchtime might be the best time to climb the crag unobserved. A glance at my watch told me I had about fifteen minutes to go to my room, collect my torch and pink sweater, and start out for an apparently aimless stroll in the sunshine before luncheon was served. How really simple it was going to be!

I reckoned without Stratford, who confronted me with fire in his eye as I entered my bedchamber, uttering a sharp yelp of displeasure at the sight of me.

"You stop that," I said. "Just because we held hands once in a stalled car, don't get possessive. I cannot take you everywhere I go."

He continued to stand, foursquare and feisty, gazing at me

163

with reproach, but the yelp was not repeated. A sort of grumbling was taking place inside his throat. I put on my sweater, checked the battery in my torch and bent to pat him. He ducked away from my hand and caught the cuff of my jeans in his teeth.

"Let go!" I commanded. "I mean it. I'm in a hurry."

He considered my command for some time before obeying it. Then he darted for the door and positioned himself so close to it that he would have to precede me into the passage when I opened it.

"You can't come with me," I said.

He didn't move, but stood with his eyes fixed on the doorjamb, waiting.

"You can't, Stratford," I said again. And again.

When I began climbing the narrow rock path up Crag Cavage, he was still with me and I was glad. I dreaded the prospect of entering the old castle again, but Stratford, small as he was, seemed afraid of nothing. His claws clicked along beside me as briskly as if we were promenading in Park Lane as we ascended the crag, approached the ugly old doorway and plunged into the chilly darkness inside.

Once inside, however, with my torch turned on, I stopped, realizing I had no idea where to look for the treasure Jemmy Cavage had allegedly brought back from the Near East seven hundred years before.

Where did Thaniel and Whitwell go after they chased me out of here? I thought. The answer was the only clue I had: *They went up to the top of the rock steps, and then a door slammed.*

I would have to go up those steps, too. I would have to open that door.

"Come along, Stratford," I said, jumping as I heard my words bounced back at me out of the stony emptiness. "This way."

The corgi and I made our way through the lofty hall of

reindeer antlers to the bottom of the crude rock steps.

There I stopped, but Stratford bounded ahead, negotiating the tall slabs of rock as a kangaroo would have: crouching on his short, powerful hind legs, then leaping up to the next step, and on and on. When I saw the ruddy fur body with the single white rear paw disappear beyond the beam of my torch, it was as if he had jerked me after him on an invisible leash. I started up the rock steps, too.

We reached the pie-shaped step and made the turn. We passed the steps where Whitwell had sprawled, sobbing and babbling, his bare feet dangling over the steep unobstructed drop to the rocky floor far below.

Don't think about the drop, I cautioned myself, *and don't even think of turning the light downward to look at it.* Even so, I remember thinking that by contemporary London architectural standards I was easily five stories above the pavement. Then my light illuminated something that was not made of rock.

About four steps further up, directly ahead of the little dog and me, loomed a wooden door with black iron hinges. The wood was oak. *A cooper made it,* I thought. *It's thick old barrel staves.* This observation served to divert me from a more terrifying reality about the ancient door.

It was not quite closed.

"Wait, Stratford!" I implored. He paused on the top step and glanced back at me, his eyes blazing like black diamonds in the glare of my torch. Then, with great calm and delibera-tion, he disappeared into whatever lay beyond the door. For all I knew, standing there alone in the chilly darkness, he had disappeared forever.

There was still time to change my mind, turn back, run down the steps and through the double file of prehistoric antlers, out into the May sunshine. It was what I longed to do.

I didn't do it. Instead, I forced myself to reach out toward the oaken surface and push the old door wide enough to look inside.

There was daylight here, a single bright shaft of it stealing through a slit in the masonry just wide enough to let an archer shoot without being seen. There was almost nothing else. This was a monastic cell, totally bare except for a narrow cot in one corner and a blackened candlestick on the stone floor beside it, just below the slit of window., The candlestick was old, old enough to have belonged to Jemmy Cavage. And the plump tallow candle it held was burning.

I did see a flame from my bedroom, I thought, *and Thaniel must have lighted it. But why here? There's nothing here but an old cot covered with sacking.*

Stratford stood transfixed by something I could not see. His ears were two pointed steeples reaching almost to my knee. His eyes and muzzle were fixed on something under the cot. Was someone hiding there?

"Come out," I said, appalled to hear how my voice was quavering. "Don't be afraid."

There was no answer, and Stratford didn't move. I would have to see for myself what had the little dog mesmerized.

I crouched on the floor and pointed my torch under the cot. Nothing there but dust. I swept the beam the full length of the space from its head to its foot, seeing only stone. Then, as I withdrew the torch from beneath the cot, I accidentally struck its crude wooden footboard, with results I cannot even now bring myself to remember without feeling the palms of my hands go wet with panic.

The cot swung slowly, silently upward till it was standing on its head, flat against the wall. Across its bottom were three sturdy slats that made it look like a ladder. A ladder leading nowhere, apparently, since it reached only halfway up the wall. Unless, by a miracle, that was where I would find what I had come to search for.

Bless you, Stratford! I thought as I tested my weight on

166

the bottom slat. It was as stout as it looked. So was the next one. I decided to climb to the top, press and pry at every stone I could reach, and work my way back down again.

I must have been at this for about five minutes when I heard the growl gathering in Stratford's throat and the scramble of his paws and claws suddenly hurrying across the slippery old stones. Then, although there was no one on either side of me, someone whispered in my ear: "You fool!"

It was as if my hands and feet had suddenly turned limp as boiled spaghetti; I lost my grip and my footing at the same instant. I felt myself falling backward into that dark emptiness where time goes on forever but the sound and pictures stop.

◦   ◦   ◦

Stratford must be locked in somewhere, I thought. *He keeps barking and barking, but it sounds so muffled. If I can ever get my eyes open, I'll go and let him out.*

It was important to open my eyes, I knew, but it was more than I could manage for the moment. Instead, I lay still and said soothing things to myself.

Someone crept in and startled me just now, and I slipped off the ladder. Now whoever that was has gone, and shut the door to the steps. Stratford is outside the door and I'm inside, lying on the stone floor . . .

I had to stop right there, because my hands were resting on velvet, not stone. There were pillows under me, not a floor. The dog's barking was too far away to be just outside the door of that small cell. I had to open my eyes quickly, and somehow I did.

I was in a vast chamber I had never seen before, a shadowy cavern that seemed to be carved from jagged living rock. The ceiling, if there was a proper ceiling, was lost in darkness high above me; the space on every side of me

167

seemed infinite in the half-light. And I was indeed lying on a heap of pillows in the midst of all this vastness: pillows that shifted heavily as I propped myself up on my elbows and felt for the pocket where I kept my torch.

It was still there, and I almost tore the pocket in my eagerness to pull it out. The beam created a small cocoon of normality around me, and I ventured to get to my feet.

"I'm coming, Stratford," I called. Then I began to cough and sneeze from the dust I had stirred up around me.

"Where am I? I thought, turning the light on the couch where I had lain. The pillows were really sacks, I saw, and the scrap of velvet, more brown than crimson, didn't begin to cover them all. *Who brought me here? Who spoke to me just before I fell? And how do I get out of here? How do I get out?*

Which way was Stratford's barking coming from? It was impossible to tell.

"Stand still!" I called to him. "Stay! I'll find you, but stay!" Still the barking seemed to come from quadraphonic speakers, ringing me in a circle of confusion, leading me in all directions at once.

There must be edges to this space, I told myself. *I'll find the nearest wall and walk along it till I find a door.*

I turned my torch to its brightest and shone it to my left. Not six paces away there was a rock wall. It was unlike the wall in the monastic cell. That one had been constructed from blocks of stone by human hands. This was a single rock face, pitted like the surface of a meteorite. There would be no doors in it, I knew before I began pacing off its length; this wall was put here by God. Somewhere, though, it might join some man-made structure. In that hope, I kept inching forward.

There's nothing to worry about, I assured myself.

I was wrong.

I am somewhere inside Castle Cavage, I continued, follow-

168

ing the beam of light forward. *Thaniel will come here this evening. He always does.*

I looked at my watch. It was almost three. Not long until sundown. Not long at all.

I'll be able to call to Thaniel when he gets here. He'll hear me as plainly as I hear Stratford now. He'll get me out of here if I haven't found my own way out long before then.

It was then that I saw what was hanging on the wall just ahead of me: the edge of a piece of cloth. Moving cautiously ahead in the enormous rock chamber, I discovered that the cloth was embroidered. Someone with unbearable memories and an infinity of time had used needle and thread as I had seen them used only once before. This hanging had been embroidered by the same hand that had stitched the great tapestry that hung among the tombs of the lords of Dair in the Cathedral: the tapestry that had shown flames behind the Cathedral, a knight with black hair reputed to be Jemmy Cavage, the archbishop who became St. Charles de Cordel, the statue of the Archangel Michael with his foot crushing down the . . .

Gazing at the tapestry that hung before me now, I remembered a single, frightening fact about the head of evil under the Archangel's foot, a fact which had escaped me when I looked at it in Dairminster Cathedral. Its tangled hair was exactly the same bonfire red as Alaric Meade's.

Madness! I told myself sternly. *Any resemblance between a thirteenth-century representation of evil and Rick is absolutely impossible!*

Yet there was the bonfire-red hair again, stitched into the terrifying tapestry in front of me. It showed beneath the helmet of an armored knight who stood on the road beside the River Dair. Three men with broken swords lay dead at his feet, but he stood with his back turned to them, watching one of his henchmen swing an ax which would momentarily cut a young boy's hands off. Behind him, from a high

169

window in Castle Cavage, a blonde woman holding a baby watched the scene.

Who is he? I asked. *What does this mean? Is that poor lad Crinsley?*

There was another tapestry hanging beside the first one, and there was more bonfire-red hair in it. The knight with red hair was riding his armored warhorse up the rocky path on Crag Cavage, dragging the handless boy behind him in the dust of his horse's hoofs. The blonde woman in the high window had her hands clasped in prayer.

Were those three dead men relatives of hers? I wondered. *Was Crinsley? Are there any more tapestries here?*

There were indeed, but the next one raised more questions in my mind than it answered. It showed the knight with black hair, the one Thaniel had introduced as Jemmy, first Knight of Cavage, when we had first seen him in the Cathedral's tapestry. Here he was riding away from Castle Cavage in Crusader's garb. There was no sign of the knight with the bonfire-red hair. In fact, there was no other person in the entire tapestry. Except the woman with the baby in the window of Castle Cavage.

But she's not the same woman! I said to myself. *She's a brunette.*

Maybe that was dust and cobwebs. I tried blowing them away, but the hair on the tiny embroidered head stayed black. Another color surfaced, however. Behind the swaddled baby she held in her arms, her dress was blue.

What had Old Billy's letter from France said about a little woman with long black hair? Had it said anything about a blue dress? Or was that just Clewys chatting me up? "The one I've heard about," Clewys had said, "always wears blue." *Nonsense!* I said to steady myself. *There's another embroidery next to this one.*

This one made no sense to me at all. It was virtually the same scene as before. The knight with black hair was riding

170

away from Castle Cavage. The embroidered surface was very dark, and I blew on it industriously, but the needleworker had meant it to be black as a night with no stars or moon. I studied it intently before I saw that the knight had a sack slung over his back, and that there was a small head poking out of the sack: a child's head with a mop of black hair.

How peculiar, I thought. *Maybe the next one explains it.*

In the next one, splendor and glory reigned supreme. The knight with black hair sat astride a huge black horse. A child with black hair was on the saddle in front of him. There were banners flying and crowds massed all along the river road. In the forefront, I saw the knight with the bonfire-red hair, his arms extended in welcome. On either side of him was a woman with the same red hair.

Why is each of the red-headed women making a curtsy? Who are they, anyway?

Whoever they were, the knight with black hair was ignoring them. His gaze was directed steadfastly upward. Was it to God or to Castle Cavage's highest tower? I could not tell. I knew only that it was the finest piece of needle-work I had ever seen.

It was then I stumbled over something on the floor. I turned my torch down quickly and saw a bit of cloth clamped inside an embroidery hoop. I knelt to look at it. The dust of centuries had collected on it, and I had to lift it and invert it before I dared blow on it. Then I could see what was there: a great square of bare canvas with embroidered figures in the very center only. The figures were a man with black hair and a small boy with black hair, both patting a dog that looked like Stratford. There were a few stitches in the unfinished portion, too. They might have become a blue skirt. There was no question that the next stitches made in the tapestry would have been blue; a bone needle with a wisp of blue thread hooked through its tip still rested on the canvas.

171

Whoever said there was treasure here was right, I told myself, beaming my light back at the rock wall. There were no more tapestries hanging there. I had come to the corner. Now I must turn to my right and see what awaited me. I replaced the old embroidery hoop on the floor, thinking *I wonder who made these; I wonder what they mean; I wonder why they're here?*

As I turned my back on the five tapestries, I thought *Did someone once live here? Was this the Cavage cave when they were cavemen? Where am I?*

I was on my way into new dark depths and the wall beside me was still a slab of living rock, but the roof over my head had suddenly grown lower. I might have been picking my way through a tunnel in a coal mine.

Mustn't lose my bearings, I told myself, swiveling to point my torch to where I thought the heap of pillows should be. I had apparently traveled farther than I knew; the beam of light didn't stretch back to my starting point. Suddenly desperate to find my way back to the only landmark I had, I began to run across the huge rock platform that served the cavern as a floor. My foot struck something that turned over and fell with an iron clang which echoed and re-echoed all around me, and I stopped dead in my tracks until the echoes died away. Then I lowered my torch to see what the obstacle had been.

There was a box shaped like a miner's lunch pail lying at my feet, and its rounded top had fallen open—whether centuries ago or mere seconds, I couldn't tell. Jemmy Cavage would have called such a box a coffret and stored valuables inside. In fact, perhaps he had. As I bent to look, I remember being suddenly aware that Stratford's barking had stopped, leaving me in almost suffocating silence.

"Stratford?" I called. No answer.

"Stratford?" I started to scream.

Stop that! I told myself. *Stop that this minute! It won't do*

172

to scream yourself hoarse before Thaniel gets here. You've got to make him hear you. Now quiet down and check the time.

It was ten past four. Thaniel could be expected within the next hour or two. He would be far from pleased to find me here, of course, but perhaps the contents of the iron box would interest him sufficiently to take his mind off the fact that I had once again disregarded his instructions to stay away from Castle Cavage.

I seated myself on the rock floor and beamed my light at the gaping interior of the smashed coffret, hoping some fair-sized jewels would have the decency to beam back. Instead, I saw what appeared to be somebody's forgotten diploma.

Well, I'd look at it before resuming my walk along the walls; in Jemmy Cavage's day every parchment scroll was not necessarily a diploma. I picked it up and began gingerly to unroll it, a fraction of an inch at a time. The words were Latin, of course, and therefore almost meaningless to me, but they had been so exquisitely inscribed that I continued unrolling the parchment simply to admire the archaic patterns of the lettering and the interesting shading of the scarcely faded ink.

I had scanned perhaps a hundred lines, understanding not a syllable along the way, when suddenly the language changed. The letters took on new shapes and shadings. I followed them in astonishment to the very bottom of the scroll, where I found the only things on the page that I could comprehend.

One was the date, in Roman numerals.

"One thousand three hundred and eight Anno Domineye," I said half aloud.

The other was the signature, in the same strong hand I had seen on the marriage certificates that hung in Whitwell's bedroom: Cordel.

I am not a medievalist, alas. I could read the classical languages if I were. And I have never regretted this gap in my education more than I did that ghastly afternoon, as I sat pondering the document signed by a saint, wondering what it said and why it required two of the most hallowed languages of all antiquity to say it.

XII

I watched the parchment scroll fall from my fingers. I saw the lighted torch land on top of it, then roll slowly away over the rock floor. I was powerless to pick up either of them, because the voice that had whispered "You fool!" was hissing at me again.

"Deb-or-ah," it said, with no more timbre than the wind, "lisssssssssen."

I listened. Intently. Yet I could not tell whether the sound was coming from far back in the darkest depths of the cavern, from overhead—or from right beside me.

"You will die," it informed me, "tonight. Someone is coming for you now."

"Who?" I screamed. "Who are you? Where are you? Who is coming for me? Answer me!"

I must have screamed for quite a long time, but there was no reply. At last I quieted down, retrieved my torch from the floor and tried to think. So my murderer was coming for me. My murderer might, in fact, have just spoken to me. Yet I

175

could not identify that eerie stage whisper. Did it belong to someone male or female, alive or dead? I did not know.

I did know it was no time to sit still. I must redouble my efforts to find a way out. I must continue exploring the edges of the cavern. I would find a door somewhere, a tunnel, a rat hole, anything. I would not just crouch there and wait for my approaching murderer. And so I stumbled over the rocks, hunting for the heap of pillows where I had regained consciousness and trying to guess whose whisper I had heard just before I blacked out.

Kendra! was my first thought. *The drunken little Duchess of Dair maneuvered me into visiting Castle Cavage against the Duke's strict orders. I wouldn't have come within a mile of the place if it hadn't been for Kendra.*

That was too simple, however. Physically, how could it be Kendra? She was so very tiny, and surely someone strong must have lifted me from the floor of the cell and carried me into this place. Kendra must have had help from a man. A man with reasons of his own for wishing me dead.

Considering who that man might be was one of the most agonizing thought processes I have ever had to force myself through.

Could it be Rick, redheaded like the demon under the Archangel Michael's foot, redheaded like the killer knight in the embroidered hangings I had just seen? Something made me think Rick had been inside Castle Cavage despite all Thaniel's prohibitions. While he and I were still on the train to Dairminster hadn't he offered to show me the Old Place on the crag? Was this the fate he had had in mind for me even then? Was this what he had meant when he said, "There will be so many things you don't believe, Milady Deborah, but all of them are true?"

But Rick is my friend! I told myself. An ugly little stab of truth sped through my head and caught up with that statement. *He is also Kendra's friend,* it forced me to admit.

176

And he's a playwright, so inventing a story about Crusaders' treasure would have been ever so easy for him.

No, it couldn't be Rick, I decided. Rick had warned me to be very, very careful of Kendra. It had to be somebody else. It had to. But who else could it be but Thaniel?

I had been fighting that thought, but there it was, confronting me in the black emptiness of that rock chamber, and it wouldn't go away. It was only too terribly easy to construct a damning case against Thaniel, and I did.

I know something that I should not know, I told myself. *I know more than anyone except Thaniel's father and his son about why he visits Castle Cavage every night. And still I know so little. Perhaps there is Crusaders' treasure hidden somewhere. Perhaps there really is a Lady who walks, a ghost.*

And then, still venturing along the treacherous stone floor a step at a time trying to get my bearings, the thought flashed into my head: *Maybe from time to time she demands a sacrifice!*

What was it Dr. Darsey had said about an ancient ritual of human sacrifice associated with the disposition of the Maypole? I couldn't remember. I wouldn't try. It was nonsense. The cold fact was that Thaniel didn't want an auction at Dair. As I knew better than anyone else after last night, Thaniel would do anything to prevent that auction. And for sheer effectiveness, it was hard to think of anything to beat killing off the auctioneers.

But it couldn't be Thaniel. Last night he had trusted me with a terrible truth. Last night he had lain in my arms and wept and let me comfort him. Last night ...

That was last night. The little truth-telling needle inside my head jabbed through the sweet memories to the bitter fact. *Last night is over.*

Only it wasn't over for me.

No, it couldn't be Thaniel. He hated Kendra. He wouldn't

help Kendra harm me. Or would he? I had to stop thinking about it.

For one fleeting moment it entered my mind that the person who wanted the auction least of all was Dair's Dowager Duchess. Whatever she kept locked up in the Picture Gallery would be taken away from her, shown to the world and sold to the highest bidder. But Thaniel's mother, like Kendra, lacked the strength to lift my unconscious body from one room to another.

Just then Stratford began to bark again, and a new voice began to echo from some unpinpointable place over? under? inside? the rock chamber where I stood trapped.

"Deborah!" it called. "Deborah? Answer me if you're here! Godammit, answer me!"

I was not sure whose voice this was, but I knew I must answer it or I might never hear another.

"I'm here!" I shouted back. "Help!"

o   o   o

By my watch, the tapping and pounding lasted only fifteen minutes, but it seemed a lifetime. For all I knew, it was the end of my lifetime, and as I listened to the mingled barking and tapping and pounding that seemed to come first from one direction, then from another, I stared at my watch and tried to think of Gavin. For some reason, I couldn't summon his face very clearly; it kept getting mixed up with Thaniel's and Rick's. *The knight with black hair and the knight with red,* I thought idly. *How foolish!* I chided myself immediately. *You're getting lightheaded from the dust and lack of air in this place.*

I felt the rush of air before I saw the square of daylight materialize in the darkness. But when I saw where the light was coming from, I knew my suspicions of Kendra and the Dowager had not been baseless. The ceiling over my head had opened, and from where I cowered below I could clearly

178

see the up-ended cot whose slats I had climbed. It stood just where I had left it, against the wall in the monastic cell directly above me.

I fell into this place, I thought. *Nobody had to carry me.*

Someone's silhouette blocked my view of the cot. Someone who was hastily lying down on the floor above my head and extending both arms down to me. Someone who was trying, and failing, to speak to me over the corgi's frenzied barking. It was Thaniel. I realized I had no choice but to grasp his hands and let them lift me to—what? Safety or sudden death? Tucking my torch back into its pocket, I took two hesitant steps forward, swung my arms straight up and felt Thaniel's strong hands close around my wrists. As he pulled me out of my prison, I remembered what Dr. Darsey had told me on May Day.

Whoever decided where the Maypole should be put up also decided who would be sacrificed when the Maypole was taken down. And did the sacrificing, of course, he had said. And here was I, quite literally in the clutches of the man who had thrown the great sword Wilva to decide the location of the Maypole every year since he had become head of the House of Cavage. Had Thaniel also committed a murder every year? I had not allowed Diana's garrulous maid, Augusta, to tell me how Hugh Gafford had died. I wondered now if he had died in May. I wondered if I must die in May. Was the Duke of Dair my rescuer or my murderer? I had only a moment in which to decide.

He was very angry. His face was white with rage, but whatever he was shouting at me was quite inaudible over Stratford's booming bark. And so, the instant he set me on my feet, I turned and ran away from him. I ran out of the cell and down the rock steps, but he was right behind me. I felt him reach out and try to take my arm. Terrified, I turned and moved to the outer edge of the step to elude him. For a second I felt stone under my heel and thin air under my toe; I was almost over the edge. Forbidding myself to look down,

I succeeded somehow in pivoting and running back up the steps. I reached the top a few paces ahead of Thaniel. I gained another step or two along the narrow passage that led past the barrel-stave door of the cell to yet another coil of steps going up. I took these two at a time, but still I heard the baritone echoes of Stratford's nonstop barks drowning out whatever Thaniel was shouting at me, and I felt pursuing footsteps vibrating through the ascending blocks of rock under my feet. And then I saw where I was: outside in the scarlet twilight on a narrow ledge high above the swift, glittering currents of the River Dair.

Oh, no! I thought. *The voice that called me a fool understated the case. This is exactly where he wanted me to come. I'm actually helping him to kill me.*

Then Thaniel stepped out on the parapet, too, and began inching toward me, with the barking dog right at his heels. Out in the open the barking no longer echoed and I could at last hear what the Duke of Dair was bellowing at me:

"You are going to fall and kill yourself!" he roared.

I heard myself scream back, "Oh, no, I'm not!" *You are going to have to throw me off this tower,* I resolved silently, *if you want to play Bronze Age games tonight.*

But I was soon backed off to the very last inch of footing on the ledge. Now there was nothing to do but wonder. Would he miraculously slip and plunge into the river before he reached me? Or would he, inevitably, come within arm's length and give me the light, lethal tap that was all it would take to push me over the edge? I waited like a stone statue to find out.

When at last Thaniel was near enough to do as he saw fit, he grabbed my wrist so hard it hurt, again shouting, "You are going to fall and kill yourself, you little maniac! For God's sake, stand still!"

Then, as if I were just so much fishing line, he reeled in first one, then the other of my arms, until both my hands rested on his shoulders. Next thing I knew, he was carrying me as if I were a baby, along the narrow stone ledge and back inside the old tower. Once there, I was uncertain whether to weep or swoon, so I did neither. Stratford, however, decided to fall silent. Thaniel did not.

"I warned you not to come here!" he roared at me, carrying me down the coil of rock steps, back to the open door of the monastic cell. I made no attempt to answer him, deriving a curious reassurance from the nearness of his heartbeat, the protective, encircling warmth of him, even the rough wool of his turtle-necked fisherman's sweater. When he finally put me down, I remember wishing he hadn't.

The cot was still up against the wall like a ladder. The trap door in the stone floor was still open. But now the fat tallow candle was guttering in its blackened holder. Thaniel spoke to me softly for the first time.

"I dare not let this flame go out," he said. "You can find your way back to the house from here, can't you?"

"Alone?" I protested. "No, I certainly cannot go back alone! The voice said I would die tonight. It said someone was coming to kill me."

"Voice? What voice?"

I told him. "That's why I ran from you, Thaniel," I finished. "I thought you had come here to kill me."

"Not so," he said, his dark eyes deeply troubled. He might have said more, but footsteps were approaching us from somewhere below and I quickly hid my face against the cream-colored ribbing of his thick pullover, whimpering something about murderers. The corgi grumbled briefly but spared us his bark. Thaniel whispered to me, as gently as if I had been very ill, "Hush, Deborah, it's only Whit coming to meet me. I'm here a bit early tonight because this mad dog of yours came tearing after me and insisted that I follow him. But now Whit's here, and you must leave us."

"Can't I wait for you?" I implored.

Thaniel simply shook his head, turned me around and faced me toward the steps leading back to the corridor of antlers, the low door, the narrow rock path down Crag Cavage and the trees and gardens of Dair. My murderer might be approaching me through those very gardens now. My murderer might be closer than that: already inside Castle Cavage, just waiting for me to pass by alone.

"Thaniel, no!" I cried. "I can't go alone. I'm afraid."

Whitwell's astonished face was looking up at me from the pie-shaped step where the flight curved out of sight around the thick masonry wall.

"What's wrong, Mrs. Guest?" he said.

"Name something!" his father thundered at him. "Mrs. Guest can't seem to stay away from here, though God knows we've done our level best to persuade her it's off limits. Now she's afraid to take herself back where she belongs, so we've got to convoy her. And we've only a spare minute to do it in, so mind you don't trip on one of these blasted rocks, Deborah."

Angry though he was, Thaniel had taken my hand and marched down the rock steps ahead of me while he spoke. Whitwell had turned and walked at his side. The little dog played about our feet. As we reached the bottom step, Thaniel said, "I hope you can run, Deborah. Usually women can't."

Before I could remind him of the run he and I had made from his mother's apartments to the sitting room with the Joseph Davis clock, he sprinted into the darkness, pulling me along after him as if I were his skating partner. We ran, the Duke of Dair and I, with Whitwell and the corgi close behind us, at the desperate speed with which one runs in dreams. The crag was stained blood red by the sunset, but the clump of trees at its base was already locked into the dark embrace of night. The white statuary in the formal gardens looked almost blue in the last of the light. The long rows of boxwood hedges were tall enough to shield a regiment from view. The rustling yew trees clipped in

182

grotesque shapes cast grotesque shadows. In minutes, we had left them all behind.

I knew why we were running so fast. Thaniel had to get back to Castle Cavage before that candle went out.

Why? I asked myself. *What does he do up there when he lights that candle? What does he say? To whom does he say it? Why is it a secret?*

The lamps had been lighted behind the long windows of the great house. *Golden spangles on a dark blue backcloth,* I thought as we raced toward them. Then, just as we reached the edge of the vast North Courtyard, Thaniel stopped. For half a second both his hands encompassed my waist.

"You'll be all right from here on," he said. "Here."

He bent, swooped up the corgi and deposited him in my arms. Then he took Whitwell's hand as he had taken mine, and they vanished into the first of the moonlight, racing against a candle in an empty cell.

XIII

Dair's North Courtyard is enclosed on three sides. I stood on the fourth, facing the long line of lighted windows in the great house. At my left, the moonlight shone on a row of some twenty stone archways. Under each arch I thought I could discern the gleaming bonnet of an automobile. No, I was mistaken! The arch in the very center was only a black void. One of Dair's celebrated cars had not yet come home.

At my right, directly opposite the garage, was a stone wall with a gate of lacelike wrought iron in its center. I decided to cleave close to that wall. Perhaps no one would see me. Unless, of course, someone had been watching the sunset turn Crag Cavage crimson while our frantic little party clattered down its rock-strewn path.

I took a first cautious step to my right, felt Stratford twist abruptly out of my grasp and hurtle to the paving.

"Come back here!" I called after him, but the click of his claws died away in the general direction of the terrace that ran the length of Dair's north façade, just three or four stately steps above the courtyard.

Ah, well, I could move faster without twenty pounds of panting dog weighing me down, I told myself, hoping it would make me feel less deserted. And now that I had cried out after the dog, I had better hurry. Anyone might have heard me.

The tall iron gate in the middle of the wall stood wide open. As I hurried by, bent almost double to make myself less visible, I saw the light green two-seater parked on the broad allée that ended at that gate. The sight of the car made me quite reckless with rage. I had to know if the Duchess of Dair was inside. Or if she had once again lent this automotive treasure to her friend Alaric Meade. I had to know if either, or both, of them sat inside the car waiting for me. So I pulled my torch out of my pocket and aimed it at the windscreen just where the driver's seat would be.

Turn it on, look and run! I commanded myself, pressing the switch.

I was running up the terrace's broad, shallow steps before I allowed myself to think again. *Easy, old girl,* I thought then. *That car was empty.* Nevertheless, I could not stop running. I had no idea which room I was entering; I simply reached for the handle on the first door I came to. There was lamplight glowing behind its glass panes, and that was enough for me. The handle moved efficiently under my fingers, the door pushed open and I stumbled inside; to safety, I hoped.

A face confronted me. It was unimaginably pale and looked quite ludicrously frightened at the sight of a stranger. The face was my own, reflected in a delicate oval mirror with twin candles gleaming at its base. *Candles.*

Candles. Thaniel. Little stone cells over huge rock caverns. Five embroideries hanging all in a row. Parchment scrolls in iron boxes. In seven hundred years, none of the Cavages had ever been killed in battle, yet a voice inside their ancestral castle had assured me I would die tonight. Well, I had a lot to attend to first.

Just below the oval mirror, on a small satinwood table, I saw the one thing I wanted more than food, drink, soap and water or a shoulder to cry on. It was a telephone, and it was only about six steps away.

Six steps can be a very great distance. I had only taken one of them when I heard a sharp, snapping sound. Someone was apparently shaking the moisture out of a very thick bath towel, but there was absolutely no one in the room except me and my pallid reflection in the mirror. Or was there? As I turned to look at the sea of brocade-covered furniture that made an island of the fine Savonnerie rug on the floor, a cushion toppled over the arm of a sofa and landed almost at my feet. It was closely followed by the imperious corgi named Woodbine, who landed on it, then shook his thick red fur vigorously, repeating the snap I had heard.

"Are you on duty during Stratford's dinner break?" I asked him, wondering momentarily where Stratford had got to. "If so, I hope you enjoy monitoring phone calls."

There are many stories in circulation about Mr. Singleton and more of them than you might guess are apocryphal. No matter what anyone tells you, he cannot appraise your diamonds from across the room; thus he had absolutely nothing to do with the arrest and subsequent deportation of that Latvian soprano a few years back. The painting that hangs behind his desk is not from the hand of Leonardo, and his house in Swan Mews was not built for Beau Brummell. As to whether he was in his youth a croupier at Monte Carlo, I doubt it very much. But one thing in the vivid legend that surrounds Mr. Singleton is unquestionably true. He enjoys some very close friendships at Scotland Yard.

I placed the trunk call to his office, half-praying he had not yet left for the day. Woodbine sat at my feet, beaming encouragement. My eyes roamed the long room restlessly, ticking off details from force of habit. Absolutely first-rate

186

French furniture: a bit massive for my taste but Le Roi-Soleil had not been given to understatement. One of the best rugs the orphans in the soap factory had, to my knowledge, ever made. And the two inky-blue vases on the table between the windows could only have been manufactured at Sèvres for La Pompadour. All in all, a rather grandiose setting for a small dog and a woman in a disgracefully dirty pink sweater and blue jeans, but ...

"Walter Singleton speaking." His voice came crackling across the miles from the auction rooms behind the Brompton Oratory, and I began to cry.

"Oh, it's you," he said, not unkindly. "What's wrong?"

I wept harder.

"There, there," he said. "I received your note in today's post. If they're planning to sell up everything at Dair, how many more people do you think you'll need?"

"I need help!" I bawled.

"Exactly my point, Mrs. Guest. Now suppose you tell me what's the matter."

"I think someone is trying to—"

Someone is trying to kill me was what I had to say. I did not say it, because another face appeared beside mine in the oval mirror, paused there long enough to see that I was making a phone call and promptly glided out of sight.

It was the face of Alaric Meade.

"Trying to what, Mrs. Guest?" Mr. Singleton asked.

I turned away from the mirror and watched Rick's beautifully tailored back move slowly, reluctantly away.

"Yes, indeed!" I said firmly. "I particularly need someone with a knowledge of classical languages."

"Easy enough. But you said someone was trying to do something or other. What did you mean?"

Rick had stopped. Was he out of earshot or not? I decided he was not, although he stood with his back to me, apparently studying the contents of the bookshelves.

"It defies description," I replied.

187

"Try," Mr. Singleton countered.

"An excellent idea but quite impractical," I said.

Rick chose a book and dropped into a brocaded chair to examine it. At his feet, Woodbine slumbered, snoring lightly. Had Rick planned to sit exactly there or was it purely accidental that I could not reach the doors to either the terrace or the passageway without walking in front of him?

"I take it you're not alone," Mr. Singleton said. "Would you care to answer a few questions yes or no?"

"Gladly."

"Are you meeting with a lack of cooperation?"

"Yes. I suppose you could call it that."

"Have you quarreled with someone?"

"No, I haven't."

Why couldn't he ask the right question? Why couldn't he say "Are you in danger?" or "Has someone threatened you?" or "Do you expect to be murdered before midnight?" Why couldn't he ask something fundamental like that?

I knew the answer, of course. Mr. Singleton was far too sane even to imagine a situation in which one of his employees had to deal with disembodied voices promising sudden death.

"Mrs. Guest, would you like to be relieved of this assignment?"

Still the wrong question. I watched Rick steal a glance at his wristwatch, then return to his book.

"I rather think I shall be," I quavered into the telephone, "before the night is over."

There was a split-second of dead silence from Mr. Singleton. When he spoke, he said the right thing at last.

"Is it a matter for Stillwell?" he asked.

"Indeed it is," I told him, feeling such relief that my legs began to wobble and Rick's shock of fiery hair seemed for a minute to blur.

Although I had met him only in his capacity as an avid

bidder for antique maps, I was well aware that Mr. Milton Stillwell was a Detective Chief Inspector in the CID.

"Then I shall ring off now and tell him so," Mr. Singleton said. "Will that be all right with you?"

Rick was consulting his watch again.

"Yes," I said, hesitantly.

"Very well. Goodbye for now," Mr. Singleton said, speaking quickly. I heard the connection broken. Now only hollow silence hummed in my ear, but I clung to the receiver for dear life.

"There appear to be three El Grecos here," I said, describing them in great detail.

Is Rick to be my murderer? I wondered, watching him rise, replace his book on its shelf, look at his watch again and stroll to the window. *It wasn't Thaniel. Is it Rick?* What was he taking out of his pocket?

"And a superb Reynolds that I never even heard of before," I babbled on. "A family group in a garden!"

Rick had taken a notebook and pen from an inside pocket and was scribbling something. Now he was walking in my direction, staring straight at me without a flicker of a smile. He couldn't kill me while I was talking to Mr. Singleton on the phone; he couldn't and he wouldn't try. What was the little white slip of paper in his hand going to tell me? To ring off?

I'm going to keep right on talking, I resolved.

Rick held the slip of paper in front of my face.

"Excuse me, Mr. Singleton," I said to the dead phone in my hand, "Alaric Meade of *Nobility* is here, and he appears to have an emergency. What is it, Rick?"

The note was impeccably lettered and very brief.

DIANA IS HERE, it read, FOR THE NIGHT.

So that's why the green car was parked outside the gate! I thought. *He brought Diana here from Esty Hall. But was that wise?*

189

Rick's face was asking me the very same question, as he folded up the little note and seated himself on the nearest sofa. *Murdering me is the farthest thing from his mind,* I decided. *He's afraid some spook is after his little girl. And maybe he's right.*

At any rate, he clearly meant to wait until my phone call ended. Perhaps it would be safe for me to end it now.

"Yes, please do," I said. "I'll be right here all evening, Mr. Singleton, so do ring me back as soon as you know. Very good. Thank you. Goodbye!" And I set the receiver back in its cradle without a sound.

By now Mr. Singleton has spoken to Inspector Stillwell, I reminded myself as I sat down on the chair directly facing Rick. Woodbine opened one sleepy eye to check my exact location, then closed it again and resumed the nap he was taking right beside Rick's foot.

"Sorry that took so long," I said breezily.

"Sorry I hung about so, Deb, but Thaniel's mother sent me to find you. She's decided to have supper with Diana and Whitwell, and she'd like you and me there, too."

"Oh, Rick, I simply cannot."

"It's not for an hour. Once you change, you'll feel more like it."

I wasn't sure I had the energy to change, but certainly I hadn't the strength to argue.

"Perhaps you're right." I sighed. "Where is Diana now?"

"Meeting her new governess. That's why this whole thing has happened, I'm afraid."

"What whole thing?"

"Oh, you remember, Deb. I promised the child she could spend the night at Dair as soon as she had a governess. Apparently, she told the Dow what I'd said."

"The Dow?"

"Yes. That's what we call dowager duchesses in the irreverent pages of my little rag."

190

"Oh."

"At any rate, the damned nanny arrived on the four o'clock train and Diana insisted that all promises be kept this very night. So Grove met the nanny and brought her here, and I went to Esty Hall and collected Diana and her toothbrush, and I hope to God it's all right with the Cavage ghosts."

So do I, I thought. *So do I.*

"I could swear I saw little Dwain turn pale when I asked her to show Diana to her room," he continued, running a nervous finger inside his crisp yellow shirt collar. "But would she tell me one word about the supernatural situation around here? Not Dwain!"

"One of the maids at Esty Hall is less discreet," I said. "She confirms what I've already told you. There's someone or something named Crinsley who patrols the woods that separate Esty Hall from Dair. She says he's visible only to Gaffords, and she is very much afraid of him."

"Go on."

"She told me Diana must never go into those woods after dark, because Crinsley would kill her as he killed her father before her."

"But Hugh Gafford didn't die in those woods, Deborah. He jumped from the top of Castle Cavage one fine summer's night, screaming blue murder."

"What was he doing there?"

"Nobody has the slightest idea."

"Maybe Crinsley comes out of his woods if he finds Gaffords trespassing in other places. What was it Clewys said?"

"Only that Cavage land is a dangerous place for a Gafford to be after dark," Rick said. "But that's all he'll say."

"Well, Diana is here now, and she's perfectly fine, and I'm convinced that you and I are talking utter nonsense."

"But since we are, who was Crinsley?"

191

"Oh, Rick, how would I know? Diana did show me an old letter that mentions his name. Doesn't say anything about him, though, except that the writer didn't care to tarry with him."

"Tarry where?"

"I'm not sure. It mentioned someone named Jemmy having gone to Jerusalem, leaving the writer alone with Crinsley. Is that any help?"

"Jemmy, if my guide to the Cavage crypt in Dairminster Cathedral is accurate, would have been the first knight, the one who rode to the last Crusade. No doubt he did leave a girl behind."

"Or more than one. There are two unsigned marriage contracts hanging over Whitwell's study table. A Jaymes Cavage shares top billing in both."

"Really? I've never seen them."

"I wasn't able to read them, not knowing Latin. However, it appears that two different girls named Gafford tried and failed to wed the elusive Jemmy around about twelve-ninety Anno Domin-eye."

"At *Nobility* we'd call that proof positive of the existence of a third girl."

There it was again: the question neither Whitwell nor Thaniel had been able to answer. Who did Jemmy Cavage marry? And why, after seven hundred years, did it matter?

"Rick, as you can see, I've had a rich, full day. Now, if I'm to have dinner with the Dow, as you call her, I'll have to get dressed. Not that I have a dress, you understand, but I must put on something cleaner than this."

"Tell me the name of the maid at Esty Hall before you go. While you're changing, maybe I can ride over there and try to find out if she knows who Crinsley was."

"Don't you think it would be better for you to stay here? In case Diana sees him."

Rick's gray eyes had never looked more exactly like

Diana's than when he said, "If only Gaffords see him, Diana might not."

It seemed entirely natural for me to say, "You mean because she's your child, not Hugh Gafford's?"

Something kindled inside his eyes as he answered, more softly than I had ever heard him speak before, "I have always hoped so."

I had been standing, ready to go to my room. Now I sat down again in silence.

"You never met Lacey, did you?" Rick said at last.

"No, I never did."

"Of course not. She and Hugh had been married for quite some time before Gavin started bringing you here and there. I still saw her, of course. I loved her. I'd loved her all my life. Although I really couldn't blame her for marrying into the peerage when she got the chance. It was a great deal better than trying to go on being a model until I became the toast of the West End. She told me Hugh rather reminded her of me until he opened his mouth. But what the hell, she said, imagine me being a countess! Which I could well understand. Look at me. I dearly love the lords and ladies, too. Especially their stately homes. A not unusual compensation for orphans, is it?"

"Orphans? Who are we talking about, Rick?"

"Lacey and me. We had a true *jeunesse dorée*. We grew up together in a sort of children's jail just outside Brighton. That can be quite a tie if you have no others."

"I had no idea. It must have been hell."

"Not really. We didn't know anything else. And there were some good old spinster ladies running the show. God only knows what kind of fantasy lives they led, but they certainly thought up lurid names for their foundlings. Just imagine calling a helpless infant Alaric Meade. And then turning around and naming the next one Lacey Raindollar—"

A missile covered with fur the color of fire was in the air,

193

hurtling up from floor level at high speed, so swift and silent I sat motionless with disbelief. This could not be happening! But it was. Woodbine, who had been sound asleep at our feet, had awakened and leaped from the ground with all fangs bared to sink into Alaric Meade's throat.

He wants to kill Rick! my nervous system finally succeeded in telling my brain. At that instant, one of the dark blue vases from Sèvres burst into jagged shards against the dog's fiery fur. Had I thrown it? I wondered as I watched Woodbine freeze, then fall, carrying half of Rick's crisp yellow collar with him in his shockingly sharp white teeth.

I had not thrown it. A man with black hair, wearing a turtle-necked fisherman's sweater, must have done it, because he was now holding the furious dog in his arms while Rick cautiously picked himself up from the cushions where the dog had momentarily knocked him flat on his back. The man was Thaniel, but he had raced through the terrace door so suddenly that my already overburdened senses had taken an extra beat to recognize him.

"Where did the nice doggie learn *that?*" Rick asked, fingering his ripped collar.

Thaniel replied, "If I knew, I'd know who killed Lacey Raindollar."

Woodbine sank his teeth into the thick ribbing of Thaniel's turtleneck with such ferocity that Thaniel was thrown off balance. If I had not rushed to his side, he might have fallen, but I managed to put a steadying hand between his shoulder blades just in time. Rick must have pulled the dog away from Thaniel by using all his strength; when I dared to look, after all the growling and cursing subsided, I saw Woodbine pinioned in Rick's left arm, his muzzle clamped shut by Rick's right hand, his eyes still rolling with rage. Thaniel's sweater was ripped apart from his chin to his collarbone. I saw no blood, but the horror on Thaniel's chalk-white face was somehow equally distressing.

194

For what seemed like an hour, no one spoke. Rick sat staring at Thaniel. After a while, Thaniel sat down beside him.

"I guess we know the magic word," Rick said at last.

Thaniel picked up a sofa cushion and covered the old corgi's wild eyes. Then he tapped the hand with which Rick held the dog's muzzle. Rick let it go, and Thaniel pounced. For a moment he appeared to be wrestling with a cushion that had two flailing red fur hind legs. Then the flailing turned into scratching and even that grew sporadic.

"You're suffocating him!" I protested.

"I ought to," Thaniel admitted. "But I still need him. Would you mind ringing for someone, Deborah?"

I found a golden bellrope and pulled it desperately. Behind me, I heard Thaniel say, "Mother's poor old poodle knew that magic word, too."

Then Grove was in the room with us.

"Grove," Thaniel drawled, as easily as if he were about to ask if there were any spare Scotch in the house, "do you remember when my mother's poodle killed Lady Esty?"

"Yes, Your Grace."

"Woodbine was alive then, wasn't he?"

Grove thought, then nodded. "Yes. The accident was ten years back. Woodbine is six months older than Whitwell."

"Nearly twelve, eh?"

"Yes, Your Grace. I think that's right."

"Now here's the hard part, Grove. How many other dogs have we still got that were alive at the time of the—er, accident?"

Grove's lips moved silently for a while as he concentrated on his answer.

"I'd say there's five left."

"Five?" Thaniel continued his slow, tea-party drawl, as if nothing at all had happened. "Which five?"

"None of the big ones, sad to say. But there's Tex and

Jingle and Bonnie. And Rip. And—ah, it's on the tip of my tongue, Your Grace, but—"

"How about Bard?" Thaniel inquired politely.

"Bard! That's the one I was thinking of! Bard!"

"Good. Please round up all five of them right away. Put them all in one car, and be ready to drive it away in a hell of a hurry."

A thousand questions animated Grove's large face. He permitted himself one. "Is something wrong, Your Grace?"

"Yes" was Thaniel's answer. It hissed like a whip. Again, I watched Grove make his surefooted way out of the Duke of Dair's presence by walking backward.

"Are you thinking the same thing I'm thinking?" Rick asked Thaniel.

Thaniel nodded slowly. "We've got to prove it, of course, but I think she taught them all."

"To hell with proving anything!" Rick was shouting. "She didn't want Hugh to marry anybody. So when he married a woman a thousand times her superior in every conceivable way, this was what she did! My God, Than, she's a murderer, and she murdered my Lacey!"

Thaniel's face was anguish itself, but all he said was, "We have no proof."

"Haven't we?" Rick roared. Then he seized the dog from Thaniel's grasp and ran into the passageway with him.

"Stop!" I called after him. "Rick, come back here!" Then I was running after him. I remember turning to look back just once and being surprised to see that Thaniel was not right behind me. Instead, he stood before the candlelit oval mirror, rummaging for something inside the table that held the phone.

Rick was careening up the passageway like a madman, wildly opening doors right and left, muttering something over and over. When I finally got close enough to hear what it was, I discovered that he was saying, "Revenge is sweet but sometimes slow, revenge is sweet but sometimes slow, revenge is—ah, ha!"

He had found his quarry at last.

Not every actor is a playwright, but most playwrights I've known could have become excellent actors. Of them all, Rick gave the best performance I have ever seen when he strolled into Dair's North Gallery that evening, half his collar torn away, a glowering but silent old corgi under his arm, and me, still resplendent in my dusty sweater and jeans, following after him. Despite these impediments, he entered as jauntily as if Noel Coward had sent him.

Kendra was alone, a dandelion on a green sequin stem, almost microscopically small in this soaring room with its row of tall, arched windows facing the North Courtyard. She sat near the farthest of these windows, ankles demurely crossed, rocking back and forth very slightly, sloshing the champagne in her glass as she swayed. I had not seen her wear a tiara before; this one was a rather modest affair of amethysts and pearls, but it served to make her look even tinier, a child dressed up in some duchess's finery. She inclined her head regally as Rick and I approached her, but continued to sing, "Love is a simple thing, love is a silver ring, shiny as a ribbon bow ... soft as a quiet snow ... love is a pink balloon ..."

Rick couldn't have seemed calmer or more casual as he sat down beside her, the sullen dog perched on his knee. He got right to the point.

Smiling his roguish best, he confided, "Kendra, I've had a damnable lapse of memory. I simply cannot remember Lacey's maiden name."

Kendra transferred her glass from one hand to the other and patted Woodbine's head. "And I can't remember this nice corgi's name," she said, smiling a gorgeous smile that was careful to stop before it included me.

Rick pressed on. "I must know Lacey's name better than

197

my own," he said. "Now, damn, what was it? Lacey Rain-shilling? No. Maybe it was Lacey Rainpenny."

Kendra's smile was frozen in place. She did not speak. She did not move.

Rick continued. "Could it have been Lacey Rainruble?"

And then he freed Woodbine from his grip, sat back and said, "We'll think of it any minute now, I'm sure. Could it have been Lacey—"

Just then the late Lacey Raindollar's daughter, Diana, skipped into the room with Whitwell close behind her and volunteered this statement: "Lacey is one of my middle names."

XIV

Rick grabbed for Woodbine a split-second too late. The corgi had jumped to the floor and pattered over to greet the children.

"I'll bet I have a lot more middle names than you do," I heard Whitwell announce.

"Here, fella," Rick was calling. "Come here, boy." He was stalking the haughty little dog as intently as a hungry hunter, but Woodbine easily eluded capture, daintily reversing his field and diving under pieces of furniture whenever Rick came too close. "Deborah, head him off for me," Rick said, "I don't want him to hear Diana's full name. Do you understand what I mean?"

I understood. One of Diana's other middle names must be Raindollar. I joined the deadly little chase, moving slowly, trying to guess which way this unleashed killer dog would decide to turn.

"Whitwell Thomas Richard ..." Whit was reciting, as Diana counted the names off on her fingers. "... James ..."

"Diana!" Rick said sharply as Woodbine again danced out of reach, smiling at the game. "Go and fetch your governess! This very minute, please!"

Diana looked at him with a trace of pique. Clearly, she was as unaccustomed to having her conversations interrupted as to all the more agreeable forms of parental attention. Then she looked back at Whit.

"What comes after James?" she said.

Rick threw himself at the spot where Woodbine stood beaming at him. Woodbine executed a sort of bullfighter's pivot and escaped once more.

"William. And Nathaniel. That's six," Whit said.

"Whitwell," I called, watching the corgi disappear under an exquisite little Hepplewhite bench not ten paces away from Diana. "Whitwell, I must have this dog's collar and leash straight away. Will you please go and get them for me?"

"It's not six," Diana was saying. "Whitwell isn't a middle name, so it doesn't count."

"I want that collar and leash immediately!" I said.

Whitwell opened his mouth to reply to Diana, then sighed and turned to me. "All right, Mrs. Guest," he said. "I'll get them for you, but they won't do you any good. Woodbine won't let a stranger put a collar on him."

The icy shiver of Kendra's glass shattering on the marble floor almost prevented me from hearing what Woodbine would not do. Kendra had jumped to her feet at the sound of the dog's name, and the glass had slipped from her fingers. Now she stood like a sequined statue, staring at the corgi with uneasy eyes, because his game of hide-and-seek had ended the instant she stood up. She had his undivided attention.

It's not for the first time, either, I thought.

"He can't count Whitwell as one of his middle names, can he, Mr. Meade?" Diana asked, seating herself on the little bench. "I have six names not counting Diana."

Rick's only answer was "Hush!" Miraculously, she did. And so it was in silence that we all watched Woodbine take up a position directly in front of Kendra, Duchess of Dair, and begin his homage to her. He rolled over, first to one side, then to the other, just missing her green sequin hem. As she continued to stand absolutely motionless, he rose to his hind legs and took two faltering steps before falling back on all fours. Then he sat up on his haunches, gazing intently up at Kendra, waiting proudly for—was it praise or further orders? It was very plain that at some time in his long life he had received both from her. But now Kendra did not speak to him. Now Kendra did not touch him. Puzzled by her failure to respond, Woodbine whined briefly.

There was a new voice in the room now.

"Why don't you pat the poor dog on the head, Kendra?" Thaniel inquired as he entered the great room carrying a dog's collar and leash. *So that's what he was rummaging for in the table under the mirror!* I thought.

Only Kendra's eyes moved. I watched them. They were snapping with fright.

"After all," Thaniel continued, "you taught him everything he knows."

Then he whistled and the corgi went to him.

"Every single thing he knows," Thaniel continued, kneeling to fasten the dog's collar. "My bride, my dearest dear, my prairie belle, my little dog trainer."

Then he rose to his feet again and bowed formally to Diana, saying, "Don't let me interrupt, milady. You were, I believe, about to tell us your full name. Please continue." And, looking at Kendra pleasantly, he gave the handle of Woodbine's leather leash a debonair little flip.

"I was only saying that I have more middle names than Whitwell," Diana began.

"Never mind," said Rick, lifting her from the bench and heading for the door.

"We want to hear them," Thaniel said.

201

"No!" said Rick.

"Yes!" said Thaniel.

"Diana Merle Lacey Raindollar—" said Diana, and everything happened at once.

Woodbine sprang for Diana. Rick rushed her out of the room. Thaniel swooped down on the corgi, who was straining his leash to the limit, and clamped his jaws shut with the hand that wore the signet ring. And Kendra began to walk slowly and gracefully away from the rest of us, toward the magnificent chimneypiece.

Why had I never looked at it carefully before that moment? Perhaps because my only previous visit to the North Gallery had been that singing walk-through with Clewys when all Dair's State Apartments had been deserted and depressing. But now I looked at the North Gallery's chimneypiece hard. Robert Adam had left it uncharacteristically stark, and successive generations of dukes and duchesses had apparently refrained from adding any fancy trimmings. So there could be no doubt that Kendra was making her way toward the bare white marble mantel in order to be within reaching distance of the great sword that hung above it.

"Thaniel," I heard myself saying as loudly as I dared, "she's going after Wilva."

Thaniel ignored me. From the floor, where he lay soothing the dog, he spoke to Kendra instead. "Here's what I don't understand," he said. "With a trained crew like Woodbine here and all the other dogs, why the hell did you make Hugh Gafford jump off the top of the Old Place?"

"I didn't make Hugh Gafford do anything," Kendra replied. "You know yourself he was always talking about how you had some treasure from the Crusades hidden away over there. Well, I guess he decided to go look for it, and Crinsley got him."

"Perhaps," Thaniel replied amiably. "Did you know we still owned five dogs of Woodbine's vintage, Kendra?"

"I wouldn't be surprised if you did, you brainless British meathead."

"And as old as they are, all five of them go in for the kill on the same signal. Isn't that interesting?"

"What's interesting about it?" Kendra was edging closer to the mantel now and her face was almost as pale as its white marble.

"Don't you remember when you taught them to do it? It was just after Hugh married Lacey. You told me you were worried about kidnappers taking Whit out of his nursery. You said you thought all the house dogs at Dair ought to be trained to protect him. So you started training them. I thought you were being a marvelous mother, imagine that! I used to watch you teaching them to leap at that dummy you rigged up, hour after hour. But I always watched through binoculars, because every time I came close enough to hear what you were saying to the dogs, you stopped the class. Remember, Kendra? You didn't want me to know you were training the dogs to kill at the very mention of poor Lacey's name. In fact, didn't you tell me the command to give them in case of dire emergency was 'New York'?"

"No, I did not!"

Thaniel released the corgi's muzzle then and said to him, "Hey, Woodbine—New York!" Woodbine rewarded him with so enthusiastic a face-washing that Thaniel was obliged to clamp his muzzle shut again.

"I suppose the other five remember that signal, too," he observed, beginning to pick himself up from the floor.

"You're an insane liar!" Kendra snarled. She was close enough to Wilva to lift it from the wall, but she stood with her back to the mantel above which the golden sword hung.

"Why, Kendra, how can you say such things to me?" Thaniel was chuckling, standing up now, cradling the red dog in his arms. "I was there. I remember your trainees. One of them was Woodbine. And one of them was my mother's poodle. Remember her? My mother's old poodle, Oma, who

203

was sitting in the Italian Garden the day Lacey brought her baby over for the first time and told my mother the baby's full name."

"You're crazy!" Kendra screamed.

"It was very shrewd of you to train them to kill at the sound of Lacey's maiden name. It was a safe bet she'd give it to one of her children sooner or later and come over here and mention it to my mother sooner or later. And if one of our house dogs happened to be present, that would be her death warrant. Well, it all worked out, didn't it? Poor old Oma killed Lacey for you, just the way you taught her to do."

"Lies, lies, lies, lies, lies!"

"Don't waste time trying to deny this, Kendra. I have all five of your other pupils rounded up in a car right now, and Grove is just waiting for my signal to drive them into Dairminster. I expect they'll perform for the police much the way Woodbine just did, and—"

"You wouldn't. You can't. You're my husband, God damn you! I am the Duchess of Dair!"

Slowly, deliberately, Thaniel set Woodbine down on the marble floor, straightened up again and stared at the chalky face, the yellow hair, the amethysts and pearls, the garish green sequins for a long moment.

"Here's one way out, Kendra," he said quietly. "The dog is yours to command."

"So are you!" she roared. "I am the mother of your son!"

Thaniel stood staring at his duchess, dark fires playing across the face that had once been handsome. At last he spoke, in a curiously flat, collapsed sort of voice.

"Exactly," he said. "And you now have precisely one hour to pack your tiaras and get the hell out of here."

Woodbine heard Whitwell coming before any of the rest of us did. He trotted toward the doorway suddenly, his short legs moving up and down like red fur pistons, his leash trailing behind him.

"I see they found your collar and leash," Whitwell said to the dog. Then he turned to me, holding out another set and saying, "Sorry I took so long, Mrs. Guest. I had to hunt all over for these."

"You shut up!" Kendra screeched at him, beginning to slither back into the center of the great room. "Just follow me, boy, because we are leaving this dump, you and I, effective now."

The boy turned his usually expressionless face to his father, and I watched a terrible question form there.

"Must I?" Whitwell asked.

"No," Thaniel answered.

"Oh, yes, you must, you little prig! You're coming with me, so shake a leg," Kendra screamed, flouncing back almost to where her shattered champagne glass lay on the floor. But there she stopped abruptly, for her son had carefully walked to the far side of the Hepplewhite bench and seated himself with his back to her.

"You march!" she shouted.

Whitwell didn't move.

A green sequined rocket hurtled in his direction.

Does she mean to hurt him? I thought. *Or just to drag him off that bench and force him to follow her?*

I never learned the answer, because Thaniel seized her before she could touch their son.

"You now have fifty-four minutes," he told her, as pleasantly as if he were presiding at a debate.

For answer, she wrenched away from him and fled back to the white marble mantel. She had to jump to get her hands on Wilva, but in a split-second the great golden sword was hers. Pointing it at Thaniel, her green eyes glittering with rage, she lunged forward.

And then it happened. So fast that I could barely credit my senses then and scarcely trust my memory now. I retain only the unshakable conviction that a figure in blue leaped between the Duke and Duchess of Dair, uttered a strange

205

cry that seemed to begin with the word *"Lout!,"* then vanished at the very instant the sword fell from Kendra's hand.

A bolt of green lightning smashed against the carved door that leads from Dair's North Gallery to the terrace and the North Courtyard beyond: Kendra, gasping with panic, fled outside and slammed the great door shut behind her. Thaniel could have overtaken her, but he paused for one moment to toss Woodbine into a deep chair. It gave me time to reach his side and take his arm.

"Let her go!" I implored him.

The Duke of Dair's dark eyes became two glittering pistols pointed at my own, and suddenly his voice was gunfire.

"My God, woman!" he roared. "Do you think I have no pride?"

Then he was gone, and the great carved door to the North Courtyard closed with a crash between us.

The moment haunts my dreams. Even now.

Floodlights went on outside the long windows facing the terrace and the courtyard, silhouetting a small, trembling figure who stood watching in silence just a few steps away from me. I joined Whitwell at his window and ventured to put an arm around him. He continued silently to shiver, although the night was warm. Outside, at the right of the brightly illuminated North Courtyard, all twenty arches of the carriage house suddenly lit up, too. A flash of green sequins sped past ten of them to find the eleventh empty. Kendra's flying fish was gone.

"That's where her car should be," Whitwell said gravely. "Mr. Meade must have borrowed it again."

He's driven Diana home to Esty Hall, I thought.

Kendra wasted no time staring at the empty space where her car should have been, but immediately flung herself into the car garaged under the next arch. I have since been told that this was a 1925 Bentley 3 Litre touring car, and that W. O. Bentley himself had made some modifications in it to satisfy Old Billy. But that night, as I stood at the long window beside Old Billy's trembling little great-grandson, I knew only that Kendra had come lumbering out of the carriage house at the wheel of a shiny black open car with an extremely long bonnet and enormous wire wheels. She was heading toward her only avenue to freedom: the wrought-iron gate in the wall directly across the courtyard from the carriage house. The gate was open, but there was one obstacle to driving through it. Thaniel stood in front of it as if daring his duchess to run him down. But Kendra neither stopped nor slackened speed.

Doesn't she see him? Or doesn't she care? I asked myself, aware that my throat had turned to ice again and my feet were nailed to the floor.

Then I heard Whitwell say, "She can't find the brake!" and saw him run out into the night shouting, "The brake is on the running board! Reach outside the door! Outside! Stop! Stop!"

Perhaps she couldn't find the brake. But she understood the use of the steering wheel perfectly, as she proceeded to show us. Thaniel suddenly darted to his left, preparing to spring at Kendra as she drove through the gate. She made no attempt to drive past him. Instead, she swerved sharply away, pointing the old car directly at the slight, running figure of her son.

Then she must have pressed the accelerator to the floor, because the car literally shot forward. She was certain to hit Whitwell in the space of my next breath, I knew. And then I saw a flash of blue, a swirl of long black hair and a slender, upraised hand. They materialized between the boy and the oncoming car with the blinding clarity of a photographer's flashbulb and lingered in my astonished eye for one stunning moment after they had disappeared. Then it was all over.

The crash was so loud it toppled a jardinière on the terrace just in front of me, but when I stepped outside the door it was into a terrible, total silence.

Thaniel knelt beside his son's motionless body. Beyond them, crumpled like a concertina, the black car had ended its last race by plowing into a stone wall. Woodbine stood at attention beside it, his leash dragging on the pavement. It was some time before I realized I was screaming for help. By then, I was at Thaniel's side and Whitwell was saying, "Please go away, Mrs. Guest. This doesn't concern you."

Thaniel looked at me, but I knew he did not see me.

"Son?" he breathed.

"Yes, Father?"

"Did you see the Lady just then?"

The boy looked up at me before replying, but I could not tear myself away any more than I could stop sobbing the single word "Help!" over and over again.

At last he turned away from me in defeat.

"Yes, Father," he said. "Twice."

"Did you hear what she said?"

"Yes. But I didn't understand it."

"What did it sound like to you?"

"Back in the Gallery she said 'Law!,' I think."

Not true, I said to myself. *She distinctly said "Lout!"*

"And what did she say just now?" Thaniel's voice was almost dreamy; his eyes had never looked so enormous before.

"I thought she said *'Sairt sook,'*" the boy replied. "Does that mean anything?"

"We'll ask," Thaniel told him.

I was babbling like an idiot. "I've asked Mr. Singleton to send a language expert here," I began, "and he told me—"

They paid no attention.

"Something *'sairt sook,'*" Thaniel repeated, dazed.

"Yes, Father. Excuse me, please. Something has happened to Mother."

Grove was lifting a rag doll out of the wreckage of the shiny black car: a doll dressed in sequins. He hid her face against his dark jacket as Whitwell approached.

"Phone for Dr. Darsey, Whit!" he said, and the boy ran to do so.

Thaniel had gotten to his feet while my head was turned, and the dream was gone from his eyes.

"Grove!" he called. "How bad is it?"

Grove paused on the first of the low steps to the terrace and silently shook his head.

º   º   º

We were a strange, bedraggled funeral procession: Thaniel, Woodbine and I, mutely following Grove's broad, black-uniformed back through the North Gallery, into the central rotunda, up the violet marble stairs to the landing where they divided in two. One flight, I knew, led to Thaniel's mother's apartments, but Grove led us up the other. Soon we were in a broad corridor I had never seen before, shuffling across a thick carpet of white fur. Someone had surfaced the walls in gleaming black patent leather and painted the doors to look like slabs of jade. I looked up. The chandeliers had been removed and bullet spotlights perforated the ceiling as if it were a sieve. One of them was trained on a portrait: Kendra, Duchess of Dair, hung with emeralds, smiled at us with faint disdain.

The double doors at the very end of the passage were faced with mirror. Thaniel stepped ahead of Grove to open them. Then we were inside a tremendous ring of mirrors. At their very center, a circular bed stood on a low, white-carpeted platform, its green satin coverings reflecting into infinity in all directions. As Grove placed his sequined burden on this bed, an unthinkable sound split the silence.

Beside the bed, on a mirrored cube, an ornate gilded telephone was ringing.

It might have been ringing on the moon for all Grove and Thaniel knew. They stood with their backs to me on the platform that held the bed, gazing fixedly at the tumbled

209

heap of sequins while the little bell sounded over and over: stubborn, furious, insistent.

Something inside me screamed for it to stop, but it didn't stop. I began to count the rings. On the eleventh, Dr. Darsey entered the room.

"Wait out here, Whit," he ordered at the door, then closed it firmly behind him. The first eye he caught after that was mine.

"Answer that phone!" he said.

I ran to the base of the little stage on which the emerald satin bed was set, and he mounted to the bedside where Grove and Thaniel stood. Then I reached up and lifted the shrieking phone from its cradle. A mad puppet was inside, cackling out of the gilded earpiece in a frenzy of rage. I tried to muffle the sound against my sweater without notable success.

"Where the hell are you?" I heard.

Dr. Darsey lifted the jeweled wrist of the Duchess of Dair, held it for a while, then put it down again.

"God damn you, answer me!" the outraged voice on the telephone squawked into my soiled pink cashmere.

I did.

Raising the receiver to my lips for the first time, I whispered "Not now," and broke the connection.

"I am extremely sorry, Your Grace," Dr. Darsey rumbled, covering what remained of Kendra with one edge of the satin coverlet. "There is nothing—"

The telephone rang again.

I picked it up instantly. A man's voice was roaring out of control into my ear.

"Who the hell do you think you are, you little bitch? You're twenty minutes late already. Now get out of your cozy little bed and—"

Distorted though it was by anger, loudness and the faintly tinny sound of telephone transmission, nevertheless I knew this was a voice I had heard before.

Oh, God, I silently asked the mirrors that ringed me in. *Is this how Rick sounds when he's lost his temper?*

"—don't waste time on the pretty river road and the Avenue of Lights this trip. Our shortcut's clear again. They dragged that goddam tree away this morning. Do you hear me? By God, answer me!"

"I can't," I must have said, because the voice went into a gibbering fury.

"Oh, yes, you can, you tramp! You get here fast, and you bring every last thing I told you to bring, or the little girl's going to follow in her father's footsteps. Straight off the top of the tower! You're not the only one who can make things like that happen, you little—"

Thaniel's head turned for the first time. He was looking at the mirrored surface that was the door to this bright, dizzying room. It had burst open and someone was standing just inside it, blinking in the reflected glare. It was Alaric Meade.

Then who is this man on the telephone? I wondered. *The one who just threatened Diana.*

"—the police might have a lot of questions to ask about that," the voice on the telephone snarled, "and I might have a lot of answers. So you bloody well stop whatever you're doing, no matter who you're doing it with, and get over here fast!"

Then he rang off with a crash.

Thaniel stepped off the platform and walked quickly toward the doorway.

"She's dead, Rick," he said, as matter-of-factly as he might have said it was raining.

"I hear she did her best to take you and Whitwell with her."

In one of the mirrors I saw a strange smile cross Thaniel's face. "Her best wasn't good enough," he said. "Now I must go to my son."

Rick watched the door close behind him, then started

toward the platform where Dr. Darsey, Grove and I still stood.

"I wouldn't look at her if I were you, Mr. Meade," Dr. Darsey said.

"Fear not," Rick replied. "However, I must honor my contract with the late Duchess, which stipulates that *Nobility* will report any and all social functions at which she presides."

As he spoke, he was prying my terrified fingers from the gilded telephone, one by one.

"I think you'll agree, Doctor, that her funeral should be included in the agreement. After all, she paid *Nobility* a very handsome fee. And so, if Mrs. Guest will just let go of this—"

"Rick, listen to me," I began.

"—I will phone the news to a waiting world—"

"Be quiet," I implored, but he had begun dialing.

"—and who knows, there may be dancing in the streets tonight!"

"Will you please shut up?" I screamed.

His gray eyes were twin seas of pain, but at least they looked at me.

"Why should I, Deb? She killed my Lacey."

"Because if you don't, somebody may kill—"

"Hello, Elisa?" he said to someone in London.

"—Diana!" I finished.

"Put Cummings on," he told London. "I just took Diana back to Esty Hall," he turned and nodded to me, "where she belongs." Then he began to speak to Cummings.

There was only one chance now.

"Grove," I called. The big man was slow to turn around and when he did, I was distressed to have disturbed him. He had been crying.

I'm glad somebody loved Kendra, I thought.

"I'm sorry, Grove," I said.

"It's terrible, miss. Terrible," he muttered in his Boris-like basso, stepping from the platform to the white-carpeted floor. "Forty years, man and boy, I kept that Bentley humming like a bird and shining till you saw your face in it. And now it's a heap of rubbish."

He was mourning for a motor car.

"I want to hear all about that Bentley," I assured him, "while you drive me to Esty Hall."

"Ah, miss," he shook his head sadly, "the Duke's told me to stand by with five dogs, which I've got in a van, waiting."

He wasn't going to help me. Rick wasn't going to help me. I was going to have to drive to Esty Hall alone.

"Tell me how to take the shortcut through the wood."

"It's blocked, miss. The tree fell."

"No, it's been cleared now. Where's the entrance to it from this side?"

"Behind the carriage house, miss, but stay off it. It's not safe!" he called after me.

What is? I thought.

I ran all the way to the North Courtyard. Through the tall iron gates I saw Kendra's green flying fish parked at one side of the broad allée, where Rick must just have left it. I wrenched one of its doors open, threw myself inside, slammed the door shut and ascertained that what I'd hoped was true was true: Rick had left the key in the ignition.

The car was already moving when the door on the passenger's side swung open and Rick leaped into the seat beside me.

"Where the hell are you going?" he panted. He had run all the way, too.

"To Esty Hall!" I screamed, gunning the green car through the wrought-iron gates, past the wreck of the Bentley, across the full width of the vast North Courtyard into the empty archway where the Bentley had been parked.

"Well, this isn't the way," Rick informed me, but I kept on going. The Dukes of Dair had built their carriage house with a courtyard façade almost as impressive as the Bank of England, but behind those twenty stone archways there was

213

nothing but a tall stone shed with a big door in its back wall. Fortunately, it was a wooden door. Unfortunately, it was closed.

"Duck!" I instructed my passenger, and drove through it.

Countless horses stabled at our right and left woke up and protested my action, but I ignored them. Over a gravel track I sped toward the wood ahead, wondering where the bridle path began, straining to see a broken branch, a trampled shrub, a milestone, anything but uninterrupted forest. The gravel guided me to the right place. I followed it to the base of a gigantic oak tree, made a hairpin turn around the enormous trunk and felt a thousand oak leaves brush my windscreen clean of splinters from the carriage house door.

"There's nothing happening at Esty Hall. I just left there. Slow down," Rick said.

"There's a lot happening there. Someone's been waiting there for Kendra for almost half an hour. He phoned her just now and raised hell. He said she'd better hurry, and she'd better bring everything he had told her to bring, and she'd better take this shortcut, not the river road. Otherwise he'd kill Diana. Now you know as much as I do."

There was no reply. I shot a glance at Rick and very nearly lost my grip on the steering wheel. His face was contorted in a wild grimace. Both his hands were pressed against the windscreen as if to prevent it from caving in on him. His eyes were riveted to something directly ahead of us.

I looked into the long beam of the headlamps and saw nothing ahead of us.

Then Rick screamed and crumpled over.

He's had a heart attack, I thought. *He shouldn't have run all that way just now. Maybe he's dying. But maybe Diana is also dying. And what ever is the right thing for me to do now? Shall I keep going full speed ahead to Diana at Esty Hall? Or shall I back up and take Rick to Dr. Darsey at Dair? I can't do both.*

It was as if the car decided for me. At that very moment it

214

brought me hurtling out of the wood to the side of the empty stone stables of Esty Hall.

Faster. I had to go faster. I was racing death now. It was impossible to go fast enough. I took the green car flying across the cobbles toward the great doors to the Barons' Hall. Someone inside had recognized the car, because the great doors were opening to admit me.

Now I was going to have to slow down. Soon I was going to have to stop. Suddenly I realized I was not going to be of any help to either Rick or Diana. The minute the motor stopped, I was done for.

The whispering voice in Castle Cavage had told me I would die that very night, I reminded myself as I glided slowly into the fathomless, shadowy depths of the Barons' Hall. Yet everything there looked as it had looked on past occasions. A fire blazed in the hooded stone chimney corner, and Mrs. Travis stood waiting at the foot of the massive stone steps.

But there's something different about her, I thought. *The night I met her she was the great respecter of rank who fell all over little Whit, although he wasn't injured, and paid no attention to Grove, who was. Yet here comes a Jaguar that belongs to a duchess, and Travis isn't even smiling.*

"No," Rick moaned. He had fallen forward, and his red head rested on his knees. "Help!"

Thank God, I thought, slowing the car. *He's alive.*

"Where's Diana?" I called to Travis from my open window as my front wheels crept the last few yards toward her, bringing me close enough to see what she was wearing around her raddled neck. One look and I took my foot off the brake and drove the green car straight up the stone stairway to find Diana for myself. There are not enough emeralds of that size in all the world to make two necklaces like the one Travis was wearing, but I had seen its exact duplicate only minutes before. Kendra had worn it in her portrait.

Travis ran after me, of course, screaming something or

215

other, but she was on foot and I was driving a twelve-cylinder Jaguar.

Let her shout, I thought. *If Diana's here, she'll come out to see what's the matter.*

Now I was driving down the paneled corridor toward the new staircase and the door next to it, which I knew to be Diana's. But another, nearer door was opening, and it was not Diana's face I saw there.

No ambassador to the Court of St. James's could have been more splendidly attired for the evening than Mr. Hookham, who seemed to be sparkling all over, from the studs in his snowy shirt bosom and the large ornament in his satin lapel to the row of bright rings on his plump pink fingers. I stopped the car in front of his open door.

"Where is Diana?" I asked him across Rick's bowed back.

His dimpled little pig's face went pale at the sight of me. "So the Duchess sent me one of the help, did she?" he bellowed. "Well, wait till she sees how I send you back!"

Then he jerked open the door on the car's passenger side and Rick rolled out on top of him, taking him entirely by surprise, literally bowling him over.

But Rick just had a heart attack, I thought, watching the two of them flailing about on the floor. *He mustn't do this. He'll die.*

I had to put a stop to the fight so I leaped out of the car, took my torch from my pocket and lifted it high over my head, waiting for the moment when Rick would have to surrender the seat he had taken on Mr. Hookham's diamond-studded chest, relax the grip he had on Mr. Hookham's pink ears and stop banging Mr. Hookham's head against the floor. The moment never came. Instead, something crashed against the back of my skull and I went reeling over the two men's thrashing bodies into the room beyond, so stunned that I felt neither pain nor anxiety but simply lay where I had landed, passive and detached.

216

The room I had been thrust into was prepared for a romantic assignation in the grand manner. Silver candelabra lit a round table draped with pink taffeta where goblets glistened and a bottle of champagne lay cooling in a porcelain tub. There were chairs for two: the beautiful burl walnut chairs like Mr. Singleton's. And there was a bed waiting in the shadows. A bed that was already turned down. Were those real roses in the bowl beside it? Groggy as I was, I knew the bowl was real Ming; its yellow sang to me. Gazing at it was blissfully peaceful. I could gladly have gone to sleep just knowing it was there.

No, I couldn't. A man's shadow appeared on the far wall of the candlelit room: a dozen times larger than life and rocking back and forth drunkenly, shaking its huge head. Then the shadow lurched to one side and vanished, and the man who had cast it staggered into view.

"Did she hurt you?" Rick asked, bending down. Someone had very nearly cut his left cheek to ribbons.

"I think I killed them both," he sighed, picking me up and putting me into the nearest chair. From this vantage point I could see the doorway and the green car parked just outside it. Mr. Hookham lay propped against one wheel. There was blood on his shirt and one leg appeared oddly twisted, but his fists were still clenched. Mrs. Travis, however, lay inside the room, on her back, motionless, while the candles turned her necklace into the Northern Lights. *How*, I wondered stupidly, *did she manage to get the champagne out of its cooler without my seeing her do it?* The foil-wrapped top of the bottle still lay in her hand, all its edges jagged and deadly.

"Dramatist, editor, mass murderer, that's me," Rick said, taking the broken bottle away from her before he allowed himself to drop into one of the burl walnut chairs and begin swabbing his face with an enormous dinner napkin.

How could I tell him that, out in the passageway, Mr.

217

Hookham's eyes had opened. Perhaps if I could stand up . . .

I could stand up. I could walk. So I stepped over Mrs. Travis and pointed a finger at Mr. Hookham.

"Where," I said, in what seemed like a very loud voice because it reverberated so painfully inside my head, "is Diana?"

The pig's face was swollen and the mouth was a fair copy of a butcher's cleaver. The only answer I got was a sizzling consignment to hell from the furious lttle pig's eyes. I didn't flinch from those eyes, but suddenly I found my finger pointing at the spot on the carpet where the Northern Lights were going off.

"If you don't tell me," I informed him, "I shall take this emerald necklace back to Dair. The Duke and his mother will be most interested in knowing how it found its way here."

Still no answer.

Rick was at my side now, one hand holding the napkin to his cheek, the other wielding the jagged bottle top.

"Answer the question," he said quietly, "or I promise I'll kill you."

He meant it. Hookham knew he meant it. He answered.

"She's right where you left her," he said. "Tucked up in her bed, no doubt watching her telly. As for the necklace, if you fancy it, take it. There's more where it came from."

Moving my feet with great caution and precision, I began picking my way down the corridor toward Diana's door.

"No, thanks," I heard Rick say. "I think you stole it."

"Stole it?" Hookham protested. "The Duchess of Dair gave it to me with her own hands. Ask her. She'll tell you."

"No, she won't," Rick said. "She killed herself an hour ago."

Then I was out of earshot, walking through sheer willpower toward the last door before the new stairway. It took a very long time to reach, but at last I got there, opened it, stepped inside and switched on the light.

The bed was empty. The television set was dark and silent. There was not so much as a telltale chocolate wrapping.

Diana wasn't there.

o   o   o

The self-styled mass murderer, Alaric Meade, was again seated at the pink taffeta table when I came stumbling back. He was refereeing the quarrel between his two supposed victims. I began to hear it when I was still a good fifty yards away.

"Did you think you could hold a gun to her head till the end of time?" Mrs. Travis was raving. "She gave you money. She gave you your precious American car. She gave you whatever you fancied. But no woman born could ever give you enough to suit you, Jack Hookham, and—"

"Will you shut your bloody mouth?" he said.

"Diamonds! Emeralds! Wines! Cars! Candlesticks! China! Nothing but the best for you, while I kept warning you. Enough's enough, but not for you."

"You liked the arrangement well enough until I started taking her to bed, as well," he commented.

"Once in a month," Mrs. Travis sneered as I found my way through the doorway.

"Whenever I pleased!" he thundered back, his face livid.

"Once in a month! Though you even threw a knife at this auctioneer woman to please your little duchess."

"Shut your fool's mouth! I threw no—"

"Diana isn't there," I said weakly. It stopped them.

"What have you done with her, Hookham?" Rick asked. The bit of broken bottle glinted in his hand.

"Tell them where she is, Marie," Hookham muttered.

Above the incredible emeralds, Mrs. Travis's face was as tan and lumpy as piecrust. And as blank.

"She was in her bed. Augusta put her in her bed before going to visit her sister in Dairminster."

219

"Well, she isn't in her bed now." I was almost in tears.

"Did you harm her, Jack? I warned you, but all you had on your mind was your duchess. Your duchess that treated you like every other bill collector, paying you off every thirty days!"

Her voice had risen to banshee level when Rick took her wrist.

"Do you know where Lady Esty is at this moment?" he demanded.

She didn't, and she was frightened that she didn't.

"It's not my fault," she whined. "It's him."

"Then far be it from me to interrupt your conversation again," Rick said, dragging her to her feet, across the room to a door I had not previously noticed. "Come here, Hookham," he called, opening the door. "Hurry."

"I can't walk."

"Then crawl."

Hookham crawled, not fast enough for Rick, who pulled him across the last few yards of carpet with vigor that amazed me in a man who had perhaps just suffered a heart attack.

The door closed behind Travis and Hookham, and Rick locked it.

"Here, Deb," he said, loping across the room and handing me the big iron key. "Throw this away."

I put it in the pocket where my torch had been.

"What shall we do?" I asked him.

"Phone the police, of course."

"I think I've already done so."

"Good. When will they be here?"

"I rather think they'll go to Dair."

"What's the point of that? The child is missing from here."

"I was at Dair when I asked Mr. Singleton to get in touch with them."

Rick climbed into the driver's seat of the green car and

220

motioned me to get in on the other side. Then he turned his ravaged face to me for one shattering moment.

"Of course," he said. "I'm forgetting about Kendra."

It wasn't Kendra I was worried about when I told Mr. Singleton it was a matter for Detective Chief Inspector Stillwell, I thought. *It was me.*

"We'll go back to Dair," Rick said, "if I can turn this bloody thing around, which I don't think there's room for me to do, although—"

There was. Just. We drove down the stone steps as if they weren't there.

"Now fill in the blanks for me," Rick said as we sailed through the Barons' Hall and the great door that Travis had left wide open. "How did you get out of that jolly little forest unscathed?"

"I almost put my foot through the floor. I thought you'd had a heart attack."

"I'm astonished we both didn't, with that curious woodland creature running alongside us. When he threw himself at the windscreen and I saw he had stumps instead of hands, I guess I blacked out."

We had almost reached the stone stables where Crinsley's Wood began. Those same stables had housed an Irish hunter belonging to the celebrated ladies' man who had once been Earl of Esty, hero of the Malay States. *How many by-blows had that Lord Esty sired?*

"Don't go this way," I said. "Take the river road."

"Nonsense. This is much faster. And that poor devil can't take us by surprise twice, whoever he is. Just lock your door."

I threw myself between Rick and the steering wheel, pulled the emergency brake and rocked the Jaguar to a stop not ten feet outside the threatening forest.

Rick was so startled, he laughed. "If you're afraid I'll pull another of my girlish faints, I can't blame you," he said. "I'm

221

sorry it happened, but I swear it won't happen again. Meanwhile, every second counts."

"I will explain what I'm afraid of," I told him with the great calm that accompanies great weariness, "when this car is on the river road."

"You're absolutely crazy, you know," he barked at me. But he backed the car away from the moonlit branches and pointed it toward the Avenue of Lights and the river road beyond.

"And you," I began, "are a Gafford."

XV

We found the allée that leads to Dair choked with official vehicles, so we left the green Jaguar some fifty yards from the North Courtyard's iron gates and went the rest of the way on foot.

"Mrs. Guest?" a policeman inquired. "Mr. Alaric Meade?"

"Yes."

A pair of arms wearing navy blue reached through the gates to unlock them for us.

"Please come with me."

Exploding flashbulbs lighted our way to the terrace as the police photographed the wreck of Grove's beloved Bentley. Then the carved door opened for us and we stepped into the North Gallery.

Inspector Stillwell rose to greet us. There was a strange-looking urchin behind him, possibly a chimney sweep but certainly the grimiest creature in England, who rushed forward to greet us, too. I was clutching Mr. Stillwell's hands in both my own before I realized the wall behind him was mirrored. The chimney sweep was me.

"Mrs. Guest," he said. "What has happened to you?"

"We must find a lost child!" I replied.

"Ten years old," Rick chimed in. "Curly black hair. Answers to the name Diana."

"She has gray eyes," I babbled, "exactly like Mr. Meade's here."

"You had better sit down," Mr. Stillwell told me. "Stillwell, CID," he said to Rick, whose face was still bleeding. Rick nodded. They couldn't shake hands. I was determined not to let go of Mr. Stillwell's hands. Recognizing this, he sat down beside me.

"I sent a man to Esty Hall to look for you," he assured me. "A chap named Grove said you had gone there rather suddenly. Why was that, Mrs. Guest?"

"Because of Diana," I said. "A man phoned the Duchess of Dair, not knowing she was dead, and threatened Diana."

"With what?"

"He said, 'The little girl's going to follow in her father's footsteps. Straight off the top of the tower.' "

"Let him question the swine himself, Deb. Give him the key."

I did so, saying, "He's locked in a closet at Esty Hall with Diana's housekeeper, and she's wearing an emerald necklace."

"It's a bathroom, actually," Rick said.

"It's too good for them," I told the inspector, and saw him glance quickly at the policeman who had conducted us to him.

"Yes, it is," Rick agreed. "They're blackmailers. Now, there are two things they might have done with Diana."

"There are a thousand!" I interrupted.

The policeman was leaving the North Gallery.

He's not going back to the courtyard, I noted. *He's going into the house.*

"I am quite sure they didn't push her off the top of the tower," Rick said, a trifle too heartily.

"I'm not," I said, so softly that only Mr. Stillwell could have heard me.

"Because somebody here would have seen something or heard something," Rick went on.

Not until morning, I thought. *Maybe not until Thaniel's sundown trip to fetch the wine.*

"So it's more likely they've got her hidden somewhere over at Esty Hall," Rick continued.

Alive or dead? I wondered wretchedly. And then a terrible thought occurred to me.

"Although," Rick said, "knowing Diana, she might have given them the slip and—" The same thought dawned on him and struck him dumb. He and I looked at each other in horror.

"And what, Mr. Meade?" the inspector inquired.

"Once before," Rick said, "the child rode over here alone on her bicycle."

"Through a shortcut," I said.

"But that was in broad daylight, Deb. And now it's night, and that thing is roving about looking for Gaffords, and—oh, my God, no!"

He had the carved door open before I could cry out "Stop him!", but two policemen materialized from the terrace outside and wrestled him into a chair.

"Let me go!" he shouted. "Just the sight of him could frighten her to death!"

"Please," I said to the inspector. "Send someone to look for her on the bridle path. I'll show them where. But don't let Mr. Meade go. It's perfectly safe for me, but not for a Gafford."

"A what?"

"There isn't time to explain."

"I'm sure you understand that I can't take any action unless you do."

I'll go alone, I resolved. *Now.*

"You're quite right," I said contritely. "Of course I will explain. But first, will you excuse me just for a moment?"

Courtly as always, Mr. Stillwell stood up and bowed me out on my supposed way to the loo.

The instant I reached the corridor I prepared to sprint back to the green car through the terrace doors of a room further down the line, but I never took the first step. Instead, I stood frozen in place for rather a long time. For the policeman who had opened the iron gates for Rick and me was coming back to the North Gallery. Behind him was a stout woman I had never seen before. Holding this woman's hand and smiling up at her virtuously was Diana.

"Why, it's Mrs. Guest," she exclaimed, treating me to one of the better garden-party smiles of my admittedly limited experience.

"How did you get here?" I inquired, rather belligerently, as I remember.

"Dear Miss Harmon arranged it," the silvery little voice trilled. "Have you met Miss Harmon, Mrs. Guest? Miss Harmon is my new governess," she graciously explained to me. "Mrs. Guest is an auctioneer," she graciously explained to Miss Harmon. They moved on, royalty with yet more rabble to greet. I tagged along behind them.

". . . Mr. Meade is an editor," she was telling Miss Harmon as I re-entered the North Gallery.

"How did you get here?" he demanded.

"I will explain," Miss Harmon said, displaying an accent so upper-class as to put the Queen to shame. "Lady Esty and I met for the first time only this afternoon, but we both knew at once that we could trust each other completely. Isn't that true, my dear?"

Diana nodded.

"And so, if you will forgive my saying this, Mr. Meade, when you took it upon yourself to return the child to Esty

Hall—without my knowledge and against her will—you cemented the bond between us."

This poor woman is all wrong for the part, I thought.

"Lady Esty telephoned me within minutes of her, shall we say involuntary, return to Esty Hall. I was with Her Grace, the Dowager Duchess, as I had been for an hour, when the poor child's cry for help came. Her Grace rang for a motor car, and I drove to Esty Hall at once."

"Why didn't you stay there?" Rick asked. Inspector Stillwell had, I noticed, absolutely no expression on his face. I had the dust of centuries on mine.

"Mr. Meade," the governess replied, "it is one of my cardinal rules to accustom children to knowing the schedule and sticking to it. I felt that since Lady Esty had been scheduled to spend the night at Dair Manor, the whim of a casual visitor should not be allowed to interfere."

Rick underplayed nicely. "I'm not a casual visitor," he said.

Miss Harmon turned to the child she knew she could trust completely and said, "Didn't you tell me Mr. Meade was—?"

"No," said Diana. "I didn't."

"Was what?" Rick pressed on.

"A gossip columnist," Miss Harmon finished, with loathing.

"Diana has just introduced me as an editor, Miss Harmon."

"A courtesy, I would assume. Earlier, when she phoned me, she was more specific. Weren't you, Diana?"

The storm burst. "You promised!" Diana raged. "You promised when I had a nanny I could spend the night at Dair! You broke your promise to me, Mr. Meade!"

"It was for your own good," he told her.

I turned away, pitying Miss Harmon.

The decibel level was rising as the Gaffords aired their opposing viewpoints, and Mr. Stillwell was forced to raise his voice also. It made my head ache all the way down to the roots of my back teeth.

"Was there anything else you wished to tell us?" he asked.

Yes, I thought, eyeing the great golden shaft of Wilva which still lay where Kendra had so abruptly dropped it. *I want to tell you that someone in a long blue dress appears out of nowhere when the Duke of Dair is in danger. And that there is a room carved from living rock under one of the floors in Castle Cavage. And that a voice warned me I would die tonight. Only I really haven't the strength to speak.*

"I know how tired you must be," the inspector said. "But Mr. Singleton told me the matter was urgent. This decanter, by the way, seems to contain whiskey. Suppose I pour you some."

I accepted the glass gratefully, swallowed rather more than is my custom and was rewarded with a little glow of returning vitality. My mind slipped easily into the pedantic rut which makes me, as Gavin always put it, an utter bore when sloshed. I decided to begin at the beginning.

"Inspector," I said, "whatever is wrong here has probably been wrong since some time in the thirteenth century...."

o   o   o

Stratford woke me with an urgent combination of muffled woofs and jabs from his red forepaws.

"Go away," I responded. The woofs became yelps.

I opened my eyes and shut them again quickly. I had fallen into bed so tired that I had never drawn the curtains. Now blinding afternoon sun flooded the room.

Oh, no! I thought. *They've let me sleep too late. They've gone to Thaniel with everything I told them, whatever I told them. And now everybody knows what the scroll in the iron box says, and what the tapestries mean, and what's inside the Picture Gallery and maybe they even know who Jemmy Cavage married.*

All I knew was that I was unimaginably dirty, and that there would be no auction at Dair. I had been in the tub for a good ten minutes before it crossed my mind that Thaniel wasn't married anymore. It was a very pleasant realization, possibly for all the wrong reasons. But it got me out of that tub very fast.

As usual, there was no one in sight in the little corridor outsidè my bedroom. Beyond the black door that led to the central rotunda, it was, as always, deserted as an airport on Christmas Day. Stratford's claws clicked in brisk march rhythm on the marble floors.

"You are a very good dog," I told him as we reached the door of the lift, "with really excellent vocal cords. If you hadn't made all that noise, I'd still be trapped in that cave. I want you to know I appreciate it, Stratford."

Was I imagining things or did he bow his aristocratic head in acknowledgment before preceding me into the little lift? Fortunately, when we reached the level where the busts from classical antiquity glowered out of their violet marble niches, I stepped out of the lift first. Someone in white swooped down on me instantly: Mrs. Mackleroy, all teeth and temper.

"Idiot!" she greeted me. "The Dow's expected back any minute, and you bring a dog into the entrance hall! Get him out of here straightaway!"

"I'm terribly sorry," I began. "Here, Stratford. Come here. Oh, no. Did you happen to notice where he went?"

"No. I have better things to do. But he'd better not turn up anywhere around the old lady or I won't be responsible, I'm sure."

"I'll look for him," I said. "Though I must point out to you that a corgi named Woodbine seems to have the run of the house, and another dog just dropped a litter in the Duke's boot cupboard. So Stratford isn't the only—"

"I'm sure you know much more about the Duke's boot cupboard than I do. Though, if what I hear is true, you won't be getting to know it any better."

The great synthetic smile that appeared on her face like a

229

quarantine notice encouraged me to turn on my heel and walk away without further conversation. A section of Robert Adam's paneling slid aside as I passed it, and Dwain looked out at me.

"You're just in time for lunch with your friends!" she called. "Here, come this way. You'll save yourself steps."

"Which friends do you mean, Dwain?" I asked, stepping out of the marble magnificence of Dair's central hallway into the drab, tan-painted confines of its servants' passages: the network of narrow corridors that lay behind Dair's splendor as blood vessels lie behind the skin, invisible, indispensable, never at rest.

"The two gentlemen who arrived from London last night," Dwain said, leading me through a maze of mops, brooms and parked vacuum cleaners. "They wanted me to wake you because they don't know what they're here to do. But Dr. Darsey wouldn't hear of it."

She stopped beside a finger-marked partition and tapped it with her little fist. It swung backward so sharply that I had to jump out of the way to avoid being struck. Through the opening it left in the wall, I looked into a small oval room painted deep blue and furnished with two sturdy card tables of bronze-colored metal with folding chairs to match. One of these tables had been set for luncheon, and the manservant I had last seen at the Dow's elbow was now setting plates before Sir Thomas Lynbrook and Eustace Yount.

"Surprise!" I said jauntily, stepping through the partition and sitting down with them, suppressing the amusement I felt as Eustace's fork fell from his startled fingers.

"High time you showed up," he grumbled, retrieving the fork from the mound of mashed potatoes where it lay. Sir Thomas nodded absently, cutting up a chop.

"Now, Eustace," I said. "It's not so frightfully late. I only slept until one o'clock, and I'm sure they told you how tired I was."

"Yes, but you do know, don't you, that it was night before last that you went to bed?"

I stared at Eustace in blank amazement.

"What do you think Mr. Singleton would say if he knew you had spent thirty-six hours of salaried time sleeping?" he continued,

The manservant set a plate and cutlery before me, and I looked at the food as if I had never seen food before.

"I had no idea," I sighed, "but I believe you. The circumstances were a bit unusual."

I loathe Eustace Yount, and I regretted that, on the one occasion in my life when I had slept an entire day away, he —of all people—had arrived to clock my performance. Eustace and I agree on only one point: that he is good at evaluating domestic artifacts. Mr. Singleton hired him away from a post as Assistant Keeper of the Laces or some such thing at the Victoria and Albert Museum, and he is very astute about textiles as well as old bottles and pots and whether or not furniture brasses are original. However, he was the last person I would have chosen to examine the extraordinary tapestries I had seen in Castle Cavage. Although he would know, or take pains to find out, all about the needle and the thread and the nature of the dyes, and could be depended on to talk about the five old embroideries as tirelessly as if they belonged to him instead of the Duke of Dair, I was quite sure the intensity of the passion which had guided the needle would escape him entirely.

"Extremely unusual, I should say." He smirked at me now. "Our beloved client, Her Disgrace, gone to her reward, Detective Chief Inspector Stillwell creeping about the premises and a veritable army of police lurking in every corner. By the way, is it true about the Duke and you?"

Thaniel, too, would dislike Eustace thoroughly, I decided, devouring my chop.

"Now don't be coy, Deb. If you've hooked a big one, I'm

231

sure it's quite all right with me. Though I must say he flies into a towering rage when things don't go his way."

I won't reply, I thought. *Eustace will tell me what he meant by that whether I want to know or not.*

"How have you been, Sir Thomas?" I said.

"Puzzled," Sir Thomas told me very gently. "I have no idea what I'm supposed to be doing here."

"Nor do I," Eustace said, taking center stage again. "Mr. Singleton only said you wanted an expert on tapestries and someone with a knowledge of classical languages pronto. So we rushed up here and Inspector Stillwell and his bobbies told us it would all keep until you'd had your beauty sleep. There is to be no auction. Did you know that, Deborah?"

I nodded.

"Then you really shouldn't have sent for us. As I am sure Mr. Singleton will soon tell you in no uncertain terms."

I had not eaten for days, but suddenly my appetite vanished. Eustace probably earns no more per diem than I do, but Sir Thomas Lynbrook's time comes high. An Oxford don, he has been called the most learned philologist in Britain. But I suspect it is the fact that he also looks like the most learned possible Oxford don that has made him a fixture on this nation's television screens, expressing his gentle opinions on subjects as far afield from philology as the value of vegetarianism or the menace of pornography. With his fine-boned, narrow face and its crown of wavy white hair, Sir Thomas bears a strong resemblance to William Blake's sketches of God, and he seems able to translate absolutely anything. Well, there was indeed something for him to translate inside the iron box I had stumbled over in Castle Cavage, but I had never had the chance to tell Thaniel about it. Or about the five tapestries, either. Had I mentioned them to Mr. Stillwell? I tried to think back through the fog of pain, fatigue and whiskey, but I could not be sure I had.

"Quite a treat, actually," Eustace babbled on, "watching a peer of the realm have a tantrum."

Small wonder Thaniel had been enraged. I had never had the chance to tell him I had summoned the CID, either. Suddenly my distress escalated from having lost my appetite to being in imminent danger of losing my lunch. I would have to leave the table without a minute's delay, so I stood up and headed for the nearest doorway. It led into a small, windowed sitting room.

"The Duke is hardly a lavish host," Eustace continued, oblivious to my departure. "Where did he put you up, Sir Thomas? I'm told this little cubbyhole was Mr. Gragg's suite, whoever Mr. Gragg was. A Spartan, probably."

I'm in the butler's quarters, I thought, closing the door behind me. *That's why there's such a good view of the front entrance.* Through the window at my left, I saw an immensely long maroon limousine glide past the curving colonnade and come to a stop. It was the car that was built for the Czar, and Thaniel was out of it even before Grove. Mrs. Mackleroy came flying out of the house just as Whitwell and Dr. Darsey emerged from the huge automobile. Then Grove appeared from the far side with the Dow in his arms.

Why are they all wearing black? I wondered. *They look as if they had been to a—*

Of course. Among other things, I had slept through Kendra's funeral.

○   ○   ○

They stood in the violet rotunda, oblivious to me, waiting for the Dow's silver golfing cart. The total blackness of their clothes made me glad I had put on my black velvet jeans and sorry I hadn't a black pullover as well. The Cannes Festival T shirt wasn't quite the thing, I knew, but there was no time to lose. I must speak to Thaniel as soon as possible. However, I waited until Grove had seated the Dow in her jaunty little vehicle before I started forward. To my surprise, the Dow

233

waved to me as I emerged from the shadows. What could I possibly say to her?

I mumbled something about my condolences and watched her bite back her laughter. I turned quickly to Whitwell to say something similar, but Thaniel spoke first.

"Ordinarily," he said, in what seemed to be a rather exaggerated Etonian drawl, "all of us would thank you, Mrs. Guest. Not only for your gracious expression of sympathy, but also for your thoughtfulness in summoning to this house a high official of the Criminal Investigation Department at Scotland Yard, and a blithering little maggot of a chatterbox with a knowledge of embroidery, and an old man I last saw lecturing about the Sanskrit roots of the English language when I was an undergraduate."

Dr. Darsey was staring at his shoes, but Mrs. Mackleroy was gazing directly at me, her eyes flashing with pleasure.

"Even my late wife, gregarious though she was, rarely assembled such a guest list for Dair. And so I feel it is I, poor country bumpkin though I am, who should thank you for having put me in touch with people I might never otherwise have met."

"Oh, please try to understand," I heard myself say. "You need all three of them, and it's all at no cost to you."

The Dow was fighting a losing battle with her smile.

"Nurse," she said, not bothering to turn her lovely head toward Mrs. Mackleroy. "Do we still employ the Frenchman who prepares the midnight suppers?"

"Yes, ma'am, I believe so."

"Tell him Lord Mabry will have an omelet. At once. Go with Mrs. Mackleroy, dear. And tell me what you honestly think of the omelet later."

This is the happiest day of her life, I thought. *She's ruling the roost again. After a very long involuntary layoff.*

"Shall we go someplace where we can all sit down?" she said as Whit and Mrs. Mackleroy dutifully withdrew. I hoped Mrs. Mackleroy was still within earshot when the Dow added, "When there are servants present, Thaniel, you simply must take care what you say."

Thaniel was in no mood to be silenced that day. As we hurried along behind the golfing cart, he continued to address me in English so elaborate it was worthy of a Restoration comedy. It slowly dawned on me that, although his face remained as solemn as his black suit and tie, Thaniel, Duke of Dair, was jesting.

"You speak of cost," he said. "It is entirely possible that your embroidery chap and your Sanskrit man can be paid out of various profits old Singleton has squeezed out of me on past occasions. But as for the police, my dear, where in hell do you think their salaries come from?"

The silver cart piloted us into the North Gallery, and Dr. Darsey helped the Dow into the very chair by the window where Kendra had consumed her last champagne. I saw that Wilva again hung high above the mantel and that the shattered glass had been swept from the floor. As we approached the long windows, more and more of Crag Cavage was revealed to us, rising out of a black thicket of trees that grew on the farthest edge of the faraway formal gardens. But not until I was seated could I see the grim old castle at the top. Was there someone on the rock path coming down? I squinted, trying to tell, but then decided I must be mistaken.

Grove's immense bulk blocked the windows for a moment as he offered sherry on a tray. Thaniel and Dr. Darsey each accepted a glass; the Dow and I both waved the tray away.

I'm picking up her regal gestures as if I were Diana, I chided myself a second later.

"I really think the first thing I must do is engage a butler," the Dow remarked when Grove and his tray had departed.

"Mustn't overdo," the big doctor cautioned her.

"And then," she continued, "I shall have some of our numerous mirrored walls replaced."

"Little by little," he counseled. She favored him with a ravishing smile.

She'll have Kendra's wing redecorated by Monday, I thought to myself. *And feel ten years younger for doing it.*

"To Scotland Yard," said Thaniel, toasting us with his sherry glass. "In general. And Inspector Stillwell in particular."

"I was told you'd had words with him," I ventured.

"A moment's misunderstanding, nothing more. After all, I hadn't sent for him. And I didn't realize you had."

"There wasn't time—" I began.

"I hope," his mother interrupted, "you made it clear to the inspector that the Picture Gallery is not to be unlocked."

"Not under any circumstances, Mother. The fact is I almost sent him packing. But we did need an official police report about Kendra's smashup. And then Stillwell mentioned something Mrs. Guest had told him about a pair of alleged blackmailers locked in a bathroom at Esty Hall."

The Dow stared at him in horror, one exquisite hand flying to make sure the jet brooch at her throat was still in place. It was.

"He had sent some men there, and he showed me photographs they had made. After I saw those, I could appreciate his interest in knowing if anything is missing from the Picture Gallery."

The old woman's beautiful face grew stern.

"He is not to look in there," she said curtly.

"No, Mother. But someone who knows what belongs in there really should check over those photographs."

He waited for her to pick up her cue, but she ignored it, so he went on.

"Kendra seems to have transported some rather choice items from here to Esty Hall. All I recognized was an emerald necklace you gave her after Whitwell was born, and a Chinese vase she once assured me a dog had smashed to bits. But there were many other things, including a nice painting that may also be ours."

"What sort of painting?" the Dow asked.

"A landscape. The police say it's signed by Turner or Whistler, I can't remember which."

Was there a momentary blink to conceal the sheer thankfulness that had lighted her eyes? I thought there was.

"There are no landscapes in the Picture Gallery," she said, looking out the long windows.

No landscapes in the Picture Gallery, I mused. *That's odd. I'd love to know what they do have hanging there.*

"Thaniel," his mother said, "did you give the police permission to visit Castle Cavage?"

"No," he said, very slowly, "I did not. Why do you ask?"

"I thought I just saw—"

"—someone on the crag?" he asked her.

"Yes."

The remains of his sherry splattered my black velvet lap as he leaped up and ran to the windows.

"Deborah," he said, "if your bloody inspector has gone inside the castle, I'll have his badge and his pension and—"

Just then four men emerged from the trees at the base of the crag. They moved quickly across the green lawns to the central walk of the formal gardens. Three of them, I noted, wore navy blue. The fourth must be Mr. Stillwell.

"The goddamned trespasser!" Thaniel began to shout. "I'll have his head for this! I'll have his badge and his pension and his bloody head!"

The rest of us sat motionless, watching the four men's progress from the gardens through the courtyard to the terrace outside the room where we sat waiting.

Thaniel flung open the terrace door for the inspector. The three policemen, left outside, looked as grimy as I had looked two days before, and their expressions troubled me.

"Inspector Stillwell!" Thaniel roared. "By what right did you and your men presume to enter Castle Cavage?"

Mr. Stillwell shot an uneasy glance at the Dow and said, "Your Grace, we should have a word alone."

"Answer my question!" Thaniel cried. "By what right—?"

"We have a search warrant."

"A search warrant! A search warrant! I will not have these intrusions, Inspector Stillwell—"

"Yes, Your Grace. Now let's have a word alone, please."

There was a ring of metal in Mr. Stillwell's voice that I had never heard there before. Thaniel heard it, too. It silenced him completely. The color drained from his face, but he led the way into the next room briskly enough. Every muscle in my body longed to follow him.

"Let's have a word alone, please"—is that what the CID says when you're about to be arrested? I thought wildly, my eyes riveted to the closed door of the next room.

The Dow's low voice was almost a moan now. "I always knew there was something up there besides wine," she said. "My husband loved the sunset so, and yet he always stopped his work before the sunset came and said he had to fetch the evening's wine. That's all he would ever tell me. But we didn't drink much wine."

Dr. Darsey's reply surprised me. "Try to be brave, my darling," he said. *So that's how it is!* I was thinking when the door that separated me from Thaniel opened, and he rejoined us, even paler than before.

"What is it, son?"

"I don't want you to get all upset, Mother. It's a matter the police will attend to for us."

"What is it?" she repeated.

"They found a grave up there."

She stared at him, almost uncomprehending.

"Do you mean—a new grave?" Dr. Darsey asked.

"No, thank God, a very old one. They can't even guess how old." Then his extraordinary dark eyes found mine and he said, "The inspector wonders if Sir Thomas can read the headstone."

o   o   o

There are times when men must cope and women must

238

wait. This was one of them, and the Dow and I both knew it. We sat together at the North Gallery's long windows watching Thaniel, Dr. Darsey, Sir Thomas Lynbrook and little Eustace Yount follow the police toward Crag Cavage. The afternoon sun was so bright it made the courtyard pavement glint like diamond dust and turned the green lawns of the formal gardens into charming little felt shapes clipped from the top of a billiard table. For a moment, it was almost possible to think of Castle Cavage as an illustration from a fairy tale, But how often do you see three uniformed policemen in a fairy tale?

"Thieving little bitch," the Dow said quietly.

I made no reply, being uncertain whether she was addressing me or referring to some third party.

"The thieving little bitch gave my emeralds to a blackmailer. She would have had all of Dair sold up and given the money to him. She must have been more than just a thief to have to pay that kind of blackmail, don't you agree?"

"I daresay, Your Grace, it will all come out at the blackmailer's trial." Remembering the last time the Dowager Duchess and I had sat alone, I had no intention today of mentioning trained dogs or the sudden death of Lacey Raindollar.

"Who is he, do you know?" she asked.

"A man named Hookham, Your Grace. He used to guide the tours at Esty Hall."

"Hookham," she said. "He was poor Hugh's valet. I wonder—"

I wonder, too, I thought, careful not to let the expression on my face change. *I wonder if Lacey Raindollar was the only person Kendra killed. I wonder if Kendra also killed Hugh Gafford. She might have talked him into going treasure-hunting inside Castle Cavage, then followed him as she followed me. If the strange acoustics there frightened him as badly as they did me, she might have driven him to his death just by speaking to him. After all, one whisper made me fall off a ladder. But I didn't have a valet lurking about to keep*

239

an eye on me. I only had Stratford, who is not the blackmailing kind.

"However," the fine low voice cut off my train of thought, "there are many more urgent matters I must think over before I permit myself the luxury of speculating on the full extent of my late daughter-in-law's sins."

Thaniel's black suit was a pin dot ascending the crag. The green confetti dancing about next to it must be Eustace's polo shirt. *Poor Thaniel,* I thought. *Imagine having to listen to one of Eustace's monologues at a time like this.*

"There is," she continued, "the matter of the search warrant, for example."

"Yes," I said. *They are going to be able to search your precious Picture Gallery,* I refrained from saying.

"I should so very much object if they insist on seeing the Picture Gallery. Do you think they will?"

"I can't say, Your Grace."

She toyed with the jet brooch for a moment, staring out the window, watching her son disappear inside his ancestral castle. Then she turned to me, her marvelous eyes distraught.

"Mrs. Guest, I want you to do something for me before those men come back."

Ah, I thought. *Is this where she beseeches me to state that all her stolen Rembrandts are actually worthless fakes, painted five years ago by gypsies now safely in prison? Or is she at last about to speak of Frederick Pennington?*

"If I can help you," I said warily, "I will be only too happy to do so."

"You can. You are very knowledgeable about art. I would like you to advise me."

"With pleasure, Your Grace."

"Then if you will first help me into my silver chariot—"

Apparently she hadn't the use of her legs at all. I had to lift her from her chair to the driver's seat of the cart. She weighed hardly more than a black glove, and her perfume was the most glorious I had ever encountered. I had to know its name.

"Everyone asks," she replied. "It's Norell. I'm glad you like it. Now sit here beside me and we'll drive to the lift."

We saw no one on our jaunt from the North Gallery to the violet rotunda. Something too silent about our surroundings told me Dair's servants were watching us, hidden inside their tan-painted private passageways, waiting for bells to summon them. The Dow must surely have known as well as I that each of the walls had ears, yet she seemed to feel she could speak to me freely.

"Only one painter's work is kept in the Picture Gallery," she began. "His name probably means nothing to you, although I believe I mentioned it to you when first we met."

Don't be too sure it means nothing to me, I thought, opening the door of a corridor feeding directly into the rotunda, then hopping back on the silver cart.

"Oh, it might," I said. "What is it, ma'am?"

The Nefertiti resemblance had never been stronger than at that moment, and she must have known it because she didn't look at me when she replied.

"Pennington," she said. "Frederick Pennington."

"Frederick Pennington," I repeated after her, non-committally.

"You see, I knew it wouldn't mean anything to you." She sighed. "He won a prize once. But that was in Paris, and it was a long time ago. He never showed his work again."

We had reached the lift, and I bounded forward to open its door. She steered the cart inside and I followed. After I closed the door and the metal gate, she pressed the button marked A and we began the journey up.

"Why didn't he?" I asked, as casually as I could.

"You'll see."

Dair's Picture Gallery is directly above the North Gallery, I realized for the first time as the Dow's silver cart retraced its path a story higher than before. And after she had finished with the keys and combinations that opened its many locks and chains, I realized something else. I was afraid to open its

241

massive double doors. She did it for me and preceded me inside.

It was a magnificently proportioned long room, ending in windows that admitted floods of clear north light. Outside was the same view we had just left: the courtyard, the formal gardens, the ring of black trees, the crag, the castle. But something stood in front of the windows here, blocking the view. Something I could see only in silhouette. Something as angular as a scarecrow or a scaffold.

"Please close the door," the Dowager said, and I spun around quickly to do so. The half-circle turn gave me a look at the whole east half of the Picture Gallery. The look startled me so much that I spun to see the west half when I turned back. It was exactly the same.

Not a single picture hung anywhere on the walls around us. But on all four sides of the filthy floor, dusty sheets covered what might have been stacks of old newspapers, crates of various heights, or—for all I knew—scale models of Mars.

I reached back fast, grabbed one of the door handles and made sure it opened the door. Then, somewhat reassured, I said, "Where have you brought me, Your Grace?"

"To Frederick Pennington's studio." She bent to take hold of one of the sheets, but it was too low for her to reach. "I'm afraid I have to keep the paintings covered, but—"

Of course! I told myself as breath came back into my lungs and my blood resumed its journey through my veins. *North light. Canvases stacked on the floor. And that thing in front of the windows is an easel. There's probably a canvas on it. And there's a common, ordinary bedsheet over the whole thing.*

"I would like your opinion of his work, Mrs. Guest. Could you lift this cloth away, please?"

I could and did. An unframed painting looked up at me. I picked it up and saw that a very similar painting lay beneath it. I drew the dusty sheet aside, coughing involuntarily as I did so. Another, larger, painting greeted my eye. Beyond it I saw the edge of still another. I had not seen such marvels of sheer painterly perfection often in my life: the draftsmanship and composition were worthy of the Renaissance masters, the light was so sensitively depicted that I knew how much—or how little—warmth it had generated and felt that warmth on my own skin.

Skin. One would have to go back to Ingres to find mere canvas turned into skin of such lifelike texture. And there was certainly no shortage of skin in these paintings. We enjoy what we do well, and Frederick Pennington had clearly relished painting these magnificent nudes. He had painted them superbly.

I picked up more dusty sheets, peeked under their edges, gazed at the canvases propped against the walls, glanced at the paintings propped up behind them.

There were dozens upon dozens of finished paintings. There must have been many hundreds of sketches and studies as well. All of them, as far as I could tell, dealt with the nude female body.

"Mr. Pennington was—phenomenal," I said at last, instantly regretting the banality of my praise.

"He was obsessed," she snapped.

I stared at her for a second, utterly astonished. Then the simple truth struck home. The same woman had modeled for all these masterpieces, and that woman was the Dow.

How did she keep all this from her husband? I wondered. *Did she marry one of those titled imbeciles one reads about, who is never allowed out of his nursery? Or was her husband a rake and a rogue and totally indifferent to what his duchess did?*

"Now you can plainly see why he never exhibited his work again," she said.

"No, ma'am, I really can't. Do you mean he didn't show them, because they're"—I reached for the most delicate euphemism—"undraped?"

243

"They're stark naked."

"But, Your Grace, there are nudes in every great art collection in the world."

"Not of me, there aren't! But for twenty years, that's all Fred wanted to paint. I suppose I was foolish, but I let him have his way. In the beginning, we were very young and we were in Paris, and I didn't mind so much. But then we came back here, and I really grew very tired of it."

If your husband couldn't pitch Fred out for you, Old Billy certainly sounds the sort who could, I thought, still stunned that this beautiful old woman had so little understanding of beauty. She sat atop her silver cart beside the draped easel, sadness all over her Nefertiti features.

"He returned from the war a changed man," she said. "He still painted every day, but I had had this wretched accident by then, so I had an excuse not to pose for him anymore. He didn't seem to mind at all. He had found a new model. Here. Look at her if you like. God only knows who she was, but my husband spent the last fifteen years of his life working on her portrait."

She had picked up a corner of the cloth that hung over the easel and sat waiting for me to take it from her. I moved from the door side of the easel toward the windows, saying to myself, *Her husband. This painter was her husband. Frederick Pennington, whose only known work hangs in the Louvre, was also Duke of Dair. Of course there is no law that a duke can't also be a genius, but I never even suspected it. What an utter bigot I must be.*

Eustace Yount's green shirt looked quite yellow against the infinitely greener greens of the formal gardens, but I was so stunned that I must have looked at this spot of near-chartreuse for a full ten seconds before I actually, consciously, saw it. It was bouncing along beside Thaniel's black suit at the head of a fast-moving little procession. Behind them, Mr. Stillwell held what might just possibly be a large old Polaroid camera, and Sir Thomas Lynbrook scrubbed at his hands with what appeared to be a pocket handkerchief. Bringing up the rear were two uniformed policemen with the humpbacked iron coffret between them, and two others carrying a ladder.

"The men are coming back now, Your Grace," I said, taking the corner of the dropcloth from her hand.

"Quickly, then," she cried, driving her silver cart toward the doors.

Somehow I knew what I would see on Frederick Pennington's easel before I actually saw it. What I did not know was how much impact it would have on me. And so I skimmed the cloth aside, nodding my unsurprised approval of the glorious blues in the dress, the luster of the swirling black hair, the flawless modeling of the upraised arm. And then I looked into the face. It was a face that exerted an actual physical pull, like a whirlpool or an undertow. It was a face to drown in.

"You see," the Dow remarked from the doorway, "he could paint clothed subjects very nicely. If he wanted to."

"Yes," was all I could reply.

"Unfortunately, he didn't seem to think I deserved that much respect. But she did, whoever she was. And she's not even pretty, is she?"

Neither is the Mona Lisa, I thought.

"Now, quickly, Mrs. Guest. You know about paintings. Here's what I want you to tell me."

I tore my eyes from the canvas on the easel and focused them on the Dowager Duchess. She had, I noticed, placed her silver cart so it blocked both the double doors.

"Yes, Your Grace?"

"What is the quickest way to destroy them?"

She really is insane, I told myself. *Be very calm.*

"You don't seriously want to destroy these?"

"I will not have policemen staring at them, Mrs. Guest! I will not have them dragged into a court of law! I will not let Fred shame me from beyond the grave!"

"No one need ever set eyes on them," I assured her, but she had taken something out of her pocket.

My God, it's a cigarette lighter! I thought, rushing toward her. But I was too late. She had tossed the flaming lighter on top of one of the dusty sheets at the edge of the floor. The fire was already leaping when she swung the double doors open, calling, "Hop aboard, Mrs. Guest! Quickly!"

I didn't take the time to answer her. I was running back to the easel, half a step ahead of the inferno, determined not to leave that room unless Frederick Pennington's portrait of the woman in blue left with me. I seized it and turned back to the doors, but a solid wall of black smoke barred my way. There was only one thing to do, and I did it.

I threw the canvas at one of the windows, praying it would shatter the glass, fall to the terrace and land face up. Then the smoke engulfed me.

XVI

Mr. Stillwell was waiting for us at the bottom of the ladder.

"How do you feel, Mrs. Guest?" he inquired.

"She'll be quite all right," Thaniel told him. "Do you mind opening the door to the Gallery for me? Thanks."

"What happened?" I asked, as he carried me inside.

"I heard the glass break," Thaniel said, placing me on a sofa facing one of the long windows. "So I grabbed the police ladder, went up and found you unconscious on the floor. By the way, Stillwell, how many men did you bring here? I ran into a whole brigade sloshing about up there."

"But what about your mother, Thaniel? Your mother was with me in the Picture Gallery."

He was gone before I could tell him to go back and find her.

"He has good reflexes for a duke," Eustace observed. "It looked as if he jumped out of this room in one bound."

"With the doctor right behind him," Mr. Stillwell added. "I had hoped he would attend to you first."

247

"Oh, I don't need him. I'm fine. Just help me sit up."

"No," the inspector said, "please lie still until Dr. Darsey returns. And tell me what happened to you while all of us were in Castle Cavage."

"Ah, that's a fascinating old place," Eustace said. "You must look at these Polaroids, Deb. As I said to His Grace—"

The inspector had encountered compulsive talkers before. "Mr. Yount," he cut in. "We will need your preliminary report in half an hour. In writing, of course."

"Inspector, that is not possible," Eustace protested. "Why, the workmanship of that iron coffret alone—"

"You must try."

"And it is much too soon to say anything about the tapestries except that they appear to be of thirteenth-century workmanship. But until we have thorough tests of the fibers and the dyes, I certainly will not risk my reputation by saying—"

"We want this in writing."

"Well, I might be able to say a few words about the construction of that strange little tower room. Deborah, do you realize that ceiling is a perfect whispering arch? I remember on my last visit to America, I was shown two whispering arches. And do you know, they were both in railroad stations. I said at the time—"

Mr. Stillwell tried again. "Sir Thomas Lynbrook," he said, "is already at work on his translations of the headstone and the scroll we found. Surely, Mr. Yount, in the same spirit of cooperation, you could write down your impressions of—"

"Mr. Stillwell," I said weakly, "where is the painting?"

He looked at me intently. "Painting?" he repeated after me.

"Yes," I replied. "I threw a painting through the window of the Picture Gallery. To break the glass."

"I wish that doctor would come back," he muttered.

"Where is it?" I persisted.

"Mrs. Guest," he told me. "You smashed the window with

248

your fist. That's why your hand is cut. That's why you need the doctor."

o   o   o

I lay on the sofa facing the long window and looked at the glittering reflections cast back into the room by the utter darkness outside. There was a fresh white bandage wrapped around my hand, and I had a curious floating sensation. Whatever Dr. Darsey had given me before he treated my hand had made me very calm indeed. Although I was physically present, I was many miles—or was it years?—away. And so I lay and listened and looked at the scene mirrored in the dark windowpanes.

Five men were gathered around a table where a lamp burned. No, one of them was too small to be a man; it must be a boy. Of course, it was Whitwell! He sat between his father and Mr. Stillwell. Facing them were Sir Thomas and Eustace Yount.

Eustace was speaking. "—in my experience of whispering arches, I have, of course, tested the fine example outside the Oyster Bar in Grand Central Station in New York City and the equally interesting one at the entrance to the Union Station in St. Louis, Missouri, but I can assure you that neither compares with the one we found in the tower room at Castle Cavage today. In fact—"

"About the tapestries—" Thaniel began.

"First, Your Grace, let me explain that if you stand at one side of an arch of this type and whisper, the sound travels all around the arch. Someone standing at the opposite side hears the whisper as if you were right beside him, whispering in his ear. Depending on where you stand, and how your arch is built, you can create other illusions."

And Kendra did, I thought dreamily. *Just for me.*

"Now, about the tapestries—" Thaniel said again.

"Well, first, Your Grace—"

249

"Please stop calling me Your Grace. I want to hear about the tapestries. Now."

"I simply wanted to speak of the candlestick in the window up there."

"The tapestries, Mr. Yount."

"You really are rushing me, Your Grace."

"You have very little time before your train leaves."

There was an instant of silence. Something told me Eustace had not planned to take the next train, but I was far too relaxed even to smile about it.

"The candlestick," Eustace said, "is even earlier than the tapestries and unmistakably of Near Eastern origin. One of Your Grace's ancestors may have brought it home from the Crusades. I base that opinion on—"

Now the inspector spoke. "Have you any idea what those tapestries are about?"

Eustace sighed eloquently, but he replied.

"No, actually, they're puzzling. So many of these pieces of medieval needlework deal with mythology and legend and stories everyone knew. But these appear to be in the tradition of the Bayeux Tapestries."

"The what?"

"Somebody reported the whole story of the Norman Conquest with a needle and thread in the Bayeux. Of course, they aren't as handsome as these, but they do tell the tale. I think somebody was trying to report actual events in—if I may presume to name them, Your Grace—the Cavage Tapestries."

"Actual events?" Thaniel said. "A man having his hands chopped off? A child stuffed in a sack?"

"Ah, but we are only looking at little Polaroid snapshots. When our serious photographs have been developed and enlarged, we will be able to pick out so much detail. Until then, perhaps we shouldn't try to guess what these embroideries depict, because we have only one valid point of departure."

"What is that?"

"The famous tapestry from this series, Your Grace. The one that hangs in your family's crypt in the Cathedral. Doesn't it show the Cathedral with a big fire burning behind it?"

"Yes, it does."

"Now, if that was an actual fire, it must be a matter of historical record locally. Given a few days' research time, I could undoubtedly find out the circumstances and tell you more, but—"

"But unfortunately your train leaves momentarily. Grove will drive you, Mr. Yount, and I shall await your report on the photographs and the fibers and the dyes by the earliest post. Thank you for your invaluable assistance, and goodbye."

Exactly at the conclusion of Thaniel's last spoken syllable the door closed. Now the reflection in my black windowpane showed only four people gathered at the lamplit table.

"Father?" Whitwell said.

"No. Please don't speak for a moment. I think we all need an interlude of silence. Dear God, how long did that man rattle on? Two hours? Three?"

"I've no idea," I heard Sir Thomas answer. "I was reading this, and I paid no attention."

"Your powers of concentration are remarkable."

"So is the document."

"It must be."

"Yes. I know of no other personal letter in Charles de Cordel's own hand."

"Is that what it is?"

"Yes. It is a letter of condolence. It was written to Sir Michael Cavage in the year 1308—"

Thirteen-hundred eight. Who died in 1308, Thaniel? No, it wasn't Sir Jaymes. Look at his tomb. He died in 1310. Then Michael, the little boy he brought back from the Crusades, became the second Knight of Cavage.

251

"—on the occasion of the death of his mother."

But Thaniel, you said Sir Jaymes never told anyone who Michael's mother was. How did St. Charles de Cordel know she had died?

"How very odd," Thaniel said softly. "What does the letter say?"

"That is what I have been trying to determine, but you know how tricky medieval Latin can be. And Cordel's writing is not nearly so clear as a professional scribe's. But I think I may have the sense of it. If you don't mind some paraphrasing and a bit of guesswork, I can give you a sort of reading now."

"Please."

I watched the crown of white hair reflected in the dark window beside me and listened as the words came to life again after being buried for almost seven hundred years.

" 'How well I remember the first time I saw your mother. It was a night of tragedy, of looting, burning, killing, of the evildoing of one godless man. A part of your mother's life on earth came to an end that night, for, as you well know, she was captive ever after, a prisoner of silence as well as stone. You are now nearly eighteen. It is time you knew all that happened.

" 'You are descended through the male line from the Norman knight, Sir Giles du Maine, for whom the Conqueror built the castle now called Esty Hall. For over two centuries its name was Castle du Maine. Then Edward Plantagenet rode home from the Crusades with his red-haired companion-at-arms, Rufus Gafford, to find he had become King Edward the First. He soon appointed Gafford his chief in the Welsh border country around Dairminster, creating for him the title Earl of Esty and giving him certain lands.

" 'This was not enough for Rufus Gafford. He also wanted Castle du Maine, and one night he took it. Entering its gates as a guest, he remained as its master, having forced your great-grandfather, Sir Edmond du Maine, to flee at sword's point.

252

" 'Sir Edmond took refuge with his daughter, Madeline, wife to George Cavage, in the Cavages' ancient fortress on the crag. He appealed to King Edward to restore his ancestral castle, but the King made no reply. The new Earl of Esty, his wife and his brood of red-haired daughters meanwhile entrenched themselves in their new home and set stonemasons and blacksmiths to work removing every trace of the du Maine armorial crests from the castle.

" 'One market day, Esty struck a poor country fellow to the ground for asking the way to Castle du Maine. "Castle du Maine has vanished!" he cried. "Like the family it housed. Ask the way to Esty Hall instead!"

" 'The King remained deaf to your great-grandfather's entreaties, and so at last he took matters into his own hands. One night, as Esty and his men rode past the foot of Crag Cavage on the narrow road beside the River Dair, Sir Edmond du Maine, George Cavage and George's two young brothers, Anthony and Crinsley, swooped down on them. If poor Crinsley's dumbshow account of events can be believed, Esty's party proved surprisingly numerous, well-armed and eager for battle. Sir Edmond and both George and Anthony Cavage died that night. Crinsley Cavage alone survived, his hands cut off, his tongue cut out. Thus maimed, he was tied to Esty's horse and dragged up the crag through the gates of Castle Cavage, where the widowed Madeline waited with no one to defend her. Jaymes, your father, whom I have always called Jemmy, was but a babe in arms.

" 'Jemmy grew up half wild, living on horseback, with a red dog always at his heels. Although reckless and fatally stubborn, he was unfailingly kind to his wretched Uncle Crinsley, whom he fed and barbered and with whom he seemed able to converse. I prayed many times for Jemmy and Crinsley and your unfortunate grandmother, but Esty's hold on all of them and all of secular life in Dairminster grew stronger every day.

" 'In the autumn of the year of Our Lord 1290, the Cathedral was consecrated at last. Esty resolved that one of his daughters would be first to wed there and came to me to write her marriage contract. Your father was the lad he chose for her, but he told Jemmy of his plan only after the contract had been drawn.

" 'That night Jemmy rode down from Crag Cavage at a gallop to tell me he would not wed a Gafford in any case, but he could not in honor wed at all. He recalled to me the terrible night in the winter just past, when—by order of the King—the Jews were driven out of England. On that night Jemmy had rescued a girl from Esty and the mob who had burned her home and murdered her family. I was with him when he found her in the silent, smoking graveyard Esty had made of the little cluster of wooden houses and shops just back of the Cathedral. She seemed only a bundle of blue rags on the ground, but she spoke. From my early studies, I understood what she said, and the words made my blood run cold. I never heard her speak again.

" 'Your father took her home and hid her where he vowed Esty would never find her. He did not even know her name, because she could not speak. He only knew he loved her, and he would have no other. At last he told me your birth was expected within days, and he asked my help.

" 'I gave him a letter to Steven of Amsterdam, whose party of Crusaders was about to embark for the Holy Land to aid the Knights Hospitaler in their defense of Acre against the Baibars. He was gone before morning, leaving Anne Gafford alone and unwed in Castle Cavage, where her father had already installed her and from whence he soon removed her. A few days later, in her hiding place inside the crag, your mother bore you. Your grandmother, Madeline, informed only me. She knew as well as I that Esty would have killed both you and your mother had he known either of you was alive.

" 'Your father did not return for four years. When he did, he was alone, but he rode a magnificent horse whose saddlecloth bore the insignia of the City of Amsterdam: a great blue X on a field of white. Struggling homeward, he was once nearly murdered by brigands who wanted the horse, but—as he swore to me on the night of his return—the figure of your mother, still in the blue dress she wore the day he first set eyes on her, materialized from nowhere and shouted at his attackers, so startling them that they dropped their knives and fled in terror.

" 'The night of his homecoming was extremely dark. It was bitter cold and very late. He came to my door on foot. No one saw him arrive. No one saw him leave. Thank God for that, for you might still be in hiding if anyone had.

" 'I had terrible events to relate to him, but I had not the heart to do it that night. Thus, I did not tell him that Esty had come upon poor Crinsley walking in the wood that divides your lands and there had ridden him down and killed him. Nor did I tell him your mother had sunk deep into melancholy while he was away, that she sat mute at her needlework night and day, putting it aside only for that moment at nightfall when she would lead you about with her as she lit the candles. He gave me no chance to do so, Michael. He wanted to know of you. When I told him he had a fine son, his first thought was how he might proclaim you his heir and rescue you from hiding. Together, we thought of a way.

" 'He went on foot to Castle Cavage, fetched you out in a sack and carried you away under cover of darkness to the place on the river bank where his horse was tethered. At dawn, he placed you before him on the saddle and made a triumphal entry into Dairminster, greeting everyone he met and gathering a crowd which grew to include even Esty and myself. To this gathering he presented you, saying only that you were his son and he had brought you from the Holy Land. Esty asked who your mother might be, and Jemmy said only, "Ah, Milord Esty, I mean to devote the rest of my life to praying for her."

" 'Esty had yet another daughter to offer him. I was

obliged to write the marriage contract before the day was out, but it was as before. Jemmy loved your mother and would have no other. From that day until this, he has protected her from harm, keeping the world away by leading a solitary existence. Now she is gone, and the purpose of his life gone with her, and so I ask you to try to forgive him.

" 'It may seem to you, as you have told me, that you have never seen Jemmy Cavage sober. You do not remember, but you have. You have heard his bitter memories of Steven of Amsterdam, whose lust for blood exceeded even Esty's. You have seen him rage at Esty's endless offers of gold and jewels, power and place, as dower for his daughters. You have watched him tend your sorrowing mother as faithfully as ever he waited on his Uncle Crinsley. You do not remember, but it was from your father that you had your first lessons in riding a horse, drawing a strongbow, shearing a sheep and hurling the great sword Wilva that proclaims the coming of May.

" 'I taught you only languages and logic and philosophy. Now you must teach yourself the last, best thing, which is to love.

" 'I weep that your mother's death, like her life, must be kept secret. However, this does not mean it is to be ignored or forgotten. She seemed always to want you at her side when she lit the candles at sundown. This suggested to me that it was an occasion for prayer, and so I taught you a Psalm of David in the language of David when you were but a small boy. I trust you still remember it and charge you to recite it in your mother's memory.

" 'If your year at the university at Cambridge has dimmed your memory of this, I shall copy it out for you below. I, too, shall pray for your mother. Poor girl. The only words I ever heard her speak were *Lout sairt sook.* To which I can only add *Amen.*

" 'May her immortal soul rest in peace.' "

Nothing I saw reflected in the black windowpanes moved for a moment. The silence around the lamplit table was total. Then Sir Thomas said, "The letter ends with the Twenty-Third Psalm, lettered in Hebrew. Below that is the signature of the saint himself."

At last someone spoke.

"Sir Thomas," Thaniel said, "what is the meaning of *Lout sairt sook?*"

"Thou shalt not kill," Sir Thomas replied.

Nobody noticed as I slipped out of the room.

o   o   o

Mr. Stillwell's brigade had mopped up after itself in the Picture Gallery; the floor barely felt damp under my rubber soles. I could not find a light switch so I left the double doors open. The chandeliers in the corridor helped me find my way to Frederick Pennington's easel, which stood exactly where I had first seen it and was again shrouded in a sheet. I fumbled until I found the sheet's edge and, at the instant that I flung it aside, all the lights went on overhead and around me. I heard the Dow's lovely, low voice say sadly, "There. Now you can see her clearly."

Before me on the easel, as if I had never touched it, was the portrait of the woman in blue. This time a detail of her costume which had previously escaped my notice seemed to leap at me. An oddly shaped yellow patch was sewn to her sleeve just above the elbow. The shape looked like an open book.

There are five sentences lettered on either side, I realized. *My God, it's the Ten Commandments!*

"I have tried everything," the Dow continued. "I did so hope an expert like you would know of some way to destroy that piece of canvas."

"I'm glad I didn't," I told her.

"Once," the old woman confided, "I slashed it with a knife, but the next day it was just as you see it. I gave my

257

little daughter-in-law quite a nice gift to cover it all up with green paint for me. But the paint flaked off in a week."

The painted face had a message to give me, but I knew I would have to spend the rest of my life gazing at it before I understood it all.

"However, I'm sure I'll think of something," the Dowager Duchess of Dair said brightly. "I succeeded in getting rid of lots of those horrid nudes today. You'll see; that wench in blue isn't indestructible. I'll think of a way."

Her silver cart's little engine started up and she buzzed away down the corridor, leaving me alone with her husband's masterpiece. The portrait's eyes looked right through me to something beyond. Almost against my will I turned to see what was there.

Through the empty panes of the window I had broken, I looked out at a starless sweep of navy blue sky. Silhouetted against it was the black hulk of Crag Cavage, still wearing its hideous old castle like a jagged black crown. At the highest point of that crown, behind a narrow window I knew only too well, a candle burned.

XVII

At first it seemed odd to look to my left to watch Thaniel drive, but he had insisted on taking me to the train in the flamboyant stretched Eldorado from Detroit. Over his shoulder, the River Dair sparkled in the afternoon sunshine. Ahead of us, the glorious lily window of the Cathedral throbbed with a thousand colors. But I concentrated my attention on Thaniel's rugged profile because I would probably never see it again.

"To think," he was saying, "that I have actually flown through blinding snowstorms in order to climb into a freezing tower precisely at sundown, light a candle and recite the Twenty-Third Psalm in Hebrew. Inconceivable!"

"The Lady in Blue seemed to appreciate your doing so," I reminded him.

"True. And I am most grateful to her. I also feel damned guilty."

"Why?"

259

"Well, why should I have a guardian angel when all those people in the concentration camps had none?"

"I suppose because you have been blessed."

"Indeed I have, and it's a damned uncomfortable feeling."

"Does that mean you intend to stop lighting the candle and reciting the Psalm?"

"Oh, hell, no. After seven hundred years? I wouldn't do that to her. But—"

"But what?"

"Do you think she'd allow me a night off now and then?"

"I don't know, Thaniel. She might think you were neglecting her. She really hasn't anyone except you, has she?"

"There's Whitwell. I was thinking that if he did the honors alone this Saturday night, I could stay in London."

And celebrate the fact that you are now a free man, I thought, *with your own true love by your side.*

"That's right. You do fly down on Saturdays, don't you?"

"Stay here another two days and you can fly with me."

"Oh, thank you, but now that Eustace is back at work I feel sure my absence is not going unnoticed."

"Very well, but after I get through with the dentist on Saturday, perhaps—"

"Dentist?"

"Yes."

"Who is your dentist?"

"What difference does that make? I'm talking about afterwards. I thought we might—"

"No, really, Thaniel, I would like to know about a dentist who is worth flying through blinding snowstorms to keep appointments with."

"Oh, all right. She's not exactly a dentist. But I will be through with her Saturday before tea time."

"Permanently through? Or just until Saturday week?"

"That depends on you, Deborah."

We were pulling into the parking lot that separates the railroad track from the river.

"Aren't you the same man who recently told me there was nothing he wanted quite so much as his freedom?"

Thaniel cut off the engine and turned to me. I shall never forget his eyes.

"I meant my freedom from Kendra," he said.

"The train is here."

"Oh, Deborah, I didn't expect any encouragement from you while Kendra was alive, but it's different now. You know I want you."

"Why me?" I asked, gathering up my document case and my tape recorder. "You could have anybody."

"Because," he said, helping me out of the huge car, "you are the first woman I can remember who hasn't set out after me with rod and gun, looking to bag a title."

It was only a few steps to the railway carriage I was to ride in, and we said nothing on the way there. But once inside my compartment, Thaniel took me in his arms.

"I may be the loneliest man you have ever met," he said. "I was married for years, and I've had many charming companions to help me forget about it. But I have never been loved, and before it's too late I want a woman to love me as much as the Lady in Blue must have loved Jemmy. So that seven hundred years from now she'll still love me, and she'll still be keeping an eye on our kids. You could love a man that much, Deborah. You could love a man forever."

I once tried to, I thought.

"I never had a wife. Whit never had a mother. We both need you, Deborah. Stay with us. Please."

His arms were very strong, but his voice was trembling. What was I to tell him? Only the truth would do, but what was it?

Suddenly it burst out.

"You only say you need me, Thaniel, not that you love me."

For a moment there was blank bewilderment in his eyes. Then, to my horror, he began to laugh at me.

261

"You mustn't laugh," I said, feeling the tears gathering. "Don't you realize that I was married for years, too, and that I've never been loved either?"

Still shaking with laughter, he folded me up in his arms.

"My poor darling," he said. "Of course I do."

Then the train started moving.

"Of course you do *what*?" I insisted. "Love me or just realize what I've been through?"

Thaniel was beaming as he swung the carriage door open and prepared to leap to the platform outside.

"I'll tell you Saturday," he answered. "If you promise not to interrupt."

THE END